HOT NIGHTS IN STURGIS

THE SERIES BOOK 1-4

MICHELLE LOVE

CONTENTS

The Billionaire Bad Boy Meets His Angel	vii
1. BLAZE	1
2. ANGEL	10
3. BLAZE	19
4. ANGEL	28
5. BLAZE	37
6. ANGEL	46
7. BLAZE	55
8. ANGEL	64
Angel Shows Her Billionaire Who Is Boss	73
9. BLAZE	74
10. ANGEL	83
11. BLAZE	92
12. ANGEL	101
13. BLAZE	110
14. ANGEL	119
15. BLAZE	128
16. ANGEL	137
The Billionaire Takes Charge of His Angel	147
17. BLAZE	148
18. ANGEL	157
19. BLAZE	166
20. ANGEL	175
21. BLAZE	185
22. ANGEL	194
23. BLAZE	203
24. BLAZE	212
The Compromise of the Billionaire and His Angel	217
25. BLAZE	218
26. ANGEL	223
27. BLAZE	229
28. BLAZE	238

29. BLAZE	247
30. Angel	252
31. BLAZE	258
32. BLAZE	268
33. Angel	270
34. BLAZE	277
35. ANGEL	285
About the Author	295

Made in "The United States" by:

Michelle Love

© Copyright 2020 – Michelle Love

ISBN: 978-1-64808-231-3

ALL RIGHTS RESERVED. No part of this publication may be reproduced or transmitted in any form whatsoever, electronic, or mechanical, including photocopying, recording, or by any informational storage or retrieval system without express written, dated and signed permission from the author

❀ Created with Vellum

INTRIGUE. LUST. PASSION

Blaze is a member of a motorcycle gang on their way to Sturgis, South Dakota for the huge biker rally held there every year. He's single and wants to keep it that way, but plans on taking as many females as he can to his bed while in the rowdy town.

Angel is working in her uncle's motorcycle repair shop and when Blaze comes in with a little trouble with his new ride, she finds him as interesting as he finds her.

Blaze is stricken with her knowledge of bikes and her beauty as well as her feisty attitude.

But when he asks her out, a thing he never does, she refuses.

It only serves to send Blaze into alpha-mode and he shows up at her home and makes her dinner then she takes him to her bedroom.

Both know they have stumbled onto something neither saw coming. But can Angel get past her fear of abandonment and let Blaze have a place in her heart? And can Blaze get past his idea of being single forever and let Angel into his heart? As both want to be the master of the situation, can they give into the other without losing who they are?

THE BILLIONAIRE BAD BOY MEETS HIS ANGEL

Book 1

1

BLAZE

Vibrations filled the air as the fifteen of us made the last leg of our journey to the motorcycle Mecca of the world; Sturgis, South Dakota.

After our gang met up at the Ohio headquarters of The Brothers of the Scarlet Dragon, the motorcycle club I belong to, we headed out for the three-day trip to the rally which beats all motorcycle rallies.

This is the third year that I've made this trip. I have to fool my entire family each year to be able to do this.

I'm a business lawyer. That means I push papers for the law firm that my grandfather started way back before even my father was born. Thanks to that man, we all are stinking rich.

That alone was good enough reason for me to be able to flake off my entire life. But one of the stipulations of being able to receive one's trust fund is that you have to show my grandfather your college degree.

Oh, and it must pertain to the law in some fashion!

So I had to keep my grades up in school. I had to be able to get into Harvard and that is where I stayed until I successfully completed my Master's Degree in Business Law.

A thing that I hate with every fiber of my being!

I'm the youngest in my family. My father's an only child. So the billions upon billions of dollars my grandfather has managed to make with my father's help and now my oldest brother's help too, keeps us in our fancy mansions, cars and motorcycles, in my case.

After six years of college, I was placed in the family firm. That's where I've been the last six years and I'm going completely stir crazy in the New York office.

Only a mere thirty now, I'm ready to sow a few wild oats. My family has kept my ass so damn busy, I've had little to no time for extracurricular activities, like chasing ass.

Those snooty East Coast bitches just don't do it for me anymore. Especially the ones that my family approves of.

That's another reason I hate my life revolving around the law firm. One must always keep the family name of Worthington in good standing.

My name is Benjamin Franklin Worthington of the Manhattan Worthington's. That's how I am introduced at all functions and do you think anyone is ever allowed to call me anything other than by my full first name?

No!

I am to be called Benjamin at all times, according to my stuffy grandfather, who insisted on naming my brother, and me. He got saddled with Theodore Roosevelt.

Poor man.

But my older brother is different than I am. He actually likes to be stuffy just like our father and grandfather. Mom's okay, but when Father is around, she has to act a certain way or he belittles her.

I really hate it when he does that. Thankfully, Mom has her act down pat. I can only call her Mom when no one else is around. Other than that, I must call her Mother.

Even the tiniest infraction of civilized rules and etiquette is dealt with hastily. And the ever present threat of being cut off without a dime is always in the air when anyone is even thinking about doing something my grandfather deems inappropriate.

So, as far as he knows, I'm on a learning mission to better understand the legal conditions under which motorcycle manufacturers can get by with violating the safety standards that other motor vehicles have to follow.

I came up with that whole idea all by myself!

I had to purchase a very impressive piece of machinery to make this learning mission I am on. Each year, I get a brand new bike to test. Of course, he makes me sell it afterward, but for the month of August, I get to be a free man with a badass motorcycle under my ass.

My ride for this trip is a brand new Harley CVO Street Glide in red. It s one amazing machine and a killer ride. The last three days have flown by as I do feel like I'm gliding over the road with my gang of fellow bikers.

My family knows nothing about my involvement with the gang. They would lose their shit if they knew about this!

The higher ups in this gang know about my real name and my real life. But all the others know me simply as Blaze. The badass who happens to be a lawyer too.

And when I get to be this man, the man I really feel I am, I go all the way bad.

Drinking, smoking, cussing, womanizing! You name it. I do it!

The day after Labor Day marks the end of Blaze and back I go to the slightly depressed version of myself, Benjamin Worthington.

But those first few weeks after I go back still has me feeling kind of high from all the fun I've had. And I know that this trip will be the same.

Hot ass chicks are everywhere in Sturgis with the bike rally. And they are ready to go at all times. You can get laid just about anywhere in the town that overflows with bikers for a limited amount of time.

And I plan on getting a different one every single night I'm there. I already booked myself a private motel room and had a whole box full of clothes and assorted sexual devices sent up to the motel I'm going to be staying at.

I am ready to roll!

The rumble of another Harley moves up next me and I see out of the corner of my eye it is a couple who have been in this gang for quite some time.

Rod and Ashley Manning are one of the few married couples in the gang. She rides behind him for this trip but she's got her own ride, and even rides on her own sometimes.

They have two teenage daughters and take this trip each year to get away from all the family and just be the couple they are. It's cool, I suppose. But I wouldn't want to take a chick to this babe-fest.

No way!

As they move ahead of me, another couple pulls up and I see it's the newest couple, Paco, and Phoenix. From what they said when we were camping last night, they met only three months ago and hit it off so well, they've been together nonstop ever since.

Paco's going to surprise her by going through Vegas after the rally and marrying her to make it all good and legal. I told him he should keep it easy to get the hell out of if it goes south.

One never knows how a relationship is going to work out. If I would've married the first piece of ass I got, then I'd probably be dead right now instead of cruising down the highway on a cool August morning.

Sandra Moore was my first love when I started college. We dated all through college. I kept her around mostly because she made the cut with my family.

She was from an upscale family and a law student. So much money no one can count it all, just like our family. And snooty to her very core.

I got lucky, and she found what she called a real lawyer. He took her off my hands and after the initial shock of being dumped, I found myself very relieved to be rid of her.

Playing the field in the New York scene was okay. But when you have to maintain such high standards to keep from losing your trust fund, you can't find many women who like the things I do.

After three years of that crap, I found the love of motorcycles and it took me no time at all to find this gang who took me in quickly. Like a very dysfunctional family of sorts.

There are some assholes, just like in any family. But there are some good people too. And they all accept each other for who they are. No judging is done by anyone.

I don't think it's allowed!

We're getting close to the town we've been waiting for. You can tell that by the way the whole cluster of bikes begins to speed up. Our hearts are beginning to pound in all of our chests as the excitement starts to key up.

A cold beer and a hot woman sitting on my lap are close at hand and I find myself getting nearly giddy over that fact. Not much longer until I get to put my little vacation from boredom into play.

Girls, you better watch out!

My bike makes a little bump and then I feel something odd happen. It went down a little. Something doesn't feel right.

Shit!

Looks like my plan of a cold beer and a hot girl will have to wait for me to stop off at one of the many garages they have in town.

This would be how it fucking starts for me!

This whole year has been a giant cluster-fuck. I singlehandedly lost a major client a few months ago when I dared to ask him how he could live with himself.

He's a rich son-of-a-bitch and bought the rights to manufacture the main drug used in treating AIDS. He jacked the price up so high that most people with the disease couldn't afford to buy it.

He came to our firm to seek help in keeping the product at the price he set as he was being asked by the federal government to reduce the price to what it was when he originally purchased the licensing.

Wanting our help in keeping his price, he came to us and gave a very healthy sum of money to the firm to help him. At the meeting we had with the asshole, I told him off.

My grandfather was pissed, but my father and brother, though silent, agreed with me. So I managed not to get cut off without a cent and retained my place in the family firm.

But it was a nightmarish few months with my grandfather giving me the cold shoulder.

I know that doesn't sound so bad, but my grandfather knows how to make the cold shoulder really hurt.

For instance, he bought the entire legal staff their own individual, personal drivers for a whole year. Not me, though. He also brought in gourmet lunches on Fridays, but I was not invited.

He would walk right past me, telling everyone hello who came before and after me. That kind of shit!

He finally stopped a few weeks ago and things went back to

normal. The man can keep that up for a very long time. It's probably taking years off his life.

That's what I tell myself, anyway.

Around the bend we come, and my bike is getting lower and lower. I'm glad it waited until we were almost here to do this. The first large bar we see is where our leaders pull in and I pull up alongside Rod and his wife.

We all cut off our bikes. "Hey, Rod, I'm going to catch up with you guys in a little while. I have to find a shop to see what the hell is going on with my ride."

He gives me the thumbs up so I turn the bike back on and take off to find what looks like a reputable motorcycle repair shop. I don't want to get screwed here.

Not too far away from the bar, I see a sign that says, Phil's Motorcycle Garage. The sign under it says he specializes in Harleys. So I think this might be the best place to at least start at.

Especially since the bike just keeps on getting lower.

And there doesn't seem to be a lot of people in the parking lot. Only one other bike is parked here. An older model Sportster. Looks like a chick bike.

Maybe there's some hot chick in here who can sit on my lap while I wait for the bike to be repaired!

I turn the bike off and get off to walk it into the large bay with the metal garage door opened on it. It's dimly lit in here and hard to see. But I don't see anyone yet.

Stopping to get my cellphone out of my pocket, I check the time.

Shit! It's noon. Lunch time.

I'll probably have to wait here for a damn hour before I can get any help. The hits just keep on coming. Nineteen hours of riding to get to some real fun and I have this little hitch in the scene.

I hope this isn't a sign of things to come with this trip. It's supposed to be fun after all. Not headache after headache.

A group of motorcycles blast past the garage and the entire bay vibrates with the loud noise they make. It makes my heart skip a beat. I love the growl of a pack of bikes.

I just want to be out there, having a great time with my brothers from the gang, sipping some cold suds. Instead, I'm in a dank and dark garage seeking mechanical attention for a bike that shouldn't need it yet, it's so damn new.

After the last few bikes in that group get past I listen hard and hear some tapping. Maybe a computer keyboard.

But as I look around, I don't see anyone. So I put the kickstand down and leave my bike in the bay and make my way up a set of steps.

A smell wafts past my nose and I stop and breathe it in. Fresh flowers are what it smells like. That and clean linen.

What a misplaced scent in a motorcycle repair shop. Oil and gasoline are predominating, but that little trickle of wonderful manages to seep in.

I smile for no reason other than it smells good and seems out of place in this very rugged town. Even most of the chicks around here have remnants of road dust and the oil and gas mix that comes with a pack of bikes and their exhaust systems.

The alcohol helps one not to care much about the smell of what's on your lap. The feeling is what matters the most.

More tapping and a bit of low muttering I can hear. It's a woman.

What kind of woman would be working in this grease pit?

I prepare myself to see a Hun of a female. I'll try hard not to react too unfavorably when I see the brute.

"Hey!" I shout.

But nothing comes back as my voice echoes off the metal walls of the garage.

I wait a moment then shout again, but still nothing. I'm sure I hear someone typing, though. Then the sound of a phone ringing fills the air and a female voice mutters again, "Shit!"

Maybe she can't hear well either. Ugly and deaf, yikes!

So I shout very loud in my best New Yorker voice, "Hey, a little help here, I ain't got all day!"

2

ANGEL

With the mechanics gone for lunch, the garage will be somewhat quiet for the next hour so I can actually get some work done. Parts need to be ordered and I've yet to do that as I was quietly watching Cletus work on a two-year-old Honda all morning long.

I'm in my last year of college. At the end of May next year, I'll be the proud holder of a Master's Degree in Engineering. To design motorcycles is what I long to do for my career.

Hopefully, not too terribly long from now, I can do just that. But for now, I'm working part-time in my uncle's motorcycle repair shop.

It's helping me get some hands on experience with the miraculous machines. Not that the mechanics let me actually touch any of the customer's bikes, I do watch them, though.

As long as I stay quiet and don't ask any questions, they let me watch. I've learned a lot by working here the last few years.

I grew up on the outskirts of Sturgis, South Dakota. Motorcycles kind of come with life here. I got my first one when I was fifteen. Uncle Phil gave it to me.

He was married when he was younger. No kids, though. His

wife died when she was only thirty-two. They had a real love, and he never saw fit to take another wife.

So my sister and I became like his kids in a way. He managed to get me interested in bikes, but my younger sister is much too girly.

The latest bike he gave me a few years ago is a Harley Sportster XL883L in black. It's cool enough and runs great.

My parents moved off to California last year, leaving me alone here as my sister married a marine and they now live in France. What they're doing over there is top secret, or so she told me when I asked what the hell they need our marines in France for.

Uncle Phil keeps an eye on me. I don't get into trouble, though.

I stay out of the many bars there are here. I don't really date as I think men all suck and make you think they love you but then leave you with no reason why.

Yeah, I have men issues. My first love was a hot biker with badass tattoos and a beard that was just the right amount of scratchy when he kissed me.

I thought what we had was real. He made me believe I was the girl for him. We were together for three years before he told me one day he wanted to see the world.

I was all for it. Thought I could finish college when we got done with our world adventure.

Only I didn't realize he meant he wanted to go alone. I had to watch him pack up and kiss the top of my head then he told me he hoped I had a very nice life.

A nice life!

Words couldn't come to me as he left. I was dumb-struck. I watched him ride off into the sunset and I never heard from the guy, I thought loved me as much as I thought I loved him, again.

That was a couple of years ago. I'm over him and guys in general. Who needs a man, anyway?

I have my own little house I rented at the edge of town. My little Poodle, Maltese mix pup, accurately named, Cuddles, keeps me protected. And thanks to modern technology, there are machines to do what a man can for me.

One day I will make enough money to take complete care of myself. The paltry amount I make here is enough to get me by. But just that.

With my diploma in hand, I hope to change my financial outlook in just over a year or so. I have my plan for the future. Men not need apply.

I used to dabble at the bars a little now and again, but the few guys I thought would be random one-night stands all somehow wanted more than that from me. So I stopped going to the bars.

Work and home are all I do now. My classes are all online and only once a month do I have to go and check in with a few of my professors. Life is good and things couldn't be better.

I've learned how to keep men at bay with a 'don't fuck with me' attitude. As one can imagine, I get a ton of hot biker guys who come in here with their broken motorcycles. And a lot of them hit on me.

I hit back, though, and not in a nice way!

There's no reason to act as if I might actually go out with them. I won't.

When what's-his-ass left me, I refuse to say his name ever again, I kind of broke down.

He taught me some things. First, never let yourself fall into a deep love. You lose some of yourself in that person. When they leave, like they all do eventually, you lose that piece of you too.

The second thing he taught me is how to be tough as hell. You have to be or men will come in and tell you nice things.

You'll believe their lying asses and it will end with you crying yourself to sleep way too many nights.

The third thing he taught me was how meaningless sex is. I thought what we did was special. I mean he and I found we liked the kinky stuff. A little BDSM was fun from time to time.

He'd let me be the boss sometimes, and I'd let him be the boss too. Fun, and I thought deep. I was a dumbass. It wasn't deep to him. We didn't share a special bond.

It was just sex, and it meant nothing.

And the handful of times I did it after him were very meaningless. And the guys were kind of pussy-like when I smacked them with the belt. Only one let me handcuff him to the bed.

Wimps!

And not one of them would smack my ass hard enough to make a difference. They were all, 'I don't want to hurt you.'

How could I have explained that I like a little pain in the game?

So I just ignored the men when they tried to get me to have some type of a relationship with them. My grandmother lives thirty miles away and if I couldn't get them to leave me alone, then I'd escape to her place until they moved on.

Me and Cuddles are fine alone. She's kind of a bitch just like I am. When dumbass male dogs come into the yard, she barks and goes at them like she's a Doberman.

She's the same way with the human variety of men too. My poor mailman had a package he was trying to get to my door with. She ripped his pants leg as she tugged at it to make him stop coming to the door.

He told me I needed a vicious dog sign and if I ever got another package, I could take my ass down to the post office to pick it up unless I tied the little bitch up.

I took her inside and gave her a steak and a good-doggy pat on the head.

She tried to do her job. Keep the evil, lying, no-good men away from her mommy!

Thanks to her, I never have to worry about some man getting into my house without her trying to kill them.

A large group of bikes pass by the shop and it makes the whole metal building rattle as they do. I put on my headphones and listen to a little music on my phone to drown out the outside noise.

THE ANNUAL MOTORCYCLE rally is growing very close and already large groups of bikers are coming into town. Trashy women are already showing up and strategically placing themselves on barstools in every bar and lounging around area parks, hopeful to score some biker dick.

I don't know where most of these females come from. We have a few but not as many as pop out of the woodwork when the rally is in town. It's quite amazing, actually.

It never fails to surprise me with all the ready-to-go-women, that I still get hit on just walking down the street. I'm always thinking as I'm flipping the men off who dare to bother me that there's a ton of pussy walking around, leave me the hell alone.

My uncle tells me I shouldn't dress in tight leather pants and halter tops if I don't want the men's attention. He may be right, but fuck, I should be able to dress the way I want!

I ride a motorcycle everywhere I go for Christ's sakes!

I need the leather to protect my fucking skin. If I ever fall that is.

I look around and find the clipboard with the wooden back on it and knock on it three times.

No reason to tempt fate!

With the good Lord's grace, I have never wrecked. I've come

close a time or two, but never ate it. I knock on the wood again for even thinking about it.

The computer freezes up for a moment and it scares the crap out of me that I'll have to start this parts list over. I mutter to myself, "Fucking, piece of shit."

My uncle needs to buy a new computer, but he's too cheap. This one will have to completely crap out before he'll see fit to make the several hundred-dollar investment.

And I'll be stuck having to use my own laptop to order parts until he does. The man is a notorious penny pincher.

Another thunderous bunch of bikes pass the shop, and it has me looking out the glass door at them. It's a gang all wearing matching leather jackets and looking all cool.

I've never been in a gang. Not that I haven't thought they looked kind of cool. I'm just a real loner and loners don't belong in groups.

Loners like to be alone.

Do some stormy nights have me wishing for more than my puppy as a companion?

Sure.

Does watching a love story on television have me searching for someone to love and love me?

Sure. That's why I don't watch that shit anymore.

Does the sight of a well-tattooed, bearded man with mountains of muscles get me hot?

Of course, I am only human!

But will I give a man a chance to fill those voids?

Hell no!

That leads to the heartbreak again, and that's a place I'm never revisiting.

But as I watch the pack of bikers ride past the garage, I see chicks riding bitch behind their boyfriends or husbands or whatever. And I secretly wish I could do that.

Maybe just one time. Maybe I wouldn't fall in love with the douche bag. Maybe I could keep things light and easy.

Then the phone rings and it comes through on my headphones since I have them plugged in and it scares the shit out of me. "Shit!" I scream out loud as I pull the cord out of the phone.

It's a damn eight hundred number so I'm not even going to answer it, anyway. Man, what a way to ruin a little daydream!

"Hey, a little help here, I ain't got all day!" some man shouts from the bay.

His voice is all gruff, and he sounds like an East coast, asswipe.

I WANT to yell back that I ain't got all day either but Uncle Phil talked to me just this morning about not being rude to the customers. So I don't yell anything and get up off the tall stool and go see what the prick wants.

Just as I get to the stairs that lead down into the bay I see a tall figure standing in the shadows as the mechanics turned the overhead lights off when they left for lunch.

His broad shoulders stand out against the dim backlighting. As I look past him, I see a bad to the bone Harley just inside the bay and it looks brand new.

A rich prick, I bet.

As he turns to look back at his bike and hitches his thumb, gesturing to it, I can see his long beard. "Got some bike troubles. I need to see a mechanic," he says with a gravelly, deep, sexy voice.

But I'm sure he's a cock-sucker like all men are!

He steps forward and I step back. He keeps walking forward and I keep stepping backward. All the way until we're inside the lighted waiting area and then I see him.

His hair is dirty blonde and cut so close to his head on both sides it looks almost like it's shaved. The top is a long flop of waves. His aviator sunglasses are so dark I can't see the color of his eyes.

He pulls them off and some piercing blue eyes look at me. Running over me as he looks me up and down and it sends chills through me quickly followed by heat.

Fuck me, he's hot!

His black leather jacket has red letters stitched into it. Seems he's a member of a gang called The Brothers of the Scarlet Dragon. And there's a name stitched in red just over his left very nicely defined pec.

Blaze.

Hmm, bet it's because he's like a flash of fire. Hot and then gone...

Tight, black, leather pants hug some massive legs. The defined muscles make the leather bend to conform to them.

They must be hard, like steel.

His motorcycle boots are dusty from the road. He must've ridden quite some ways to get here. Him and his gang of motorcycle riding hellions.

I'm sure he's looking for some hot action while he's in town. A wealthy banker on a little retreat from a wife and kids.

Cheater!

The form-fitting white T is sheer enough to see his six pack of abs and the lines are all so defined it almost seems unnatural.

Most likely all steroid muscles. No real work.

I'm sure he's a bunch of lies all wrapped into a nice looking package.

I see no visible tats to gauge his realness from. I'm an avid tattoo adviser and very critical of ones that don't mean anything or lend a beauty to the owner.

His caramel lips part and I can see a nice set of white teeth behind them. Then I realize I've pulled my lower lip between my teeth and hurry to let it go.

Damn girl!

For reasons I can't figure out except it's kind of hot in here and now that he's walked in it seems a lot hotter, he's taking off his leather jacket.

Fuck! His biceps are enormous and his arms are covered in art. I mean real artwork. Not just dumb tats that make no sense. He's a canvas for some very skilled artist.

I'm ashamed to admit that my body is quivering, and I just got really wet.

I SWALLOW and do my best to regain my inner bitch then say, "What can I do for you, Blaze?"

3

BLAZE

I seem to be looking at my first conquest and man is she smoking hot!

So hot in fact, I'm having a hard time forming words. "How do you know my name?"

With a nod, she gestures to the jacket I've taken off and tossed on the little beat up sofa in the waiting room. "Oh, yeah. My jacket. Um, so my bike is, um..."

Her dark brows arch up as she asks, "Making a strange noise?"

She runs the tip of her tongue out just a hair to move over her plump bottom lip. A plum colored lip gloss covers them and makes them look delicious.

I shake my head as that's not the problem with the bike but damn it, I can't recall what the problem is as she's so completely distracting. Her hand moves to her hip and she shifts her weight to her other leg.

Her long, black leather covered leg that looks so long, lean and fuckable. A pink sheer top she has on and a dark pink silk bra she's wearing peeks out underneath it.

She turns around and goes back behind the tall counter and

sits back on the tall stool there and looks back at the old computer on the top it if. She has a pair of angel wings on her back I can see underneath the sheer shirt.

Her deep, gorgeous blue eyes peer at me over the top of the old grease stained monitor as she asks, "Is it vibrating too much?"

"Huh?" I ask as I was looking at how pretty she has her black hair braided. The long braid lays over her right shoulder and the end of it rests on her boob. Her really perfect, pert and voluptuous boob.

"Is it vibrating more than usual?" she asks then looks back at the screen. "It's a new Street Glide, isn't it?"

I know the answer to that one!

"Yes, yes it is. But it's not vibrating any more than usual. I just got it a few days ago in a Harley shop in New York. Have you ever ridden one before? I could take you on a ride." I stop myself because I'm coming off way uncool. "If you want, I mean. I don't need you to go on a ride with me. But if you were wondering what a beast like my bike rides like, I could take you. On a ride that is. I could take you on a ride. Not take you. You know what I mean..."

I shut up as she looks at me with her mouth slightly open then she says, "I know what you mean. No, I don't want to ride it. I mean, it's a badass machine and I'm sure I'd enjoy the ride but not with you."

"Why not with me?" I ask as I lean on the counter and try to catch another glimpse of that sweet tattoo on her back. "Those wings on your back, any significant reason for them?"

Without looking at me she answers, "My name is Angel, hence the wings. And it's nothing personal. I just kind of hate men. That's why not you."

Of course! She's a lesbian!

. . .

"So, into women then. What a loss for men everywhere." I stand back up and turn away.

No reason to make myself sick over a girl who likes girls.

"No, not into women," she says with a huff. "Why is it when a woman says she hates men they always assume she's a lesbian? Can't a woman simply hate men without wanting to lick another chick into ecstasy?"

I turn back to look at her and stifle a laugh. "Crap! You are one verbal gal."

She looks back at the ancient monitor. "Not making a strange noise, not vibrating too much. Is it getting lower?"

Shock runs through me. "Yeah! That's it! How…"

"It's a common problem with the air ride suspension system when you're traveling over rough surfaces. It's most likely a small prick that punctured the line. I'm sure our mechanic can get it going for you fairly quickly. If you have a credit card on you, I can go ahead and write up a ticket so he can get busy on it as soon as he gets back from lunch." She holds out her hand and on the inside of her wrist there's a little angel, complete with a halo.

I take her hand and look at the tat as I take my wallet out with my other hand. "Nice."

She allows me to hold her hand and I find sparks shooting all through me as I touch her.

That's never happened before!

I let it go to retrieve my credit card and find the sparks starting to dissipate. That had to mean something.

Placing the card in her hand, I purposely graze her palm with my fingertips and the sparks come back. I notice her eyes are narrowed at me. Then she looks away quickly.

I bet she felt that too!

. . .

"So how do you know so much about bikes, Angel?" I ask as I lean back on the counter since she isn't a lesbian, and she is into men and she has such an amazing effect on me.

"I'm nine months away from getting my Master's in Engineering. I want to build bikes. Preferably ones with women in mind." She looks at me with a smile after she sees my card. "Worthington? And you are Benjamin of the famous Worthington Law Firm in New York. I had pegged you as a banker, not a billionaire lawyer. A married banker with kids. Not an extremely eligible bachelor."

And now this hard demeanor she's had will fade away like cotton candy in a rainstorm.

"You found out." I lean in a bit closer. "So how about that ride, now?"

"Ha!"

Not the sound I thought I was about to hear.

She goes to typing and not looking at me. So I ask, although hesitantly, "Why the loud, ha?"

"I see men with money around this town all the damn time." Her eyes level on me. "I can become some billionaire's bimbo anytime I want to. Thing is, I don't want to. But you should watch out for the other ladies in this town. And when I say ladies, believe me, I am using that term very loosely."

I put the card back in my wallet as she has taken off all the information she needed and placed it on the counter rather than placing it back in my hand. "You are one of the three people in this town who know my real name, Angel. No one else will know me by anything other than, Blaze. I trust you can keep my little secret."

Her deep blue, sexy as hell eyes which are framed by the darkest and thickest of lashes flutter at me as she moves her hand to her chest and says, "Me? You can completely trust me to keep your name to myself. I wouldn't want to be the one responsible for getting you mauled by the pack of hungry females which are running amuck through my hometown."

"If this is your hometown then why haven't I seen you around before? I've been here for the last two rallies. I'd remember you if I ever saw you around before." I take the opportunity to pick her braid up and finger it a bit as she's close enough to do that.

She yanks it out of my hand. "Look, Benny. No fucking around with my personal shit. Not my braid, not my mind, not my body!"

I stand up and feel kind of sheepish as she's a bit intimidating, and it's not very easy for a woman to intimidate me. But her use of a nickname for me has me wanting to laugh. And I know she'd get even more pissed if I laughed right now

"I shouldn't have touched your hair. You're completely right. It won't happen again. Unless you ask me to, of course. Then I'll run my fingers all through that silky heaven on top of your pretty little head." Her glare tells me that I have spoken the wrong words.

Those porcelain cheeks fill with red and that can only mean one thing.

Angel

"Pretty little head?" she says with a very even and low tone. It's a scary tone as I can see fire in her gorgeous eyes. "Look, I had me a biker once, and he made me believe he loved me. He made me think we had a future, and he took off and went on a world tour, alone. He broke me, Benny. I'm not a repairable person from how he left me.

So I stay to myself. I don't want a man. Especially a fucking biker with a love for the road, fast women, and booze. No offense."

"Yeah, of course. I mean what's offensive about any of that you just said? Not a thing, right? Not one thing." I tap my fingers on the top of the counter and wonder how I can repair this damage.

She pounds at the poor keyboard in front of her as she finishes writing up the ticket. Muttering indiscernible things as she does and I decide to take a walk around and look out the glass door as a group of bikers rides along the roadway in front of the garage.

"Hey," I hear her say so I turn back around and see a little smile on her face. "I'm sorry. I know you aren't just a biker in some gang. I know you're this high-powered lawyer who likes to ride once a year. I shouldn't have said all that to you. I'm a little high-strung at times."

With slow steps, I walk back toward her. "I have a feeling you don't apologize often."

SHE NODS. "TRY NEVER." She smiles again. It's a wide and genuine smile. "Please don't tell my uncle I was so harsh to you. He just gave me a lecture this morning about not being rude to his customers."

I give her a wink. "So the owner is your uncle then?"

"He is," she says and stands up and comes around the counter to fix some brochures about oil and things for motorcycles. "I'm working here part-time until I finish college and hopefully move on to working for some motorcycle manufacturer. Uncle Phil was nice enough to keep me employed these last few years."

I lean on the counter and watch her as she leans over to

straighten up some magazines on the old as shit coffee table with all kinds of stains on it. Her ass is plump and so damn round and I can hardly stand straight up as I'm getting a huge boner.

So I lean a little lower to help that not be so obvious. She seems to be calming down nicely, and I'd hate her to turn back around and see me all huge for her and get mad again.

"So you stay home and never go out? Is that why I haven't seen you around before?" I ask as I look away and try to think of things to make the boner go away.

Kids playing baseball. Eating ice cream cones. Riding on a merry-go-round.

Fuck! None of those worked!

She turns back around and says, "That's why. I'm a homebody. Work and school take up my time. The crazy bar scene is not for me."

"So, how about dinner then?" I ask as she goes back to sit on the stool behind the counter again.

A THING I'm thankful for as the hard-on is staying, it seems.

She shakes her head and laughs. "No. No dinner. No date. Nothing. Look, Benny, I don't want you to take this personal. It's not. It's just that I'm done with love."

A loud laugh comes out of me. "Damn! Who said anything about love? I was talking about getting some food and eating it. Not running away to Vegas with me to get hitched!"

Her cheeks go pink and now I've embarrassed her.

Shit!

She won't look at me as she shakes her head and looks down. "No. I know that. I didn't mean for you to take it that way. Sorry. Just no thank you to dinner. I think I hear them all coming back from lunch. Your bike will be looked at soon if you'd care to take a seat."

"How old are you, Angel?" I ask as I find her way too young to be so cynical and set on a life of being alone.

Her blue eyes shine as she looks back at me. "Twenty-four. And you're around thirty, right?"

I nod. "I am thirty. And I'm in no rush to settle down. I'm here to sow some wild oats. So I get it why you don't want to date anyone who comes in with this crazy rally."

"Good," she says with a smile.

A burly man comes in from the back with a stained up blue uniform on. "What ya got, Angel?" His voice is all messed up from years of smoking and being around harsh fumes.

She gestures toward me with an open hand. "This gentleman has an issue with his bike. It's the red one in the bay."

He looks me up and down. "In town for the rally?"

I nod. He looks back at Angel. "He hit on you?"

She shakes her head. "No, Uncle Phil. He was a complete gentleman."

"Good!" he says then turns his large body around and walks out of the room toward the bay.

ONCE HE'S out of earshot, I give her a wink as she looks at me. "Thanks for that. He looks like he packs a wallop."

With a laugh which sounds like Heaven to me, she says, "He does. And I've seen the mess it leaves. I didn't want your first night in town to be with a shiner and a busted lip. The tramps would just hate it if your pretty face got all messed up."

I lean over the counter again and smile at her. "So I have a pretty face, do I?"

She blushes and shakes her head. "You are incorrigible."

I'm smitten is what I am. I've never been smitten before, but this has to be it. "Come on, Angel. Just dinner. Just one dinner and if you hate me, then I'll never bother you again."

"Nope." She gets up and walks out of the waiting room, leaving me there alone and wondering how the hell this chick has gotten under my skin so damn quick.

I drum my fingers on the counter until she comes back. She's beaming as she goes back to her chair.

"Well, what has you all smiles?" I ask.

"Oh, just the fact I was right about your bike. Just a little pinhole. It'll be ready in about an hour."

"Cool, I get to hang out with you for another hour." I go take a seat on the very uncomfortable old sofa and grab a magazine and sit back.

"Seems so. Or if you want, I can give you ride to where ever your gang is and drop you off with them. Someone can give you a call when your bike's ready," she says.

"Nah, I'm going to hang out here with you and hopefully talk you into dinner tonight." I give her my million-dollar smile.

"That won't happen, Benny."

4

ANGEL

"Oh yeah, I forgot to offer you anything to drink," I say as I recall Uncle Phil's speech this morning on how to treat his customers. "I have a pot of coffee in the office and there's a few sodas. Or we have some bottled water."

"I was craving a cold beer," he says with a lopsided grin that's really adorable.

"Sorry, we can't keep beer anywhere inside the shop or Cletus will find it. He's got a nose like a bloodhound for anything that contains alcohol. But I make a mean coffee with caramel and chocolate." I get up and head back to the office. "I'll get you one. I'm making me one, anyway."

I need a drink myself as this man has my insides all wiggly. It's a thing I find quite annoying.

And I happen to have a secret stash of alcohol hidden in an ordinary milk carton that Cletus would never touch. After I fill two disposable cups with coffee, I open the milk container and pour some Baileys into each cup and give them a stir with my finger.

I don't think Mr. Beg Me For A Date, will mind.

. . .

As I walk back into the waiting room, he looks up from the magazine he's holding and his eyes roam all over me. It makes my insides wiggle even more and I hope this drink knocks the wiggles away.

I lean in close to whisper so Cletus won't hear, "There is some alcohol in here, but don't say anything about it or my secret stash will be history."

"Now we both have secrets to keep," he says with a smile.

"That we do, Benny," I say then tap the side of my cup to his and we each take a sip.

I watch his expression as he pulls the cup away from his very firm lips. They're as chiseled as the rest of his face is. Hard corners in some places, soft curves in others.

The man is a mixture of hard and soft all over his body. And from what I've seen so far, his personality is that way too.

"You like it?" I ask and wait.

He nods and runs his hand up my arm. "Thanks, I've needed something to knock the edge off."

His touch is making my wiggling insides go into a full roll and I take a step back, trying hard not to let him see how he's affecting me. I turn and walk back to my seat. "You're welcome."

I don't know what's wrong with me. It's not like I don't see hot guys every single day. He's just another one.

After another sip I find myself very curious and ask him, "So, being a lawyer, how have you managed to keep that beard you have there?"

He gets up and brings his coffee with him then leans on the counter. "I started growing it a year ago just for this trip. It was difficult to get to keep it. Until I came up with the reason I needed to."

His finger moves in a circle around the top of his cup and I find myself wondering what that finger would feel like as it moved in just that fashion around my nipple.

Damn it!

I look into his eyes to stop myself from daydreaming such dangerous dreams. "So what was your reason?"

"Beard products and potentially harmful effects of them. I'm supposed to be writing a legal report once my research is finished," he says with a smile.

"Is the gang a part of your legal research too?" I ask then take a sip of the coffee I wish was straight whiskey as he's doing such a number on me it's making me seriously think about accepting his dinner invitation and a whiskey would remind me that I don't date.

"No. No one knows about my involvement with them." He smiles and winks. "Now you know another big secret about me. It's time for you to let me in on another one of yours, so we can stay even here."

Looking into those piercing eyes has me feeling a bit freer than I usually do and I just say what's crossing my mind, "Pain excites me."

His eyebrows raise and he laughs as he says, "I'll bring my whip then."

I go all wet again and it makes me really mad at myself. So I add, "But I never give in, Benny. Sorry, the answer is still, no."

He sighs and picks his coffee cup up and walks away, going back to sit on the sofa. "Have you ever heard the expression, cut your nose off to spite your face, Angel?"

I nod and look back at the computer screen that's blinking like crazy so I hit the side of the old monitor and it goes all the way black. "Shit!"

"Did you break it?" he asks as he gets back up and comes right back behind the counter and looks at the black screen.

"Maybe," I say and take a step back.

He looks the whole thing over then looks at the back of the monitor and pushes the cord that's connected to it in a bit and presto, the screen is back. He looks over at me with a huge smile, like he's saved the damn day or something.

"There you go. Computer repair services are not my usual thing, but I will accept a dinner date in lieu of cash." His hand rests on my shoulder and I have to fight the urge to lean in and kiss him.

His eyes hold mine for way too long before I manage to say, "How about you give me this one repair job for free. You know, to keep me coming back for more."

"No. I want to take you to dinner. I'm done taking no for an answer, Angel." He stares hard into my eyes.

A shiver runs through me as I see it there in his eyes. He has the ability to make me do things. Bend me, form me, rule me.

"You have to take it, Benny. That's all I'm giving you. No, thank you."

My uncle walks into the waiting room and looks at us with his small dark eyes narrowed. "What's up?"

Shaking off the ominous vibe this man is giving me, I answer, "I thought I had broken your computer, Uncle Phil. But Blaze here figured out the cord was just loose. He saved you a few hundred bucks as I don't think I would've ever thought of that and I would've told you it was time for a new computer."

HIS EYES GO BACK to normal and he reaches out to shake Blaze's hand. "Thanks, Blaze. Is that what she called you? I thought I heard her calling you something else."

"She's made up a nickname for me, it seems. But Blaze is what I'm called. And you are Uncle Phil. It's very nice to meet you. I was just asking your niece out to dinner this evening," he says as he cuts his eyes back at me.

So I finish for him and say, "But I told him no. I know how you don't like me to date the customers, Uncle Phil."

My uncle looks at Blaze for a good long moment then he shocks me as he says, "This guy would be okay, Angel. You have my approval to accept his invitation."

"What?" I say and take a couple of steps back. "No! Rules are rules after all."

Blaze looks back at my uncle and asks, "What's her favorite type of food?"

"Italian. Anything Italian," my backstabbing uncle says. "Your bike is just about ready." He walks away, leaving us alone again.

"He likes me, Angel. What do you think about that? Maybe I'm not so bad after all," he says then goes back to sit on the sofa.

"You are bad. You are leaving. And you are not getting me to go with you anywhere. I'm not the kind of girl who likes to become a notch on any man's bedpost." I go back to typing in the parts I have to order as this guy has been keeping me off task for over an hour now.

"You sure do jump to some massive conclusions there, Angel. I asked you to dinner not to join me in my motel room." He laughs and picks up the magazine he's been pretending to read.

"Right, Benny. Getting me into your bed isn't on your mind at all," I say as I roll my eyes.

HE LOWERS the magazine with a Harley like mine on the cover. All I can see are his eyes. His dangerously intriguing eyes. "It's not. But it seems to be all you can think about."

My cheeks heat with embarrassment. How did the fucker get me on this end of this deal?

I've told the man I like pain and now he knows I'm thinking

about him and me in bed and fucking like a couple of rabid animals.

Fuck!

I walk out of the room and go to the bathroom to readjust myself. Looking in the mirror, I see the reflection of a young woman with a lot going on inside her head.

Maybe it's been too long since I had sex with a real man. The machines can't hold you. They can't tell you sweet words. They can't handle you roughly and make you beg them to keep going or stop.

Maybe I should get laid. Not by that guy!

Not him. I think he has the power to break my heart. I know he does as a matter of fact.

BUT MAYBE SOME other random stranger is going to be necessary to get myself back under control. If this guy can get me so hot and bothered with so little fucking effort, I must be a walking time-bomb, waiting to explode all over some poor schmuck.

With a crack of my neck and my knuckles, I walk back out to find my uncle chatting it up with Blaze who has his jacket back on and is signing the bill.

"This is a very reasonable bill, Phil. Thanks for the break in the labor cost," Blaze says as he barely looks up at me when I walk in. "You want to run that transaction for me real quick, Sweetie?"

Sweetie!

I don't say a word though as my uncle disappears back to the garage with a smile on his face. I simply punch in the price and send it to the merchant services site and wait for an approval code.

His hand is resting on the bill and I need it to write the code down on it. But I wait for him to move his hand. Which he doesn't do.

"Can I have that, please?" I ask very politely.

"Come and take it," he says.

I look at him to find him smiling with a shit eating grin. So I move my hand slow and deliberate over his and slide the piece of paper out from under his hand.

Electricity flares through me, but I try desperately to ignore it and keep my eyes steady. His blue eyes flash and his grin disappears.

He feels this too!

I watch as his lips tremble a little. "Come on, Angel. Let me take you to dinner. Just dinner. Anywhere you want. Please."

With a shake of my head, I say the words again, "No, thank you."

I can't let him take me to dinner because it will be me who makes the next move and takes him to bed. I can feel it inside me.

I want him like I've never wanted a man in my life. He's everything I want all wrapped up in a very nice package.

Gorgeous with a dangerous edge. Muscles, tats, great personality. The ability to make me feel as if I'm coming unglued right in front of him.

How he could make me scream and beg is obvious. And I can't do that.

So I just give the top of his hand a quick pat. "There are plenty of females waiting for you out there, Benny. Go pick one out and she'll give you what you're looking for."

In a quick movement, he has my hand in his as he looks at me with an unwavering stare. "Angel, I did come here with the main plan to bed as many women as humanly possible. That is a fact. But now that I've met you, I want only you. I can't explain why, but I do. I want to spend every minute I can with you. I'm not feeding you a line. It's completely true. I don't do this. I don't ask women out. I usually don't even hold any kind of real conversation with one unless I'm drinking. You do something to me. I want to spend some real time with you and see what this is all about."

He seems so genuine. And it's hard not to give in to him. But he's a walking heartbreak for me.

"You seem like a good guy, you do. Benny, I am broken. A piece of china held together by only a bit of Elmer's glue. I have to guard myself. I know you don't understand and I don't expect you to. Please understand this is not personal. If I was a different person, I'd accept your offer in a heartbeat. But I am who I am. A product of what my past has made me." I pull my hand from his and look away.

"Don't think of yourself like that, Angel. No one is completely broken. You aren't as fragile as you think you are. Maybe we're supposed to help one another. I don't know. I just know I have a strong pull toward you. Stronger than anything I've ever felt. Now, if you can look me in the eye and tell me you don't feel a damn thing, then I'll leave you alone."

I look anywhere but at him as I don't know if I can look at him and lie. I do feel a strong pull to him. It's more than a mere attraction. He's hot and all but it's deeper than that.

Dangerously deep.

My body freezes as he takes me by the chin and makes me look at him. His eyes search mine. Then the alarm goes off on my phone and we both look at it as it vibrates along with the sound and moves over the counter top.

"That's my alarm. Time to go." I pick up my phone and take a step back, breaking away from his hold on me.

I grab my keys and helmet from under the counter and spin around on my heel and take off. Without saying a word, I walk out of the shop and quickly get onto my bike.

With one quick kick, I start it and take off. I can feel his eyes burning a hole into my back.

This feels all wrong, but I'm doing it, anyway. Riding away from the man who could be the one for me...

5

BLAZE

I watch her ride away as I stand at the glass door of her uncle's shop. She leans over a bit as she leaves the parking lot and takes a right. The sound as someone clears their throat has me turning back around and finding her Uncle Phil standing there, looking at me.

"Is she still saying, no?" he asks me as he rummages around behind the counter.

"Yep." I turn back to watch her until she completely disappears. "Do I have a chance in hell?" I turn back to him.

He shrugs his shoulders. "The girl isn't into bikers. Now if you were a doctor or a lawyer, you might stand a chance."

His words perk me up. "I am a lawyer. She knows that."

"And still no, huh?" he asks with a little shake of his head. "Maybe it's the clothes you're wearing. You may be reminding her of the guy who broke her heart a couple of years ago when he up and left her to travel the world or some shit."

"Do I look like him?" I ask as I'm wondering if that's why she's so dead set against getting to know me.

"No. He had dark hair and was shorter than you. Just the biker thing. Gage, really did a number on her. The two were inseparable for a few years. I know at least I thought they would get married one day. So when he made this odd move to leave and leave her behind it threw her for a loop." He looks up at me and smiles. "But you never heard that from me. Got me?"

I nod. "Is she coming back today?"

"Yeah, it's just her lunch break. She'll be back in an hour. Why? You planning on giving it another shot?" he asks as he picks up the empty coffee cup she left on the counter and tosses it in the trash.

"I'M CERTAINLY THINKING ABOUT IT." I step away from the counter and go to the door. "See you in a little while, Uncle Phil."

"Bye, kid. Good luck," he says as I leave.

Getting on my bike, I start it up and find it feels normal again and head over to the motel to change clothes.

If she wants a lawyer, I can give her that.

The small not so fancy motel is just up the street a bit and I find Rod and Ashley pulling in at the same time I am. We get off our bikes and all go inside the main lobby to get the keys to our rooms.

"You booked a room here too, I see," I say as I hold the door open for them to go inside first.

Rod's hand on Ashely's ass has me wondering how they've managed to keep a spark going between them for as long as they have. After we all check in, the desk clerk tells us that there are free cocktails in the little lounge next to the office.

Never ones to not partake of free anything, we three head that way and find some beers on ice in a large silver bucket. I grab three, handing them each one.

"I've been needing a beer since before I got into town," I say and pour the golden miracle down my parched throat.

We all take seats, them on the love seat and me in the chair near them. Rod takes a drink then says, "So what was wrong with your ride?"

"Air suspension leak. The girl who works at the garage diagnosed it very quickly with no help from me at all. I actually forget what the hell was wrong with it when I laid my eyes on her." I take another long drink, draining the can and get up and grab another.

"She rattled you, huh?" Rod asks and looks at his wife. "I know that feeling."

She gives him a dark look and then smiles. "Me too."

Taking a seat again, I open the cold beer and ask, "So how did you know you were meant to be together? Was it love at first sight, or did you grow on each other?"

Rod's smile moves over his entire face as he looks at his wife. "I went looking on the internet for a woman who was into the same things I was. It was a thing the girl I was hung up on told me I should do. She was right, and I found this one after only minutes of looking over the various profiles. I knew she was it the second I saw her picture."

Ashley takes up the story as she runs her hand over his thigh and looks into his eyes, "He sent me a message and when I saw his picture I knew I was very interested. When I read his likes and dislikes, I knew we'd get along."

"And man did we get along!" he says as he squeezes her thigh.

Ashley looks at me with a grin and says, "From the moment this man touched me, I knew he was the one."

I take a drink and look at Rod. "Was that the same for you?"

He nods. "And every day has been the best of my life."

"So you two believe in love at first sight then?" I ask as I find this very interesting.

They both nod and then they kiss for only a moment. Rod looks back at me. "Why so interested, Blaze?"

"The chick at the shop got my plans for this trip all going out the window. There's something about her that has me feeling all crazy. When our hands met, it was like electricity shot through me. When she laughed I found my heart beating harder. The thought ran through my head that I couldn't live a day without hearing that sound. That wonderful sound." I pull the can up to my mouth again then set it back down without taking another drink.

Ashley watches me and asks, "So when are we going to meet her?"

With a sigh, I answer, "Not sure you will. She told me, no, when I asked her out to dinner."

"Damn!" Rod says then laughs. "You sure she's on the same page you are?"

I nod. "She is. I could see it in her frightened eyes. She was hurt by a biker a couple of years ago. Thought it was the real thing but one day he told her he was out of there and never came back. He left her behind and I think she thinks all men are like that."

Ashley nods, knowingly. "And you're only in town for the rally then you're gone too. I see her point."

"Me too. But I also think if she'd allow us to spend some time together that things could be worked out if we are the ones for each other. But she isn't about to even see what happens between us." I pick up the beer and take the drink I put off a second ago.

This all seems so hopeless to me. I should forget about her and go to the bar and pick up some loose chick and forget about her. Forget about Angel. Forget about what might be.

. . .

Rod stands up and pulls Ashley with him. "We're off to get cleaned up and rest a bit before tonight's crazy activities. If you want my advice, I'd say to turn up your inner alpha and don't give her a choice."

I nod as they walk past me then look at Ashley as she runs her hand along my shoulder. "Blaze, you can get through to her. If it's real, you can break that barrier she's set up to protect herself. I know you can. See you later, Brother."

"Later," I say and finish the beer, then make my way to my room.

As I walk inside, I see the box that was delivered. I open it and take the clothes out and hang them all up. Then, in the bottom, I see the shit load of rubbers and the padded cuffs.

I take them out and put them in one of the drawers then I take the small whip out and the edible strawberry panties and add them to the drawer. The tube of antibiotic ointment with painkiller I put in the bathroom, and then look at myself in the mirror.

"Who are you, Benjamin Franklin Worthington of the Manhattan Worthington's?"

The tattoos on both arms have remained hidden from my family for the last three years since I started getting them. Suits successfully keep them hidden from judgmental view.

And for a moment, I think about not giving this chick what I think she wants. A successful man who she can have faith in. Build trust in. Fall in love with.

That man is me but not exactly the real me. But neither is Blaze.

I'm this man who seems to be searching for a middle ground. Somewhere between rogue gang biker and billionaire lawyer.

The way she calls me Benny has me thinking that she just

might be the one to help me pull my two worlds together in some way.

Angel is this smart woman who's about to hold a Master's Degree in Engineering. Something that my family would respect.

But she also is this motorcycle-riding woman with no financial stability. Something my family would hate.

She'd definitely be a woman in the middle of the two worlds that I'm a part of. Smart, spunky, but also fragile and afraid.

Maybe I could help her close the gap between her two worlds. Show her that there's no reason to think of herself as broken just because some numb-nuts, who was not meant for her anyway, left her to roam the world on his own.

She was meant for someone else. She was meant for me.

AFTER A NICE HOT shower to remove the grime of the road, I put on a nice pair of black Armani slacks and a light blue button-down shirt that I think accents my eyes and I hope Angel notices that.

Back into the shop, I go in with a bouquet of flowers I stopped and bought for her. The bell dings as I enter the waiting room and find no one around.

Before I can call out, she comes up the stairs out of the bay and stops when she sees me. The way her mouth hangs open has me bubbling on the inside as I know that my new appearance is affecting her in all the right ways.

"HEY, ANGEL." I walk toward her, holding out the flowers. "I brought you a little something for your desk, or counter or whatever you call this place you work at."

She takes them from me and walks behind the counter,

placing them on it and leaning in to smell them. "These are nice. Thank you."

Not really knowing what else to do, I stuff my hands in my pockets. I thought she might get all gushy and realize she should let me take her to dinner. But she's just being really quiet.

"You're welcome. I felt like you helped me out earlier with my bike and helped me not get screwed over on the price. I owed you something nice for the nice thing you did for me."

She smiles but doesn't look at me. "It's my job, Benny."

"Not entirely, it's not. So how was lunch?" I ask, as I'm going nowhere with this woman.

"Fine. I had a turkey on wheat at home." She starts tapping at the computer keyboard in an effort to act busy I bet.

"I thought I'd try my hand at dinner again. I thought I'd show you what I'd look like when you and I go somewhere nice. Not the old biker guy. The lawyer part of me. You know that's me too, Angel." I find myself rocking back and forth a bit and stop as it might make me look a little nervous. That has to stop.

I *am* nervous but I don't want her to see that.

Finally, she looks me over and says, "You do clean up well, Benny."

"And I bet you do too, Angel. So what do you say to a nice evening out together where we can get to know one another better?" I ask as I take a step back so she can really take me all in.

WHEN SHE LOOKS at me I nearly want to jump over the counter and pull her into my arms because I see the fear there and I want to hug it out of her.

"I really do love the flowers. You keep taking this personally even though I've told you countless times not to. I don't date. End of story. You look great, both ways. Hot biker guy and hot billionaire. You're sure to find a woman, Blaze, or Benjamin, or whoever you are right now." She stifles a laugh and I find myself pissed off.

"I'm both," I say with a snippy tone to my voice. "I'm sure you aren't always Miss Motorcycle Mechanic Chick. There has to be a frilly little female inside of you that you let come out on occasion."

Those pretty eyes get hard in an instant and now I'm sorry I copped that attitude with her. One long finger points at me as her plum colored lips open and say, "Look here, dude, I don't need to explain myself to you or anyone. Be both guys. Be who the fuck ever you want to be. I'm me. Warts and all, I am just me."

"Angel, I didn't mean to make you..."

"Well, you did make me mad! You've pissed me off. Thanks for the flowers. And have a nice life. I've had enough fun for one fucking day." She walks over to the door that leads down the stairs to the bay and shouts, "I'm out of here for the day, Uncle Phil. See you tomorrow."

I hear him shout out a goodbye then she's back grabbing her helmet and keys and hauling ass past me. Taking my hands out of my pockets, I grab her arm as she comes by me.

HER EYES ARE SO full of anger it really makes no sense. "Hey, I'm just asking you out on a fucking dinner date. Shit, Angel! The theatrics are over the top."

"And I'm just politely refusing. Why can't you take no for an answer?" Her foot taps on the linoleum floor with a loud sound.

It's like counting off the seconds until she erupts again.

This woman needs to get laid so bad it's not even funny!

. . .

"ONE KISS, Angel. If you feel nothing, I'll leave you alone," I find myself saying and have no idea where that came from.

"Ha!" She jerks her arm out of my grip. "Ha!" She walks out of the door, leaving me standing there like an idiot.

I push open the door as she climbs onto her bike. "Angel, just one."

She looks at me with a smile and makes the damn one-syllable laugh again then starts the engine and peels off.

I guess I'm about to turn into a fucking stalker over this trick!

6

ANGEL

Why does this town have to be so damn busy and full of cruising bikers?

I'm mad and just want to get home and get away from all men.

Why did he have to show up there looking like a million bucks? Why did he have to show me the other part of him that I'll be missing since I can't have him in my life forever?

That man is fucking hot as shit in his tight black leather and dressed up too. It's not fair, really. Successful businessman one minute, dangerous biker the next.

It's just not fair!

And the other thing that isn't fair is how he wants to show me these two fantastic sides of him. Him! A man who will only be around a short time then poof, he'll be gone. Back to New York to hobnob with the upper class.

What a jackass!

Who does that to someone? Who shows a girl what all she can't have?

. . .

Sure, I could have him for a night. I might even have been able to hang onto him for his whole visit here. But then he has to go back and here is where I'll stay.

I'm nowhere near the class I'm sure he's expected to marry into. Not born wealthy. Not schooled in aristocratic snobbery. Not perfect by any means.

There will never be a wedding announcement in the New York Times where it reads; Billionaire, Benjamin Franklin Worthington of the Manhattan Worthington's and Angel, no middle name, Jennings of the middle of nowhere, Jennings' are happy to announce their impending nuptials.

No, that will not be a thing which would ever be allowed by such a high profile family.

So why is he so adamant in taking me to dinner? Or kissing him? Or any of it?

The damn crowd of slow-moving bikers is serving to piss me off even more and I find myself cussing under my breath constantly. Finally, I see a break and dash through it.

The traffic thins to nearly nothing as I get to the outskirts of town and see my home. My little white wood frame rental with the pink shutters on the front windows and the green front door.

THE WHITE PICKET fence surrounding the small home keeps my dog safely inside it. And there she is, popping her little body up as she hears my bike coming home.

Her happy yaps make my anger ebb and when I pull up and get off my bike, frantic wags of her short tail make me laugh.

"Hey, Cuddles? Did you miss Mommy? I was home just a couple of hours ago."

I open the gate, walk my bike up and park it next to the stairs that lead up to the small front porch that I have two white rocking chairs on.

Those are our chairs where we spend most evenings enjoying the sun which sets on this side of the house. I take mine and she jumps up on hers as I pet her soft whitish fur. "You need a bath, Cuddles."

She barks a bit as if agreeing with me. I pick her up and hug her as she licks my face. "Mommy had a very bad day. A mean man bugged her a lot today to go to dinner with his gorgeous ass. He thinks Mommy can handle having him for only a little while before she has to let him go again. But Mommy can't handle that at all."

Her little yappy bark tells me she understands completely and her lick on my lips, while gross, tells me she's there for me and always will be.

The sound of a bike coming makes me look up. Not many of the visitors come out this far. There's nothing to see out here.

I gulp as I recognize the bike and the bearded man in Armani slacks who's riding it.

"WHAT THE FUCK does he think he's doing?"

I put Cuddles down so she can try to keep him from getting through my gate. She barks and runs like a maniac to guard the gate as he pulls to a stop in front of it.

He climbs off his bike and opens one of the compartments on one side and pulls out a large grocery bag. It's green and environmentally safe. So that means he's worried about our planet.

Great, another wonderful thing about the man who will never be mine!

I watch and wait for my little dog to rip his expensive slacks as he opens the gate and then my mouth drops open in disbelief as my vicious guard poodle mix jumps up and down in excitement over the strange man.

He smiles and catches her up in one arm as she jumps into it like she's always known him.

"Who are you?" he asks in the little sweet tone everyone talks to animals and babies in.

"Her name is Cuddles, and she usually hates men. All of them," I say as he walks up the stairs.

I have yet to get out of the rocking chair. He places the dog on my lap and smiles at me, then of all things, tweaks my nose as if I'm some cute little kid. "Just like her Momma."

I set my jaw tight and glare at him. "Yep."

He cocks his head to one side.

"Well, aren't you going to let me in so I can make you dinner? I brought the things to make spaghetti and meatballs."

"I do believe I told you no about a hundred times, Benny." I continue to glare at him and he acts like he doesn't see it at all.

"You told me no to taking you out. You never said no to me cooking you dinner at your place. No, not once did you tell me no about that." He smiles and his whole demeanor tells me he's so proud of himself for coming up with the technical loophole he's found.

I stand up as it's obvious this lawyer is so ahead of me it's not even funny. As I unlock the door I say, "You didn't ask that or I would've told you no to that too." I hold out my arm as a gesture for him to go inside.

"LADIES FIRST, MY ANGEL." His smile is so wide I want to knock it right off his handsome face.

I walk in muttering to myself, "His Angel. Really!"

Cuddles bounces around his legs as he comes in and I find myself pissed at my dog for the first time ever.

"She's adorable. I usually don't like animals in the house, but she's like a little person, isn't she?" he asks as he sets the bag on the tiny countertop.

"Yes, she is like a little traitorous bitch, that one," I say as I look around the room to make sure that there are no unmentionables lying around.

I do live alone and on more than one occasion have slipped out of my bra while watching television and left it lying around. My sweep of the area doesn't show me anything I need to rush to hide so I look at my dog.

The pop of a cork makes me look at him, the man who can't take no for an answer, as he opens up a bottle of red wine. "I'll just let this breathe while I'm cooking." He pulls a six pack of beer out and breaks a couple off and hands me one after he opens it for me. "Here you go, my lady. Go take a load off and watch some television. I can find what I need in here."

With a shrug of my shoulders, I do what he's said. The beer is good and cold and goes down easy. I watch my dog helping the intruder find things.

Keeping the television low, I listen as he talks to my dog, "Cuddles, huh? I like something a little bit tougher. How about Rambo?"

"She's a girl!" I call out. "And you can't come into someone's home and immediately rename their dog, Benny." I take another drink of the beer and find him smiling.

He waves a wooden spoon my way as he says, "So how long do we have to be together before I can do that then?"

I look away and mumble, "More than five minutes."

After a little bit of clanking of pots and pans as he gets together what he needs to make dinner, he comes into the room, wearing my white, frilly apron.

I nearly spit out the beer I had just drank as he takes a seat on the coffee table I have my feet propped up on. His long fingers begin to untie my boots as he looks at me. "You've had a long day, haven't you? Let me get these off for you, my Angel."

"Yes, I did. There was this weirdo who asked me out over and over all day and made it one hell of a brutal day, Babycakes." I laugh then take another drink, finishing the beer off. "Wanna beer me again, Pumpkinhead?"

He pulls off both boots then holds his hand out for the empty can. "I do want to beer you again. And I will, after you shower."

He takes my hand and somehow leads me right to the little bathroom that's just outside my bedroom door. In he goes, pulling me along behind him.

Reaching into the small stand-up shower he starts the water. Then he turns to me. "Dinner will be ready in about a half-hour. So don't stay in here forever, my Angel."

The bathroom is very small and his body grazes mine as he walks past me to leave. I have to hold myself steady using the sink so I don't fall into his arms.

He closes the door and I fall to sit on the closed toilet as my knees give out.

What is he doing to me?

PULLING MY CLOTHES OFF, I climb into the shower and put it on straight cold water. I have got to calm down!

After a quick shower, I get out and wrap myself in a towel and head to my bedroom to find something to put on. I settle on a pair of cotton shorts and a little pullover T-shirt with the only clean bra I have left, a black lacy thing that can be seen through the shirt.

It's sexy but not over the top sexy. I could go out there in overalls and army boots and the man is still going to attempt to get into my panties. Which are black lace too.

Giving my freshly shampooed hair a nice scrunching, I make my way out to the living room with a freshly washed and make-up free face and find him sitting on the sofa, petting my dog and sipping on a beer.

His eyes go all over me and his mouth hangs open a bit. "Wow!"

I roll my eyes. "Come on, Benny! I have on no make-up. My hair's a tasseled mess. My clothes are five years old. What's to say wow about? Unless it's like 'wow, what a mess'."

He gets up and walks toward me, but I hold up my hand stopping him as he looks like he's about to pick me up into his arms and hug the shit out of me.

He stops and says, "It's a wow, you're really gorgeous. Even without a stitch of make-up or your hair in that pretty braid, you're still fucking hot as shit, Angel. I swear it's that kind of wow."

I look at him and shake my head slowly. Like I said, I could've come out in anything and he'd have acted this way.

It's just an act. He'll say all the right things in order to get to the goods.

"Whatever. So, are there any beers left?" I ask as I start to walk to the kitchen.

He turns and hurries in front of me. "Sit, and I'll get you one."

"I can..."

He stops and turns back. He's too close and I feel my heart speed up. I step back and shut my mouth.

"I know you can," he says. "But tonight, I want to wait on you. I wanted to take you out and let someone wait on you. But you refused, so now it's me who will be your personal servant for the evening."

Walking around the other way to sit on the sofa, I say, "I see." I sit down and look at the television to find he's put it on one of my all-time favorite shows that makes me laugh even when I don't want to.

He comes back and hands me a new beer. "You can change it if you want. I just put it here because I love this crazy show. It's hilarious."

I LOOK up at him and want to slap the shit out of him because the fucker is perfect for me. Instead, I say, "It's one of my favorites."

A grin spreads over his face. "Cool. See, we like the same things. I also happen to love spaghetti. And it's nearly ready. I'll bring our plates in here so we can watch the show together and laugh our asses off while we eat. K?"

I nod and sit back then watch his fine ass walk away. "You know, you're going to make someone a great wife one day, Benny!"

He laughs and says, "Thanks. And you'll make someone a great hubby who comes home from work all grumpy and has them jumping through hoops to cheer him up."

And then he goes and makes me feel bad about how I'm acting.

Motherfucker!

HE'S DONE SO many nice things for me today and I've been an uber-bitch the whole time. So I take a drink and get up and go to the kitchen to find him plating up the food.

"Hey," I say and he looks at me.

"Hey, what do you need, Angel?"

I take the three steps to close the gap between us as he turns toward me and run my arms around him and hug him.

His arms move around my body and hold me in a nice loose hug.

"I'm sorry about being such an ungrateful bitch. I really do love those flowers. They're the first ones I've ever been given. And no one has ever gone out of their way to do all this before. You're a great guy. I'll rein in the attitude and make this a lot better evening for you."

I feel a wet tongue on my toes as Cuddles licks me and gives me kisses for doing the right thing. I laugh as it tickles and let him out of the hug.

I find his expression full of sincerity. "Thanks, Angel. I know that took a lot for you to say. Let's just have a nice time then. That's all I ever wanted was to show you a nice time."

I smile then turn away to go back to the living room, then say over my shoulder, "Well, I might as well enjoy this while I can. You'll be gone soon."

"Yeah, I won't be in your hair for too long, Baby." Then he gives my ass a swift smack.

Oh hell!

7

BLAZE

The change in her attitude lets me know the girl I'm so attracted to is in there somewhere. Trapped behind the walls she built because of that idiot who left her.

I have patience, though. And when I see something I want, I have a phenomenal amount of it.

Taking our plates to the living room, I place them on the coffee table then go get the wine and a couple of glasses. As I fill the glasses, I catch her gazing at me.

"Not quite the guy who came in the shop this afternoon. That badass biker was searching for some easy chick to play with his ding-a-ling. Not waiting on an uber-bitch hand and foot," she says and I flinch with her blatant honesty.

I sit down next to her. Close but not so close our legs touch. Holding up my glass, I gesture for her to pick hers up. She does and I tap mine to hers. "Angel, what you say is true. I came to Sturgis for all the wrong reasons, but then I found you and now I know why I was called to this Mecca in the middle of nowhere. It was you I was always drawn to this place for and nothing else."

. . .

She looks at me for a moment and her eyes go soft then she smiles and nods. "And you, my sweet prince on a bike from Heaven, came to find this lonely wretched woman who longed for you to find her and take her away from the lonely existence she had placed herself in."

We tap the glasses once more and take a drink. She places her glass on the table then pats the top of my leg. "Let's eat. It looks great, Benny."

I know those words we each said may have come out kind of like we were making them up and joking. But I think we both meant what we said.

I stab a meatball and hold it to her lips. She smiles then opens her mouth and takes it. A growly moan comes out of her and she nods as she chews. "It's good. Did you make these in my kitchen? There's no way!"

"You're right. There is no way," I say with a laugh. "I bought them already made and simply heated them in the oven."

She laughs and bumps my shoulder with hers.

"At least you're honest. I'd have accepted the compliment and lied about making them."

"Nah, you wouldn't have," I say as I take a bite of one myself.

"Yes, I would. At last year's Christmas party at work, I didn't make anything and when Uncle Phil told me I had to bring a pumpkin pie, I went and bought one. I put it in a pie plate from home and took it. Everyone was talking about what a great pie it was and what was my recipe. I told them it was a secret my grandma had passed down to me. The secret was it was made by Mona from the local bakery. All I added was a tub of store bought whipped cream!"

Her laugh makes me want to kiss her and I wish it didn't. I want so badly to just hang out with her tonight. Let her know I really want to get to know her. The real her, not the front that she puts on to scare away pursuers.

"Minx," I say instead and tweak her cute little nose.

She wrinkles it up as I do and smiles. "I'm not a little kid."

No, she is not!

"I KNOW. But you're adorable and your laugh makes me feel good inside. You're sweet when you want to be." I take another bite as she watches me.

She takes a large forkful of spaghetti noodles and crams them into her mouth. A thing my family would find appalling. I find it funny as she just can't figure out when to stop twirling them around her fork.

So instead of showing her how it's done, I load my fork up and take a huge bite too.

She quirks one brow up and says, "Wanna see who can get the most meatballs to fit into their mouths?"

I nod. "Bet I beat you."

"Bet you don't." She stabs one and places it in her mouth.

I do the same then she places the second one in and so do I. A third one goes into her small mouth and I find a knot slipping down her throat and quickly chew mine up and swallow.

I point at her. "Cheater! I saw you let one slip down your throat!"

She chews the others up and swallows. "Damn! You're the first to catch me doing that!"

I want to kiss her long slender neck so damn bad it hurts. But I don't.

"So now I know, no more food challenges with you."

She shrugs her narrow shoulders. "I'm a sneaky one. You have to watch me."

"I can see that." I take a sip of wine and find we're both trying to grab the remote as one of the funniest parts of the show is coming up. "This is funny," I say.

At the same time, she says, "Have you ever seen anything so hilarious?"

We stop reaching for the remote and look at one another. Her lips are halfway pulled up to the left and her deep blue eyes aren't droopy like they were when she was at work.

Then she turns her head and looks at the television, only I can't stop looking at her. She watches the show and bursts out laughing and all I can do is look at her.

Watch her erupt into laughter. Watch her light up like a firework on the fourth of July.

Why on Earth would that dumbass leave her?

I'm glad he did, though. Because now I can make her mine. All mine, and forever, if she'll have me.

I finally turn my head to watch the show and we find ourselves laughing at the same times, over the same things. Taking bites and drinks at the same time.

We're like a couple of people who were part of the same puzzle but the pieces got mixed up for a long time then they finally figured out we belonged together.

Sitting back at exactly the same time as we've finished dinner, I look over at her to test our sameness. "I have a container of gelato in the freezer. You ready for some?"

She lays her head back on the sofa and rolls it toward me. "Not yet. It was so good, I'm stuffed. Later on, it would be great."

I knew it!

I always wait for a couple of hours after eating to eat desert too.

"Okay, let me know when you want some." I lay my head back too and look at her as she gazes at me.

"It's just that I always eat the sweets a bit later. So I can really enjoy them once my food has all settled. But I get it if you want to leave and get to the bar with your friends. I mean gang. Or whatever you call them. This was very nice of you, Benny," she says then puts her hand on my thigh.

Not in a, 'I want to grab your cock' kind of way. In a real way that says thank you for being nice to me.

"I'd like to hang out with you if you don't mind. You're a lot more stimulating than anyone out there." I place my hand over hers.

She stops rubbing my leg as her lips form a hard line. I think she's about to tell me to go. And I so do not want to go.

Then they soften and she smiles. "I'd like it if you stayed for a while longer."

Inwardly I'm hoping up and down with joy, outward I say, "Cool. Let's see what else is on tonight."

So my first night in Sturgis is going nowhere near what I had planned. First, I spent most of my day in a stinky garage. Second, I cooked for a woman who made sure I knew she didn't want to spend any time with me. And third, I will not be getting laid tonight.

It should feel like it all has gone wrong. But instead, it all feels more right than anything I've ever felt in my life.

She picks up the remote and searches for a movie and when she stops on my most favorite movie of all time, I don't say a word to let her know that.

With a look like she knows I'm about to make fun of her, she asks as she shakes her head, "You probably don't like the Johnny Depp, Willy Wonka, right?"

"I do."

Her face blossoms. "Want to watch this then?"

I nod. "Want to scoot over here and lie your head on my shoulder?"

She looks very wary. "Do you really like this movie? Like you aren't just telling me, yes and you secretly hate it?"

"When I saw you stop on it I was about to ask you if we could watch it. It's my absolute favorite. I shit you not."

With a press of the button, the movie comes on and she moves over next to me as I throw my arm along the back of the little blue sofa. Her body is close to mine. Her head is against my shoulder and I feel more at home than I have ever felt anywhere.

Including my own home!

I want to kiss the top of her head but don't. Her hand moves over my chest then she looks up at me.

"Benny, do you really want to be here, watching a silly movie rather than down at the bar having a crazy badass time?"

I nod. She just keeps looking up at me for the longest time. Then she places her head on my chest, near my heart.

Moving my arm, I wrap it around her and hold her tight to me. Then I do kiss the top of her head. "I like being here with you so much more, my Angel."

She sighs and turns up the television.

An hour into the show she sits up and stretches. "I'm getting kind of tired, Benny."

Shit, she's going to send me away!

"I see. Okay, well..."

She places her hand on my chest. "I don't mean you have to go. I mean can we stretch out on the couch. Lie down. Lie down on the couch together."

"Oh! Yeah, of course." I say as I kick off my shoes and get up so we can get more comfortable.

She stands up and looks me over. "You got underwear on?"

I nod. "Why?"

"You could get more comfortable. You know, get out of those clothes. They'll get all wrinkled if you don't," she says as she walks away. "I have to pee. Get as comfortable as you want. I'm going to grab a blanket I cover up with when I'm watching television on the sofa."

"Hey," I call out, making her stop. "If I'm stripping down to my underwear, I want you to as well. I don't want to be nearly naked all alone."

She hesitates then nods.

As soon as she disappears into the bathroom, I jump up and down and do a few fist pumps into the air. A very soft, "Yes," comes out of my mouth as I quickly undress.

Right down to my tight black, show it all off, boxer briefs. I lay my clothes out nice and neat on the chair and lie down on the sofa on my side, waiting for her to come back and slip into my arms.

Nothing has ever sounded more enticing than knowing I'm about to hold her as we watch the ending of Willy Wonka.

I know it sounds lame as shit. I know this. But damn it, I've never been more excited about anything in my life.

Nothing!

The light in the hallway goes off and she comes back with only the television giving off any light. My heart feels like it has stopped beating for a moment as I see her in a little black bra and panty set.

My dick gets hard immediately. So I take one of the pillows from behind me and strategically place it in front of my erection so when she lies back against me it doesn't make her jump up and decide that this is a bad idea.

Because this is a fucking awesome idea!

She tosses a little purple blanket over me then I fold it back and she lies down in front of me. I pull the blanket over her and cover her then drape my arm over her body.

"NICE LINGERIE SET," I say very matter of fact like. "I saw it in a Victoria's Secret catalog on some skinny ass blonde. You're pulling it off much better than she did."

She giggles a bit then says, "I didn't know Armani made underwear."

I give her a little squeeze. "If one can wear it, Armani makes it."

I lie my arm out and she lays her head on it. "I love this part when the girl gets fat and purple," she says.

"Me too. She's such a brat."

"Aren't they all! Except poor little Charlie."

Her skin is soft against my chest and stomach and my dick is growing in leaps and bounds.

This was an awful idea!

I don't know why I said it was a good idea. It was a terrible idea.

"My feet are cold," she says. "Mind heating them up for me real quick?"

She puts her ice cold foot between mine. "Whoa, that is cold." I pick up one leg. "Stick them both between my legs here. They'll be warm in no time."

They will, I'm sure, because she's making me hot without even trying!

"Thanks, Benny." She puts her feet between my calves and they're cold but it's like the best cold ever because she needs me. She needs me to warm her up in more ways than one.

I run my hand slowly up and down her arm as she lies on her side in front of me. She turns her face back a little. "You're very nice. You know that?"

"No, I'm not. You bring out this part of me that I really don't have normally."

SHE TURNS OVER. Her tits are right there, looking up at me just like her eyes are.

"Benny, do you have any want at all to kiss me?"

"I do," I say probably admit way too quickly. But it's the truth.

She licks her lips and I lick mine then I ease down until our mouths touch. It's amazing as sensations zip through me as if I'm being turned on for the first time.

Parts of me buzz that have never done that before. And I'm not what you'd call inexperienced.

I ease the kiss and look at her. She makes me so damn happy as she says, "Benny, you want to watch the rest of this in my room?"

Fuck yes, I do!

"If you really, really want to, I do," I say as I run my hand over her cheek.

She gets up and takes my hand then leads me to her bedroom. The door opens and there it is. Pink curtains and a fluffy pink carpeting. And a canopy bed with a black sheer cloth hung over it and a black bedspread with pink pillows at the top.

That is when I spot a set of silver handcuffs off the metal headboard. "Who are you inside, Angel?"

She says with a grin, "A little bit of Heaven and a little bit of Hell."

8

ANGEL

"Here's the deal, Benny," I tell him as I pull him further into my bedroom. "I know this can't last. I know you have to leave and go home or you may decide this night will be the only one. I know that. I understand that. But for tonight, I want to pretend."

"We can do that," he says as he fiddles with my bra strap. "But what if I don't want this for only one night, Angel?"

"We'll cross that bridge if and when we come to it. For tonight, I want to pretend you love me and will never leave me." I look straight into his sparkling blue eyes to gauge his reaction.

"Not a problem," he says with no sign of fear in his eyes.

"Okay, then. I like to get rough, so our safe word is ratatouille," I tell him and watch his eyes light up even more.

He unclasps my bra and pulls it off as he gazes at my breasts. "Got it. So if you're done with the talking we can get to the action."

I push his boxers down and see what I felt earlier. "Oh, yes. Let's stop talking now."

My hands move over the large and gorgeous appendage he

has as I go to my knees to worship his gift. His hands feel strong and demanding as they move through my hair.

My lips touch the tip and it makes him growl, "Yes, Angel."

Opening my mouth, I slide it over him and relish the soft skin which covers his steely hard cock. I moan as I move back and forth, licking and sucking in a gentle fashion.

No reason to get frantic yet. Who knows when I'll get to do this again after all?

He's very long and thick and only half of him fits. Until I take him all in and his cock moves down my throat after an initial gag reflex is overcome. His low moan tells me he likes it.

Up and down I go until I taste his pre-cum, then I move faster and suck harder. But he pulls my hair back hard, jerking me back. His eyes are dark as he looks down at me.

"I don't want to lose it just yet, my Angel."

I nod and wipe my mouth with the back of my hand as he pulls me up. He holds me tight to him as he breathes heavily. "That was very nice."

Running my arms around his neck, I lean in and press my lips behind his ear and whisper, "The moment I saw you I craved to feel the sting of your hand on my ass, Blaze."

TAKING A HANDFUL OF MY HAIR, he pulls my head back and grazes his teeth along my neck until he makes it all the way up to my ear. His breath is hot as he says, "I can make that happen for you, Baby."

Picking me up in his strong arms, he goes and sits on the edge of the bed and expertly turns me over and places me face down on his lap. I bite my lip in anticipation of the first strike.

His warm palm moves in a slow circle then it goes to one side of my panties and he rips it. Then he rips the other side too and pulls the torn panties off me. I flinch with the action that makes me ache. It's been so long since I was handled this way.

Small circles I can feel him rubbing all over my ass, prepping it for the first smack which I'm finding myself tensing up for. Finally, his hand leaves my ass and then he brings it down hard and fast.

"Again," I hiss.

He does it again and I go all wet inside and shaky with need. Then he makes three in rapid succession. Suddenly, he picks me up and tosses me on the bed.

"I have to taste you, Angel," he says with a husky deep tone, and I find him moving my legs apart and his face is quickly buried.

His tongue darts in and out of me as he moans. It sends a vibration through me and I have to take the sheet in my hands and pull at it to keep myself still so he can work his magic.

"Oh my God, Blaze!"

His fingers press into my ass as he lifts me up so he can go in deeper with his intimate kiss. I can't stop moaning then his mouth moves up, and he takes my swollen clit between his teeth and gives it a nip then runs his tongue back and forth until I can't take it anymore. "Benny!" I scream just as the climax takes me over.

His tongue goes back inside me to taste the juices then he's back up and looking at me very hungrily. "Please tell me you're on birth control."

I smile and say, "Please tell me you're free of diseases, motorcycle man."

"I am. I had a check-up a month ago. So we're good to go." He moves up my body as I draw my knees up.

With no hesitation at all, he moves his large cock into me and I moan louder than I ever have before.

It's like Heaven with him between my legs. His tight and

chiseled abs press against my stomach as he presses himself into me. "My God, Angel! You're so fucking tight. It has been years, hasn't it?"

"Not years," I moan. "A year and a half."

"You feel amazing." His lips touch my neck as he pumps himself into me.

It's been so long since I felt an actual flesh cock inside me and I never want it to end. I was kidding myself that a machine can do anything a man can. It's just not true.

His hot body glides over mine with every hard stroke. It feels so much better as his weight knocks the air out of me and I have to gasp to regain it.

His mouth on my neck is wet and hot as he bites and sucks it. He's going to leave marks all over me but that's okay. I decide to leave my nail tracks all over his back and rake them over him, making him groan.

My body begins to shake and I don't want to let it go yet so I say in a near-breathless voice, "Turn me over."

As he pulls back, I see his teeth clench and find myself thrown over and on my hands and knees. Then he slams into me, sending a scream out of my mouth.

I bury my face in a pillow and lean down. His cock goes even further into me, hitting new places with each savage thrust. It's beyond anything I've ever experienced before and I'm going to hate myself for letting this happen.

I will never be the same again.

But I'm not about to let the fact he won't always be mine stop me from appreciating this moment. The sounds he's making are animal-like and I have a feeling he's liking this a lot himself.

The way his hands feel as they grip my waist makes me feel like a rag-doll in them. He's all muscles and all man. And right now, he's all mine.

My body shudders as I hold back the orgasm that's knocking

at my door. I don't want to let go without him so I pull my head up and say, "Benny, turn me over and make love to me."

He pulls out and I lie on my stomach. Gently he turns me over and pushes my hair back off my face.

The way he's looking down at me makes my insides even meltier. His lips touch mine very softly as he moves his cock back inside me and makes long slow strokes.

I run my hands up his arms, resting them on his large biceps. His tongue moves over my lips, tracing them. I part them for him and he moves inside and twirls his tongue around mine.

It's slow and easy and perfect. My heart is pounding and aching and I really want to cry because if he wants to do this more than this one time, I am going to start falling in love with him.

I know I will.

He pulls his mouth off mine and looks at me. Then it happens as I look into those penetrating blue eyes, a tear escapes me and he sees it.

A SWEET KISS on my cheek takes it away. I whisper, "Tell me you love me, Benny."

His lips touch my ear. "I love you, my Angel."

"Tell me you'll never leave me, Benny."

"I'll never leave you, my Angel." His lips press against my neck as more tears slip away from me and I know I'm lost in this man.

And for reasons I cannot understand, the tears grow in quantity. Rivers flow out of me as he moves so slowly in and out of me then I feel the first jerk of his cock and my insides go crazy.

"Harder," I hiss.

He moves harder and faster then I feel the wave crest and once it crashes, his does too.

The first spurt of hot cum shoots into me after more than a year. My body falls completely apart as it does. The orgasm will not quit. I pulse and writhe under him to get him to release everything he has.

Every hot spurt, I can feel inside me. And then I'm sobbing. Hard and heavy, I'm crying and it's loud and awful.

My entire body is going against me. Letting it all out like it never has.

"Shh, it's all going to be alright. I have you, Angel," his words are soft against my neck. "I won't leave you. I promise."

I cry harder with the lies that he's telling me but I hold him tight to me. I want to believe him, but I know he's just saying what he thinks I want to hear.

"Let me up, Benny," I manage to get out of my crying mouth. "Let me go."

"No," he says as he holds me. "I'm not letting you run away from this. You need this, Angel. You need me."

"No!" I shout and cry harder somehow. "Don't make me need you! Damn it! This was a terrible idea!"

"Shh. It was the best thing in the world for you, Baby. I'm the best thing in the world for you." Gentle kisses he trails over my neck and face until he gets to my trembling lips.

My mouth is very traitorous and opens in want for his kiss. My hands I also find going against me as they move over his head, holding him to me as I kiss him hard and wanting.

My body wants his so completely, and it's making me furious.

I knew this would happen. I knew it!

The tears dry up as he kisses me hard. Finally, he pulls back and looks at me with a fire in his eyes.

"Angel, this is not over. Do you understand me? This isn't a one-time thing. And I am not a man who shares. You are mine."

"Benny..."

One finger is pressed against my lips. "You are mine. This is not over."

I blink and look off as I have no idea of what to say. This will be over sometime. It will end. Am I to play the girlfriend role for however long he's in town then go back to my normal and very lonely life?

"Say it," he tells me with a very stern expression. "Tell me who you belong to, Angel."

I swallow hard. "But..."

He smacks the side of my ass hard and it sends a jolt of pain and heat through me. His eyes go very hard as he says in a low growl, "Who do you belong to?"

"You," I say and want to smack myself for being so forthcoming with him.

So quick to hand myself over to him and he will torture me for it. Some of it will be sweet but in the end, it will hurt like hell. And he's not a man that I will get over easily at all.

He kisses me again. Hard and hot. My hands run down his back as his cock grows inside me again.

Moving back and forth inside me, he stokes the fire again and I'm arching up to meet every savage thrust he gives me. When his mouth leaves mine it is because neither of us can breathe worth a damn. I find myself screaming, "Fuck me, Blaze! Fuck me!"

My entire body is on fire for him. In and out with hard thrusts he goes, then one word comes out of his mouth. "Cum."

Like it's been conditioned to do what he's said, my body explodes on his command. I shriek with the ecstasy that's flowing through me and find him climaxing as well.

Our bodies are sweaty and the smell of sex is heavy in the

air. I can taste the salt of my tears and feel satiated. For the first time, I feel completely fulfilled.

"Now I want to hear you tell me that you love me, Angel."

I want to argue, I want to tell him to go to hell, and I want my heart back. I know he'll leave and take the chunk he's managed to so quickly get a hold of. But my mouth opens and the words he wants to hear come out, "I love you, Benny."

"I love you, Angel. My Angel. Only mine."

He rolls off me and my body already aches to be back in his arms. My brain is screaming not to want that. Those arms will leave me aching, hurting and yearning to feel them again.

Before I can even get cooled off, he's on his side and pulling me tight into his arms again. His lips touch the side of my head. "Can I stay the night?"

"I don't see why not."

"Do you want me to?" he asks.

I snuggle into his wide chest and it feels so cozy. "Yeah, I want you too."

He leaves a kiss on my cheek and lies back. Then I realize I'm making more out of his words than he really meant.

It was me who told him to tell me he loved me and would never leave me. It was me who told him I wanted to pretend this was real.

I got myself all worried for no reason. He doesn't really love me. He's not serious about me being his.

With the knowledge that I got too much into the pretend game, I snuggle into his chest and feel a lot better that he will go away tomorrow and leave me alone.

I can go back to my life and live it as usual with this sweet little session to think about now and then.

No big deal!

But man, this guy would be so damn easy to fall in love with.

Luckily, his snooty family would never allow him to be with a commoner like myself.

I have nothing to worry about. It was all just an act. An act I asked him to do.

His arms tighten around me and he kisses the top of my head and mumbles, "My Angel. Always mine."

My heart pounds as his breathing is slow and steady and he's obviously asleep. So does that mean his words were real?

Does that mean he's going to hold me to the things he said?

Does that mean he really expects me to be his?

I can't let this happen!

ANGEL SHOWS HER BILLIONAIRE WHO IS BOSS

Book 2

9

BLAZE

Bright sunlight filters through the sheer pink colored curtain in Angel's bedroom. She's managed to escape my arms during the night and the absence of another person breathing in the small room is obvious.

Rolling out of bed, I make my way to the bathroom to surprise her, hopefully while she's in the shower. I'm going to take her out with me today. I'm not taking no for an answer this time at all.

I can shut her down with one simple kiss now and plan on doing that every time I need to.

"Cuddles," I call out, looking for her dog, as I leave the bedroom and find the bathroom door open and no trace of Angel in there.

With a quick grab of a towel off the shelf, I cover my bottom half and go into the living room, finding she's not in here either. A quick search of the kitchen shows me a note she's left on her tiny dining table.

Fuck!

She's gone!

I scan the tiny note she's left and want to scream.

. . .

BLAZE,

Had to leave town for a while. Had fun. Really, I did. Thanks for the pretend thing you did for me. I appreciate it. Hope you did too.

See you around town I guess.

Angel and Cuddles.

SO SHE WANTS to act like that was all pretend, huh? I damn well know she wasn't pretending with me and I sure as hell wasn't pretending with her.

I've never felt anything more real than what we did. Nothing!

She's scared. Afraid she's really falling for me and that I'll leave her like the jack-off did before.

But I won't.

I can tell she might well be the one for me. And I'm not about to let her go just because she has issues.

Pulling my clothes back on, I leave her house and find another note taped outside the front door that tells me to please lock it behind me. Before I do that, I go back inside and get the pen that's lying next to her minuscule note and write my phone number down at the bottom with an order to call me as soon as she gets back or I'll come hunt her ass down.

I used several exclamation points then added, 'I love you, my Angel. Yours always, Benny.'

Then I leave, lock her door and feel so damn angry inside that she didn't use the nickname she gave me on her note. Blaze is what she used and last night I noticed her saying Blaze at times and Benny at others. Each time she used Blaze, I felt like she was pretending in her mind that she felt nothing.

When she used Benny, I could feel the emotion in her. Real,

deep emotion. And we just have to get to the place where she knows I'm not a runner.

As I get on my bike and start it up, I look up and down the street. I can feel a vague hope that I can find her before she gets out of town. But it's really vague.

There's no sign of her at the garage she works at. But I stop in anyway to see if her Uncle knows where she went.

THE BELL RINGS as I walk in and Phil is sitting at the computer with a pair of old horn-rimmed glasses. He looks up at me and looks right back at the computer. "I don't know where she is, Blaze."

"Did she give you a hint when she'll be back?" I ask as I shove my hands in my pockets, feeling quite annoyed.

He shakes his head. "Nah. I think it'll be a few days."

I turn and walk out the door, calling out a goodbye to her uncle as I do. Then get on my bike and go to my motel room.

No bikes are in the parking lot so I know I missed whatever they're all doing this morning. I'll catch up to them at lunch.

A shower is in order. But to wash away her scent is a thing I don't want to do. All my plans for today are shot and now it looks like I'm going to drink this one away and the next and the one after that until she comes back.

How could she be so callous?

After getting dressed in my leather apparel, I feel more like Blaze and a lot less like Benjamin. Nothing like Benny, though.

That man only comes out for her.

ALL THESE YEARS I've been the person I was expected to be. Except when I took the month of August to be this badass biker.

And now that I think I've found the one person who can help me integrate my two very opposite personalities, she runs away.

I cruise down the main street and in no time at all, I find my gang's bikes in front of a bar. So I park and head inside at three o'clock in the afternoon.

Just like I knew I'd find, a tall, plump platinum blonde woman is sitting on the barstool closest to the door. Her arm juts out as I try to pass her. "Hey there," she says, then hands me a beer. "This one's on me."

After a moment of not taking the beer and looking right into her already bloodshot eyes, I look over to find my gang at a couple of large tables.

I look back at her and say, "Thanks. But I'm not going to be sucking down suds tonight."

As I walk away, she grabs my arm and I turn back quickly to find a pout on her large red lips. "Come on, Baby. Just one drink with me then you can go join your brothers."

I peel her hand off my arm.

"First, I'm not your baby and second, my answer to your offer is, no. Bye."

I walk away and hear her muttering about me being an asshole. Which I am most times so I don't get offended by her remark.

Pulling a chair up between Rod and Paco whose women sit on the other side of them, I think I've placed myself strategically in a position where most women won't feel comfortable coming up to me.

"Hey guys," I say and find Rod looking at me with an odd expression. "So, I saw that trick try to give you a beer, and you turned her down. Why would that be, Brother?"

"It would be because I found the one for me and I'm not about to let her catch me with another chick or it might all blow up in my face." Paco hands me a shot glass and the bottle of Jack that everyone is drinking from.

I fill the tiny glass up and drink it down. It burns and reminds me I'm alive and at the most badass bike rally in the world and need to loosen up.

But only just enough. I don't want to be plastered if Angel comes to her senses and comes back and calls me.

Rod taps the table top as he looks me over. "The one?"

I nod. "Only she has very bad men-related issues." I refill the glass and pick up the dark liquor, looking at how the light is filtered as it runs through it. "She left me at her place alone this morning. Not a word to me. She just took off like a scared rabbit, leaving me a note that said what we did was fun."

Rod smiles and pushes a tall bottle of beer to me. "Maybe she isn't on the same page you are, my friend."

"She is. I know she is. It's electric when we touch. We like the same things. You know what this badass mother-fucker did last night with her?" I ask as I look at him.

His wife, Ashely's, face comes into view as she looks around him at me. "Nuh uh, Blaze. My man doesn't get to hear about other men's sexual escapades."

"I wasn't talking about that. I was going to tell him about how I made her dinner then we watched Willy Wonka on television and it was better than anything I've ever done. Just being with her is better than a single day I've spent in my entire life." I toss back the shot then take a drink of the beer.

My heart is so much heavier than it has ever been.

Ashely mumbles into her husband's ear, "Shit! He's got it bad."

Rod nods and then shakes his head. "She didn't say where she was going? Not even a hint?"

"No. Not even a hint. She took her little dog too so I know

she'll be gone for at least one night." I move my legs out to stretch underneath the table and lay my head back in my hands.

"You know, Blaze, I've seen you in action and not everyone likes to be handled that roughly. Take it from me," Rod says. "Maybe what you two did was too intense for her."

I laugh. "Nah, she's completely into that kind of stuff. I didn't mention anything at all about liking to get rough. She asked me to do it. So that's not it. It's just that she's afraid she'll fall for me and then I'll leave her heartbroken. That's all it is. If she'd fucking come around, I could show her that's not at all what I have in mind for her."

Ashely peeks around Rod to look at me again and asks, "What do you have in mind for her, Blaze?"

"More. More than I ever thought of before. I go all dreamy as I think about all I want to do with her. Because it's like a dream to me. I've never wanted anyone around all the time before. Ever. It's making me nuts she isn't here under my arm right now." I look back at the door and find the blonde looking my way and she holds up a beer again.

I turn my head without so much as a blink at her. I won't be taking her up on her offer which starts with a beer and ends with her.

Paco pats my shoulder as he says, "Don't worry, Brother. If you want the broads to be kept at bay, I got your back."

Rod nods my way. "Me too, Brother. If you want to stay pure for this woman, then we'll make sure the ladies leave you alone. It'd suck donkey dicks if she came in and found some tramp on your lap."

Ashely says with a laugh, "Or even sitting next to you. I knocked the shit of a chick for taking the seat on the other side of my man before. Granted, I gave her a chance to realize her actions were dead wrong and politely asked her to move."

Rod's eyebrows go up high as he says, "Politely? I don't think the phrase, hey bitch, get the fuck away from my man, is considered polite."

"In some circles, it is," Ashely corrects her husband. "Anyway, the dumb broad rolled her eyes at me and maintained her seat. To which I promptly got up and removed her obstinate ass and left her with a busted lip."

I chuckle and take a drink of my beer. "Bet she never tried to sit next to Rod again."

Ashely shakes her head. "Never again. And she apologized to me on top of that."

I level my eyes on Rod and say, "You got you a pistol there, don't you?"

He looks back at her with hazy eyes and says, "I do. And that's just how I want her. Perfect for me."

Then Paco clears his throat and we all look his way. "I'd like to announce to you all that I have asked Phoenix to marry me."

Cheers ring out and shouts of congratulations are called out as Paco holds up his new fiancé's left hand with a single diamond on a gold band.

I pat the man on the back and say, "I know I told you getting hitched was a dumb idea. But in light of my new found feelings I know it's the right thing to do. I'm happy for you two."

"Thanks, Brother," Paco says as he leans over. "We'll be leaving at the end of the week and heading to Vegas to do the deed. It's going to take everything I have to do it, but I'd give all I have for her, anyway."

AND JUST LIKE THAT, I know what I want to do for them. "Let me get your room in Vegas, Paco. I'll set you up in one of the penthouses there and put the whole thing on my bill. Let me do that for you guys. For a wedding present. A week in Vegas on me. What do you say?"

"I say, hell yeah, Brother!" He turns back to Phoenix whose eyes are glistening with unshed tears. "Blaze is giving us one badass wedding gift, my love. The entire week in a Vegas penthouse. What do you say to that?"

Her face lights up and she looks at me with such appreciation. "Blaze, that's beyond amazing. Thank you so much. I hope you decide to join us for the happy occasion." Then she looks around the table. "I hope you all do."

More cheering and hollering acceptance of the invite fills the large bar and then I feel a hand on my shoulder. When I turn back, I see the very tenacious blonde is there looking at me with such a smirk on her face. "I need a light, you got one?"

I don't have to say a word as both Ashley and Phoenix get up and without a word, escort the woman away from me. I laugh and get back to drinking with my buddies.

"I owe them," I say as I look back and forth at Rod and Paco. "Remind me to buy them something nice before we leave. It's nice to have backup when you need it."

My phone vibrates in my pocket and I nearly fall out of my chair to answer it as my brother's laugh at me. But when I get it out, I see it's not Angel. It's my grandfather for some damn reason.

I shake my head and say, "Not her. It's work."

Getting up, I go to the bathroom to answer his call so he doesn't hear all the noise and give me a lecture about cutting me off.

"Hello, Grandfather."

"Benjamin."

"Is anything the matter, Grandfather?" I ask as I look in the mirror and run my hand over my long beard, making sure it's smooth.

"I'm going to need you to cut that trip of yours short this time. I need you back here to finish the Bain deal. We got him to agree to come back to us, but he wants to be sure you're on board about him. I assured him that you were, but he demanded to have a meeting with you to explain where you stand as his lawyer."

"Bain? The asshole who's selling the AIDs drug for more than people can afford?"

"The man who is selling the product he owns for what he thinks it is worth. Vulgarity is not a thing I allow, Benjamin. You are well aware of that. Now, I have set up the meeting for the fifteenth of August," he says.

But I cut him off. A thing which is never allowed, but I'm fucking doing it, anyway. "I won't be there. I won't be representing that piece of shit. As far as the law firm goes, I think it's a terrible idea to stand behind the man. I won't have any part in it."

"Then maybe you shouldn't be any part of my firm, Benjamin. Perhaps you think you know more than I do. Perhaps you think you can go it alone or something like that. Is that what you think?" he asks and waits for my answer.

"I don't want to resign my position with the family firm. I will not be a part of any team representing that asshole, Bain. Take that how you want, Grandfather. Goodbye."

As I end the call with a swipe of my finger, the tiniest bit of fear runs through me.

What would I do if I had to start over on my own?

10

ANGEL

My grandmother's words keep running through my head as I drive home after being away two nights. She and my grandfather had what she called a true love. When I told her how it felt when Benny touched me, she told me that it was because we have a connection. One, not many find in this world.

Grandad made her feel that way too and when he passed a few years ago, she knew she'd never find that kind of spark again and was never going to even look for another man to attempt to take the place of the man that she had lost to heart disease.

That alone made me think I need to stop being afraid and see what happens.

If my grandmother can live the rest of her life alone because the time she had with the love of her life will see her through to the end, then I should gain something from the time I spend with Benny.

Even if it's only a small amount of it.

The night fell on me very fast. I didn't take off until sunset because I kept going back and forth in my head about what I should do. Finally, I decided to come back home.

If Benny wants to see me again, then he'll see my bike at work in the morning and stop by. If not, then he won't. Either way, I'll know where he stands.

And that's all I need to know. After all, one amazing night is better than none.

But I pray there's a lot more of that amazing thing he and I seem to have.

The night air falls cool against my face as I drive my bike back to Sturgis. It's only about nine, I think. Maybe I should take a cruise through town and see if I can find his bike. Maybe surprise him.

But that might surprise me more. Nah, I better not do that. If I saw him with someone else, I don't know what I'd do.

It wouldn't be cool to have a hissy fit after one night of crazy hot passion. And I was the one who ran off so I couldn't blame him if he was with another woman. But I think I'd have a hard time not throwing a punch or three at them both.

No, it's best not to find him at a bar. Which I'm sure he's at. The gang most likely wouldn't let him sit alone in his motel room and sulk about some woman.

But what if he's just sitting alone in his little motel room? Lonely, sad, depressed?

I could show up and make his night. That would be awesome.

I could drop off Cuddles at home and go see if I can find his bike parked in front of one of the motel rooms.

Oh God! I sound like a stalker!

THE ORIGINAL PLAN of just going to work tomorrow and letting him see my bike there is a good one. A safe one. One where I don't make a freaking fool out of myself.

The whole thing is my fault, anyway. I could've left him my

cell number and maybe we could've talked some. But I had to go all paranoid and run off so quickly I even forgot my toothbrush and had to stop and get a new one before I left town.

And then another thought zips through my head that he might just be waiting for me at my house. Which would normally be a thing that would piss me off but now I'd love to find his bike inside my little, white, picket fence.

That would be awesome!

I could go inside and just hug him and tell him I'm sorry and we'd make love and I could spend the night wrapped up in his strong arms.

That feeling was the best thing I've ever felt. It took everything in me to move my body out of his warm embrace that early morning before the sun came up.

When I looked back and saw him sleeping so peacefully, I almost climbed right back into bed. But my damn insecurities stopped me and had me running away like an idiot.

I can't think of another woman who'd be so stupid as I was when I left him there. Alone, in my bed.

What did he think when he woke up and found me gone?

I wonder if he was mad, sad, or relieved. Maybe a bit of all three.

Surely, he realizes now that I'm very damaged. He probably knows he dodged a bullet and left there with a smile on his face.

The headlight hits the white of my little house and my heart starts really banging hard in my chest. If he's there, it'll be great and if he's not, then tomorrow will have to suffice.

As I pull up, I see no other vehicle here. So he didn't wait for two days for me to show back up. It kind of hurts that he went on. But what did I expect him to do?

LETTING Cuddles out of the doggy carrier on my back, I watch her run around the yard, sniffing like crazy. It's almost as if she's looking for something. I wonder if it's him she's sniffing around for.

The two certainly hit it off like she's never done with anyone else. I wonder if she's sad he isn't here too.

I walk my bike into the yard and park it by the porch. Then I go up the three steps and find the note I taped to the door, asking him to lock it behind him, is still there.

Unlocking the door, I still have vague hope he's inside the house. But all I see is darkness. Of course, he's not here.

After I switch on the light, I look around and find the note I left him on the table and walk over to grab it and toss it in the trash can. But I see he's written on the bottom of it and he left his phone number.

My whole body tenses as I see he's demanding I call and wrote the words, 'I love you' on the note.

So it wasn't just pretending to him!

I have fought myself the last couple of days about how real it all was. I did ask him to pretend after all.

And with these words, I see it was real for him too. But is it still going to be real since I've waited two nights to come back?

Have I waited too long? Has he found other women to fill his nights? Can I take it if he has?

Slowly, I take my phone out of my pocket and look at the number a long time. There's a lot of exclamation points on the note. It does look like he really wants me to call him.

So I press in the number and wait to see what happens.

One ring, two rings, three rings...

Shit, he's not going to answer me!

"Hello," I hear his gravelly, sexy voice say.

"Hey, Benny."

He sighs. "Angel." His voice is so quiet and the sound of all the noise fades away as he must be walking out of the bar he's definitely at. "You're back."

"I am. It sounds like you're at a bar," I say as I go and plop down on the sofa thinking he's having a good time and might as well stay there.

"Yeah, my friends are here. But I'll leave right now and come to you."

"No! No, Blaze. You stay there. Do whatever it was you were doing. I don't want you to leave your fun time to come here. That would be stupid."

"I want to be with you, Angel. I've missed you more than I thought humanly possible. Didn't you miss me at all?" he asks with a certain amount of sadness in his voice.

Should I tell him I did miss him like crazy and could only think about him these last two days?

"Blaze, we barely know each other. How could you miss me?"

"How can you say we barely knew each other? I think we got to know one another pretty damn well. So you're saying you didn't miss me at all, Angel?"

I hesitate then say, "I don't know, Blaze."

"Stop calling me that. I know what you're doing when you call me Blaze. You're not allowing yourself to like me. Or love me."

"Love is a bit fast, don't you think? I mean, you're going to have to leave soon, anyway. Why bring love into this thing we have? Whatever it is," I say and run my hand through my hair in frustration.

"I am coming over," he says with an air of authority. "We can talk all about this in person. Face to face. While we hold each other, skin to skin."

"No."

"No? Then why did you call me, Angel?"

"Your note was very demanding. I suppose I thought you might want to know I was alive and made it home. I didn't call you to drag you out of a bar where you were probably having a great time with random bimbos and make you come and talk to me about what this is we have or don't have." I get up and go to see what kind of alcohol I have in the fridge as my nerves are bristling.

"I was not messing around with anyone. I haven't touched a girl since you. Not once. Not at all. I've waited for you. I wanted to. I want you to know I think you're special, Angel. My Angel. I'm coming over," he says with a slight whisper in the last words.

"I'll see you tomorrow. It's late," I say when I find no alcohol to numb me. "I'm going to bed."

"Stop," he says with aggravation in his voice. "Just stop this. I'm going to come and see you. If you want me to leave after I take you in my arms and kiss you one time, then I'll leave. But you have to let me kiss you and hold you. I've ached to do that for what seems like forever."

"Have you really?" I ask as I walk toward my bedroom, peeling my clothes off as I go. His reminder of holding me and kissing me has my body heating up quickly.

"I have. I've barely slept and when I did manage to sleep, it was restless with dreams of you and I making love in your cute little pink and black bedroom. My God, how I've missed you, Baby. Please just…"

"Tomorrow, Benny. I promise tomorrow."

"Angel, how could you not miss me?" he asks and I don't know what to tell him because I did miss him.

"BENNY, it's just that this is intense. I need time to understand this. It's enough for me to know that you still want to see me. I've struggled between thinking it was all a pretend game and something real. So now I know it's real." I lie down on my bed, naked now and climb under my blanket as Cuddle's hurdles herself onto the bed, taking her position at the foot of the bed to guard me through the night.

"Okay, since you know what we have is real, then why not let me come over and at the very least hold you for a while? I need to see you, baby. I need to smell you and taste you. I need you, Angel. This is a thing I've never done before. I feel as if I'm pleading with you and this isn't me at all. This is the me I am with you."

"Am I making you weak?" I ask as I find myself biting at my fingernail then stop as that was a thing I did when what's-his-ass left me. I chewed all of my fingernails off and it took me some time to stop doing that.

"Not weak. It's not weak to know you love someone and know you need to be around them. That's not weakness, Angel. That's being human. I'm coming over. I need you and need to be with you."

His words are getting quieter and I know this is wearing him down. "You sound tired, Benny."

"I am. I'm so tired. You have no idea."

"Then rest. I'm tired too. I haven't slept well either. Tomorrow I'll see you. If you want to that is." I close my eyes and wait to hear what he says.

"No, I don't want to see you tomorrow."

I open my eyes and try to understand what that means. Then I hear giggling in the background and a woman's voice says, "Blaze, are you coming back inside?"

"Not messing around with any women, huh? Go back inside, Blaze! And don't even worry about tomorrow. I don't want to see you. Goodbye!" I end the call.

. . .

TEARS BURN my eyes but I don't let them fall. He calls me right back and I send it to voicemail.

I knew he was too good to be true. I knew it!

The liar. Lucky for me that chick got tired of waiting for him to go back inside and came out to get him or I'd have never known what he was really doing.

Prick! Making me believe he's been waiting for me all this time!

And for a few minutes there, I was believing his lying ass. I should've known better. I should've never even called him.

What I should've done was go find him, see him in action and leave without saying a word to him.

At least then my heart and head would agree that love sucks and ends up leaving you hurt.

The phone rings again as he tries to call me back. I send it on again and then turn my phone off.

It's obvious he won't quit.

THE THING I don't understand is why me? If he can get any chick he wants, then why does he need to step into my life and give me more pain than I've already been dealt?

I roll on my side and yank the blanket up tightly around me. Tears flow over my cheek even though I tried hard to stop them.

Fine, I'll allow myself to cry a little over the ass wipe. But only a little because I knew this was going to happen, and I allowed it, anyway.

Fuck! I invited it.

He wasn't trying to get me into bed that night. He was being a gentleman.

It was me who suggested he take most of his clothes off and lie with me on the sofa. I knew what I was doing when I said it.

And it was me who asked him to come to my bedroom. Then

I went so far as to ask him to tell me he loved me and would never leave me.

All me!

So I am an idiot. Okay, now that I completely realize that about myself I can begin to move forward. Good riddance to bad rubbish. I'm moving on.

11

BLAZE

Poor Phoenix is beating herself up for interrupting my phone call and making Angel hang up on me when she thought it was some chick I'd been hanging out with at the bar.

I promised I'd bring Angel around tomorrow so she could back up my explanation that Phoenix was only looking out for me. She wanted to make sure some woman wasn't trying to hit on me while I was outside.

But Angel jumped to conclusions and hung up on me and turned her damn phone off. So I'm on my way over there now to talk or rather, kiss, some sense into her stubborn, insecure ass.

I thought the conversation was going pretty well up until that moment. Even though she kept telling me, no, to coming over. But my plan is to bang on the door until she has no choice but to open up or call the cops on me.

I'm a little worried she might take off again so I'm hurrying to get to her house on the outskirts of Sturgis. My headlight reflects off her white picket fence and I also see the reflection of her bike near the front porch.

Even though the house is all dark, I bet she's home. I turn

the engine off and coast in so she doesn't hear me and barricade herself inside.

I park the bike and go up the sidewalk, being careful to be quiet so the dog doesn't bark and alert her. And suddenly I realize that I have a lot of stalker tendencies.

Oh well! When in love...

Slowly I go up the stairs trying hard not to let the steps creak. I twist the handle to see if by some miracle it's unlocked and find it is.

"Fuck!" Doesn't she know enough to lock her damn door?

I lock the door behind me then sit on the sofa and take off my boots and everything but my underwear and head back to her bedroom.

As I push the door open, I hear a low growl from her dog. "Hey, Cuddles," I whisper and she gets up, wagging her tail and jumps into my arms with lots of puppy kisses.

Aww, she missed me!

I'm putting her outside in the back yard so she won't bark when I shut her out of the bedroom because she thinks the bed is hers too and I don't need any company for my reunion with her mommy.

I grab her a handful of doggy treats that are in a cookie jar in the kitchen and place her little panting, happy ass out the back door. She wags her tail at me as I close the door.

IN THE LIVING ROOM, I ditch my underwear leaving them with the rest of my clothes and go stealthily back into her bedroom. Her tiny snores are still going and she has no idea there's been anyone in her house much less her bedroom.

I'm so jumping her ass about leaving that damn door unlocked but that can wait until tomorrow.

Sliding under the blanket, I can feel her warm body as I face her. She's lying on her side and her long dark hair is covering her beautiful face.

She might try to hit me when she wakes up, so I gently run my hand down her arm to hold it down, if need be. Her body shivers with my touch and mine has little shots of electricity shooting around in it.

I can't stand not to do it, so I press my lips to hers. A little moaning sound comes out of her and she scoots in close to me. Instead of hitting me, she moves her hand up my arm and over my shoulder and all the way to the back of my neck where she pulls me in to kiss her harder.

Her lips part and I run my tongue into her mouth. My cock is growing by leaps and bounds as she kisses me. The sweetness of her breath is a thing I missed more than air itself.

She throws a leg over me as I run my hands over her naked body. Seems she was most likely getting in bed and getting ready to let me come over. Until she went crazy, that is.

Her soft breasts press against my chest, then her head pulls back a little, and she ends the kiss. Those deep blue eyes are open and looking at me when I open mine.

HER VOICE IS soft and raspy as she says, "I missed you, Benny."

"I missed you. I hope you're not mad I came in anyway. And you left the damn door unlocked, making it easy. I plan on explaining that woman to you, but it can wait until tomorrow." I pull her back to me and kiss her neck as she makes a little purring sound.

"I'm sorry," she whispers.

Now it's me who has to pull back and look at her. "You're sorry. I bet you don't say that often."

She shakes her head a bit. "Not often enough. But I am sorry and I want to be different with you."

Leaving a soft kiss on her cheek, I say, "I want to be different with you too. I'm not the same man when I'm with you. I think the world is made up of rainbows and butterflies when I have you in my arms."

She giggles and bats her thick dark eyelashes at me. "You silly boy."

"I am silly over you, my Angel." I kiss her throat all the way down, over her collar bone and make her groan as I take her plump breast into my mouth.

"Damn it, Benny!"

I nip her tit then suck it hard. Popping it out of my mouth, I look back at her as her hands run all through my hair. "Don't ever run off again."

She shakes her head. "Never again."

"Where are the keys to that set of cuffs you have hooked to your headboard?"

Her eyes go wide and she gestures with a nod toward her nightstand. I pin her body to the bed with mine as I lean over her and open the drawer to make sure they're there and see the little set of keys.

Moving my body over hers, I take her right wrist and place it in the loose cuff, the other already around the bedpost. The click makes her moan and I run my fingers down her body and then inside her, and find her wet and ready.

"You won't be running off from me again. If I have to chain your sweet ass up every night, I will do it, you tenacious woman," I say as I kiss my way down her hot body.

She arches up as my hands run down her waist and my tongue runs over her stomach. "Yes, Sir."

I stop and look up at her and give her a wink.

"I like Master Blaze when I administer punishments."

"Oh yes, punish me, Master Blaze. Show me who I belong to," she hisses out as she writhes beneath me.

My fingernails make red streaks as I rake them down her sides. The sound she makes has my dick hard as a rock but I must torture the shit out of her before she gets to feel my liquid heat fill her.

She does have to be punished after all.

WITH A FIRM GRIP, I take her ass in my hands and pull her up to me. For almost a minute, I only breathe out hot breaths on her very hot and wanting pussy.

She knows enough not to ask for more. That tells me that she is practiced and knows how to obey and take what she has coming. Only she's never been punished by me, so I expect to hear her begging for my mercy before I let her have what she will be craving when I'm through with her.

One long lick I give her and her moan is outstanding. I look up and see her holding the other bedpost as she tries hard not to move.

"You need a safe word, baby?"

"I won't be using it as I deserve anything you give me. But Apple will work for me," she answers.

"Apple it is. And you do deserve everything I give you. You hurt me, you made me wait, and you made me worry." I lick her again, raking my tongue back and forth over her swollen clit only three times.

Her body is tense, and she's soaking wet. These sheets don't stand a chance.

"I know. I am sorry, Master Blaze." Her leg moves to bend her knee and I drag it back into place.

"And...," I say then give her another long lick up her hot folds, leaving a nip on her clit.

"I'll never do it again." Her body shudders with desire.

With a smile, I bury my face in her hot pussy. Licking, sucking, and bringing her to the very edge of an orgasm. But as soon as I feel her body tremble, I stop and stand up.

Her breathing is hard and fills the bedroom. I have to pace back and forth for a few seconds to stop myself from jumping on top of her and ramming my aching cock into her sweet and very wanting pussy.

"DAMN IT, Angel! Why? Why did you do this? All I wanted was to make you happy."

"I can't let myself be happy. It'll end and I can't take it."

My heart stops and I fall to my knees beside the bed. She turns her head and looks at me with tears running over her cheek. Off the side of the bed, they hit the pink shag carpet in large drops.

Face to face, I look at her crying. "Let them all out, Angel. Let those tears leave you cleansed of your fears. Let the worries go with each one that leaves your body. I am not that man who hurt you. You must trust me. You must respect me enough not to run away. Or we have nothing. And I so want something with you."

Her chest heaves as a sob comes out of her. I find it so hard not to hold her, not to try to ease her suffering. But she needs to release it.

I stay close. So close we are nearly touching, but I stay back just enough so she can begin to gain that strength that will get her over this insecurity she has.

"Cry as much as you need to." I reach into the drawer and get the key to the handcuffs. "Cry until you can't anymore. Let it go, Angel. Let that guy go. Let all that happened go. I'm going nowhere. I'm yours and you are mine."

With the click of the cuff releasing her, she lets out a loud sob. The only comfort I give her is the way that I rub her wrist where the cuff held it.

. . .

CHOKED WORDS COME FROM HER, "I thought what he and I had was love. But I was so wrong. I felt nothing for him now that I know what real love feels like. Yet it did break me when he left me. I had done nothing wrong. I kept a clean house. Kept him satisfied in bed. Cooked for him. Did his laundry and paid half the bills. What more could he have wanted? Why wasn't I enough for him? Why didn't he want to take me on his amazing journey around the world? Why, Benny, why?"

I hold her red face between my palms and place one kiss on her forehead. "Because you and he had a nice time together for a while but you didn't have an all-encompassing love. If he would've held onto you for a bit longer, then he'd have stopped you from meeting me. Your one true love, Princess."

She kind of eases her crying a bit and her eyes which are red-rimmed go big, and she looks at me with much more clarity in them. "Benny, you're right! You're right. I'd never have met you. I'd have been God only knows where and you would've never walked into my uncle's garage. You would've never touched me and sent heat and electricity through me. A thing I never knew possible."

"Me neither, Angel," I admit as I caress her red cheek.

Her eyes go soft as her expression changes to something more like wonder. "You'd never have kissed me and shown me what a real kiss is. Your body would've never held mine down with a weight I wished that I could feel forever."

I give her a half-cocked smile. "You would've never let me. So you see, not every relationship is meant to last a lifetime. But ours. Well, ours just might. We won't know unless we give it a shot."

"I want to give you a shot, Benny. I want to let the past go and give you all I have. I promise I won't run again. Can you promise you won't either?" Her eyes move back and forth fast as she looks for answers.

I stroke her cheek, softly. "I won't be running. As a matter of fact, I'd like to make this a lot more permanent. But we can discuss that in more detail after I've shown you how much you mean to me. My plans of a lengthy punishment have changed. I think you understand me now. And I think you need to feel my love."

She holds her arms open for me. "Come to me, my wonderful master."

HER TEARS HAVE DRIED up and I think she's ready to embrace this thing that we have and feel what we have for each other, leaving the old relationship behind her.

I slide in next to her and hold her to me tight as I kiss the side of her head. Then I lie her back and rest my head on my hand and look down at her as I trail my fingertips over her tits.

"Okay, we're going to get to know one another much better," I say as I circle her nipple, making it grow. "My public information I can leave out since I'm sure you have Googled me to find all that out."

She giggles and runs her hand up my arm, squeezing my bicep. "I have. So what about what you really want out of life? Because I saw picture after picture of you with your family and guess what I never saw in any of them."

I kiss the tip of her nose that's still red from crying. "A smile on any of our faces."

"That's right," she says with a tweak to my nose. "And that's a real shame because that smile you have is beyond wonderful and a thing that should always be seen. I must see it at least once every single day we're together, my love."

"Unfortunately, happiness is a thing my family isn't big on.

Respect, dignity above anything else, and the ever present power that my grandfather thinks comes along with that. And people with power don't smile. Or so he says, anyway." I move my hand through her hair as she smiles up at me and runs her hand over my cheek.

"I've heard no word about a grandmother."

I shake my head. "She passed away when my father was born. My grandfather raised him single-handedly. Grandfather was a second generation American. His parents came over from England. And they died young, leaving him alone at the tender age of twenty. That's when he found the woman he only had in his life for a mere three years."

Her eyes go sad again. "Benny, how sad. Did he ever find another woman?"

I shake my head. "He is a bit of a hard ass. Even though he's stinking rich, he's never had another woman in his life. And he says he wants it that way."

She cocks her head to the side and narrows her eyes. "Maybe that's why he's a hard ass."

Maybe she's right...

12

ANGEL

Warm lips press against the nape of my neck. "Good morning, my Angel."

I turn in his arms and see his scruffy bearded face and sleepy blue eyes and feel more than I've ever felt before. "Good morning to you."

My body begins to wake up slowly as his hands run over it. Each stroke making sensations that I was unaware were possible. "I'm taking you to breakfast."

"Benny, I can cook." I rub my eyes and stretch a little.

"I'm sure you can." His lips gently touch my cheek. "But I'm taking you to breakfast. So you don't have to."

Suddenly I remember my dog and look around the room. "Where's Cuddles?"

"Just now missing her?" He laughs. "I put her out in the backyard last night so you and I could have a little alone time."

He rolls over me, climbs out of the bed then lifts me up in his arms. "Benny! I can walk."

"I know you can." He kisses my lips lightly. "But I want to carry you."

I can see he's about to attempt to spoil me. Not an easy thing to do since I don't allow people to do that much for me. But for today, I guess I can let him have his way.

Not forever, though!

Forever?

Will this last forever?

I PUSH the thought away so I don't jinx anything. Running my arms around his neck, I lay my head on his chest. "That was nice last night. I'm glad you came."

"Me too." He puts me down in front of the bathroom sink. "You got an extra toothbrush?"

I open the medicine cabinet and produce a freshly packaged one I bought just last week. "It's pink, but it'll work."

He nods and turns toward the toilet and lifts up the lid. I turn to walk out and give him privacy. "Where are you going?" he asks as he looks back at me.

"To let you have a bit of privacy then I'll come and do what I have to do."

"Stay." He looks back to the task at hand.

"No." I take another step then feel his hand on my arm.

He flushes the toilet with one hand and holds me with the other. I look down at his unwashed hand. "Yuck, Benny!"

His eyes run over his hand. "What? My hand too dirty for you because it just came off my dick? That dick was all over you last night and you weren't saying yuck then."

"For God's sakes, Benny!" I try to pull away but he holds me tight then grabs my other arm too.

"Look, Angel, I want us to be a nice normal couple. Couples use the bathroom together."

With a shake of my head, I say, "Not this couple. I use the bathroom separately."

"I'm not saying you can never use it alone. I'm just saying

there's no reason to be shy with me. I'm not going to let you." He pulls me to the toilet and sits me down. "Now use it. I know you need to."

"Jesus, Benny! I can't go with you looking at me. At least turn around and brush your teeth."

HE SMILES and turns away and starts to brush his teeth. I'm pretty mortified and it takes me quite some time to get things moving, but I do and hop off the toilet before he turns back around.

I look up after I flush the toilet as he makes some sound and I see him tapping the mirror with his rinsed off toothbrush as he smiles at me. "I could see you through the mirror."

I roll my eyes. "Pervert!"

"Only where you're concerned." He moves past me, grazing his body against mine and sending heat through me. Starting the shower, he looks back. "Climb in here when you get finished brushing your teeth."

"Yes, Master Blaze," I say as I grin at him.

He winks at me. "And make it snappy, wench."

I give him a nod and brush my teeth and listen as he sings, "I've got you, under my skin."

After I rinse my mouth out, I get in the shower, finding his head and beard full of shampoo bubbles. He's still singing away as I step in and he moves his finger in a circle, gesturing for me to turn my back to him.

I do as the control freak wants and find him leaning me back, getting my hair wet. Then his hands move through my hair, massaging shampoo in.

I want to be mad. I want to hate this. But I fucking love it.

I've never been the least bit pampered. I'm not big on it. Or wasn't, anyway.

I could get very used to this.

After he rinses my hair out, he ends his song and turns me back to face him and kisses me. My body melts in his arms as he wraps me in them.

Man, he sure knows how to make a shower fun!

My back's against the cool tiled wall before I know it and his hands run down my legs, picking me up and just like, that he's inside me and pressing his body to mine as he holds me up like I don't weigh a thing.

Our tongues move against the others in a rough fashion as he moves in and out of me. Taking me to a place other than this shower stall.

I run my hands over his muscular back, the water helping them move smoothly and feeling each muscle that's tight as he uses them to hold me and stroke me.

Inside I'm already quivering. My body reacts to his so well.

HIS MOUTH MOVES off mine and over my neck where he sucks and nips at me. "Baby, I love you."

I moan with his words. "That sounds so nice."

He gives me a hard bite. "Is that all you have to say?"

"I love you too, Benny."

He groans out, "That's better."

The smell of the coconut scented shampoo, and him, is intoxicating. My head feels light and my body is on fire. He moves harder, pounding me with each hard thrust.

LITTLE GRUNTS MAKE hot air hit my ear as he makes them with each stroke. I can't wait any longer and my body gives in to his demands. "Benny!" I shriek with the intense orgasm.

"Yes," he moans and continues to thrust into me.

Then he makes a ridiculously loud groan and his cock jerks inside me as he keeps moving until it's all spent.

He eases my feet back to the floor. His lips touch the top of my head. "Now, it's a good morning."

I cling to him as my heart is still pounding hard and my legs feel weak. "I agree."

AFTER GETTING DRESSED, which took some time as he kept grabbing me and kissing me or smacking my ass, we're on our way out to go to breakfast. I hear Cuddles barking in the backyard and I recall that I do have a pet.

"Let me go feed her real quick, Benny. I completely forgot about the poor thing." I turn and go back in and open the back door where she promptly runs inside.

Jumping up and down with excitement, she goes right past me and jumps into Benny's arms. "Hey, there girl. Not mad at me at all for putting you outside, are you?"

She yaps a little which means she is a little mad but she'll get over it. I put down the bowl of dog food and fill up her water bowl.

"How long are we going to be gone?" I ask to decide whether I'm letting her stay inside or needing to put her back out.

"I'm keeping you all day with me, so you better leave her and her food and water outside." He moves past me, picking up the bowls and putting them outside on the back porch.

"All day, huh?" I pick up my dog and give her a big hug. "Bye, Cuddles. We'll be back tonight." I place her on the porch and she wags her tail at me. "I'll bring you a treat."

Benny closes the door and spins me around, pressing my back against it. His breath is warm on my cheek as he nuzzles it. "I'd like to give up my motel room. What do you think about that?"

. . .

"You want to move in with me for the remainder of your stay in town?" I ask as he kisses down my neck, sending trickles of heat all through me.

"I want to live with you from now on." He pulls back and looks at me with sparkles shooting through his steely blue eyes. "I don't want us to spend another night apart."

My stomach tightens and my body tenses. "That sounds very serious, Benny."

"Because what we have is very serious, Pumpkin." His fingertip moves over my lips, tracing them. "I want to wake up every morning and be able to open my eyes and look at your sweet face. I want to close my eyes each night with you being the last thing I see."

My heart speeds up. This is so quick and so unlike me. But when my mouth opens words come out without me thinking, "Me too."

"Good." He steps back, taking my hand in his and leading me toward the door. "And since we're talking about this, I want us to get something more my speed. A larger place. We can ride around and scout several out, and decide what we like."

"A larger place? Like you want me to move? I don't know, Benny. That's a little, no make that a lot scary. What if we don't work out? Then I'll have to move and that'll be..."

He stops and pulls me into a tight embrace. His forehead touches mine. "Let's don't say things like, if we don't work out. Let's keep things positive. I'm not saying this will be some relationship made in Heaven that never has a problem or a rough patch because that's not reality. We'll have our fights, we'll have our troubles, but we will get through them."

"I don't know what to say. This is all so sudden. That's all." I pull back and look at him. "We're kind of rushing into things."

"I've never been a man who rushes into things. And I know you aren't one to rush either. But this feels right. You have to agree with that."

"I do. It does feel right. But rushing is just stupid."

His fingertip moves along my jaw. "Do you want to slow things down? I keep my room and we can act like we don't want to spend every night together. Deny ourselves that. And for how long would you like to do that?"

My body aches with a need for him as only his fingertip moves over my skin. It's completely insane. "Okay, I know I want to have you in my bed every night. I know it will happen even if I try to slow things down. My body craves you now. It makes no sense."

"It does make sense. You and I were meant to be together. We found each other and want to be around one another. Not a big mystery. So it's settled then. We aren't going to say we're rushing anything. We're merely living our lives together from now on. And someday we'll decide to make that next step."

He lets me go and takes my hand again, leading me out the front door. I follow along mumbling as we go, "Marriage is on the table after only two dates. If you can call them dates."

"You can call them dates if you want to, Angel." He turns back and holds out his hand. "The key please."

I hand him my keys and he locks the door. Then puts my keys in his pocket.

"I need those. The key to my bike is on that keyring." I hold out my hand and he shakes his head.

"You're riding with me." He takes my hand and pulls me along behind him.

"No. Benny, I don't ride bitch."

He laughs and looks back at me as he tugs me along behind him. "You do now."

"Benny, for real, man. I'll ride my own bike. I've never ridden behind anyone. I think I'll feel very out of control." I pull back as he continues to tug me along.

"Good. You need to let some of that control go," he says as he picks my helmet up off my bike seat.

As he's placing it on my head, I say, "Said the control freak."

His grin covers his entire face. "You're going to have to trust me. And I'm not a control freak."

"What would you call yourself then?" I ask as he tightens the chin strap.

He looks as if he's pondering then his eyes brighten. "I'm a man who cares about you. So instead of thinking or saying I'm a control freak, you can say I'm a caring man. Who you love." He tweaks my nose then kisses it.

I have to laugh as this rugged-looking biker man in black leather, sporting a long beard and tattoos is so sweet and no one would believe me if I told them the things he says.

"I do love you." I kiss his lips for only a second and his whole face changes.

Sincerity is how I would describe his expression. "And I love you, Kitten."

My heart goes all pitter-patter in my chest. I feel heat in my cheeks as I know I'm blushing. What he does to me is awesome.

HE REACHES into one of the side compartments and pulls out two pairs of dark shades. He puts one pair on my face. "I bought these for you the other day. For when you came back. They match mine."

"So now we can match," I say with a laugh. "How thoughtful. Thank you."

He puts his on and gets on the bike then I get on behind him. "Hold on tight," he says.

"Why? Do you drive crazy?" I wrap my arms around him beginning to get nervous.

"No. I just want to feel your front against my back. So hold on tight," he says then he starts the bike, and it vibrates underneath me.

I place my chin on his shoulder and turn my head to kiss his neck. "You're very sweet, Benny."

"Yeah, I didn't know I could be sweet. You bring it out in me, Sugar."

He takes off and I hold on tighter because I've never ridden behind anyone before and I'm kind of in between shitting bricks and trying to enjoy this.

It's a thing only recently I had daydreams about after all. Now here I am behind my handsome biker, hanging on to him and feeling the wind blow over my face as he takes me away with him.

And it does feel just as amazing as I thought it would.

I just might enjoy riding bitch after all!

13

BLAZE

Her body behind mine feels amazing. And as we pull up to the café, I see some bikes from my club. I get a real sense of pride as I pull to a stop.

Finally, a real woman will be on my arm, not some tramp!

I wait for Angel to get off the bike then I do and help her with her helmet. She seems to fuss about it at first. Knocking my hand away but I just ignore her and continue.

"I can do it," she says with a pout.

"I know you can, obviously." I place the helmet on my seat and run my arm around her shoulders. "Now you get to meet my friends."

"Is it weird that I'm nervous?" she asks as she runs her hand over her white halter top and makes sure it's adjusted right.

I run my arm down to smooth out her backside, which doesn't need it. But her ass covered in tight black leather is a thing of magnificence and I just have to touch it. "No, it's not weird at all that you're nervous. They're all cool. You'll like them. I know you will."

She looks at me with a little frown on her gorgeous face. "But will they like me?"

"What's not to like?" I ask as I pull the door open for her.

She runs her arm around my waist and I can feel the tension in her body. "So many things, apparently."

"What did I say about that? Put that past shit where it belongs and become the women who has been locked up inside you for way too long. You're gorgeous, funny, and smart as a mother fucker..."

Her giggle stops me. "Smart as a mother fucker! I think I'll have to add that to my resume. Mind if I get a letter of recommendation from you with that as your opening line?"

I kiss the side of her head as I lead her toward the table my friends are at. "Of course, my Angel."

All eyes are on us as we walk up. Phoenix stands up and extends her hand immediately. "Hi, I'm Phoenix, the woman you heard talking to Blaze last night was me. I'm really sorry about the trouble I caused. I was only checking up on him to make sure no women were bugging him. Ashley and I have been keeping the bitches at bay because he was dead set on staying sin free for you. And now that I see you, I know why."

"Thank you," she says as she releases Phoenix's hand. "I had a bout of insecurities and ran like a frightened kid. I'm over it now. It's nice to meet you, my name is..."

The table full of people say, all at the same time, "Angel, we know!"

She laughs and looks at me. "Been talking about me?"

ASHELY GETS UP and holds out her hand. "I'm Ashley, and yes he has been talking about you. I have to say, I was thinking he had to be going overboard when he talked about how gorgeous you are, but he was on point. You're stunning, Angel."

Angel's deep blue eyes go really big. "Wow! Thank you. I mean, you're gorgeous yourself. That's quite a compliment."

Then she looks at Phoenix and nods. "You're also stunning, Phoenix. Is it a prerequisite to be pretty if you're to date a man in this club?"

Rod laughs. "It helps."

We take seats, I sit Angel next to Ashley and take the one between Angel and Paco. The waitress brings two coffee cups and places them in front of us. "Hi, Angel. Been a while since I've seen you."

Angel smiles at the girl who looks to be near her age. "Hey, Stella. Yeah, I've been eating at home, mostly. Does the cook still make that mean Denver omelet?"

She nods and says, "Yep. So you want that and the wheat toast? And I'll get the cream you like too." She turns to me. "And for you, sir?"

"I'll have what she's having. Since she's a local, I'm going to assume she knows the best thing to eat here." I place my hand on Angel's thigh and give it a slight squeeze.

"Be right back," she says as she spins away.

Ashley looks at Angel with a wide smile. "You have to show us the best place to eat lunch today when we take our ride. I've been searching for the perfect steak and have yet to find one."

"Freddy's is the best place. Flame-kissed magic is what they do over there," Angel says. "You'll love it or it'll be free. I went to school with the cook. Well, he likes to be called a chef, but I knew him when he made mud pies, so I still just call him a cook."

"Freddy's it is then," Ashely says. "So glad to have a local to show us around. Tell us what the others don't know, Angel. I want to see things only the locals know about."

The whole table leans in looking excited to find hidden treasures. Angel looks a little shy but her expression changes then she says, "I bet you guys like to hang around campfires and stuff like that in the middle of nowhere, right."

"Hell yeah we do," Rod says as he puts his arm around Ashley. "I love the outdoors and frankly the smoke filled bars are messing with my sinuses. What ya got, Angel?"

"My grandmother lives on a small farm about thirty minutes out. Way off the beaten path. She wouldn't mind letting us kick back at her place for the night. I'm assuming you guys have tents and stuff. Like most of the bikers who come for this rally do," Angel says as the waitress places the enormous plate filled with all kinds of delicious looking food in front of us.

Paco looks at Phoenix. "Sound like something you want to do?"

She nods. "I do. We can stop at the store before we head out and get wienies and roast them over the fire. It'll be fun."

I kiss Angel's cheek. "Looks like you're stealing the show, baby."

Her cheeks go pink and she looks down at her plate. "Nah."

Everyone chit chats and things feel comfortable. Seems Angel has a little social anxiety but seems to be getting over it well. I make sure to leave a huge tip for the waitress since she's a friend of sorts to Angel.

And back we get on my bike as the others do as well and Angel gets on behind me and we hit the road. Only this time as I ride with my brothers, I have my girl with me. And it feels better than I thought it would.

All the ass I thought I wanted is nothing compared to having Angel sitting behind me, holding me tight.

She leans with me as we make a corner and I fight the urge to kiss her as her chin rests on my shoulder. The air is the perfect temperature, and the ride seems like the best I've ever had.

My phone vibrates in my pocket and it reminds me of my grandfather and I figure it's one of my family members. Then I have to fight the urge to chunk the damn thing.

I don't bother with the phone and it stops vibrating. But it makes my mood a bit sour as I think about what the hell my family is going to say about Angel.

I CAN HEAR it all now. How could you? What were you thinking?

You're cut off without a cent!

Her lips touch my cheek and I stop thinking about anything but her. "Thank you, Benny," she says for absolutely no reason what so ever.

I give her a smile and look back at the road. A sign at the side of the road catches my attention. And then I see a dirt road with a for sale sign at the end of it. I slow down and take it, leaving the pack for a minute to see what kind of house it is.

Angel doesn't even ask as it's obvious I want to check this out. She's so cool. She just goes with the flow.

And when the house comes into view, I see her jaw drop.

It's huge. A log cabin mansion. A horseshoe drive leads us to the front of the massive home.

I stop the bike. "What do you think of this, my Angel?"

"No way, Benny. This is too much. And it's for sale. Not rent. But man, it's gorgeous, isn't it?"

I climb off the bike. "The sign said open house. Come on." I hold my hand out to her and she takes it and gets off.

She waits patiently for me to take her helmet off then we walk up the stone pathway to the Hickory wood set of double doors which make up the front entrance.

"I don't rent, Angel. That's throwing money away." I lead her up the stairs and open the door.

The wood interior is amazing and it smells fantastic. "Benny, can you imagine calling this place home? I mean, I know you live in a mansion already and have your whole life, but this is something, isn't it?"

"It is something. It's beyond compare to what I live in. Mine's nice, but so generic in the mansion sense of the word. This is real living. Real things make this place up." I gesture to an enormous fireplace. "Awesome to think about cold winter nights and that thing fired up. You and I curled up next to it. What do you think, Angel?"

We stand there in front of it and gaze at it and the Mahogany mantle over the top of it. Her hand squeezes mine. "Benny, this is too much."

"Angel, look at me," I say and she turns her head. "I have the money. I'm not going to get something average when I can get above average. So all I want to hear is if you like it or not. Don't even talk about the price."

She laughs. "Benny, what's not to like?"

"I don't know. Let's walk all around and see. We have to come up with something we aren't a thousand percent happy with so I can talk the seller down a few million or so." I pull her along and we find the kitchen.

"Well, I can't find a damn thing wrong with this," she says. "Three sub-zero fridges, a massive stove and two wall ovens. Wow! I've only seen this kind of stuff in magazines. Not even sure what some of these things are."

"We could hire a cook. And staff to keep it clean." I pull her along and look out a set of French doors. A huge swimming pool with a slide and a diving board along with a waterfall is out there.

"Staff! For a home! Benny, it's too much," she says as she leans into my side.

"No, it's what people who have money do, Baby. Do you know how hard you'd have to work to keep this place clean, even with my help? It would be a full-time job just doing that." I pull her around in front of me and pick her up, giving her a quick kiss. "Now let's find the master suite and see if that's something we can live with."

"Benny, what about your job?" she asks as I put her down and lead her out of the kitchen, toward a staircase.

THEN I SEE a set of papers on a table at the bottom. "Great, look the layout of the house. Good thing they have this here or we might get lost."

"Benny, how about you answer me about your job?" she says as she stops and holds me back from walking up the stairs.

"I don't think I want to be part of my family's law firm anymore. They're going to be representing a man I don't want to back. I've told my grandfather that and he seems intent on shoving the man down my throat." I pull at her to come on and she does as she seems a bit confused. "I can make my own practice."

"Okay. But that's kind of drastic, isn't it?" she asks.

We get to the top of the huge wooden staircase and a large picture window looks over the back side of the house. The scene is gorgeous and we stop talking and stare out the large window.

"Nah. Would you look at this, Angel? This place is perfect. There's a tennis court and a basketball court."

She takes up where I left off as she points out the window.

"An entire playground, Benny." She looks at me. "This needs to be a home for a family. Not us."

Wrapping my arms around her, I pull her close and rock her back and forth as I hold her. "Baby, what do you think I mean for us? I mean for us to have a family. We'll become a family and this place is perfect for that."

"Kids, Benny?" She smiles and giggles. "Our third day together and here you are talking about a family. Our family."

"I KNOW I'm taking much too long to bring these things up, my Angel. But I've put it all off long enough." I chuckle and she runs her hands over my bearded cheeks.

My hand moves over her shoulder and along her arm until my hand rests on top of hers. I move it to my lips and kiss it. Her eyes sparkle as she looks into mine. "Benny, you're amazing."

"You are," I say then hand her the paper I picked up of the floor plan and scoop her up in my arms and carry her. "Now let's go find that master suite."

She looks at it then points at the very end of the long hallway. "That's it down there."

Off I go passing the rest of the bedrooms, counting off five on one side and four on the other. I turn the knob on the door that's larger than the rest of the bedroom doors and nearly fall over as I see the massive room.

"Fuck me," Angel whispers. "This is too much, Benny."

"No, it's perfect."

As if on cue an older blonde woman pops out of the bathroom. "Hello there. My name's, Annie and I'm the real estate agent who has this home listed. How are you two on this very nice day?"

"Put me down," Angel hisses.

. . .

I DO as she's asked as I look at the agent and wish like hell she hadn't heard me say that. "Hi, we're the Worthingtons. I know you overheard the word, perfect, but I haven't seen it all yet so don't go thinking I have to have this home or anything like that."

She reaches out to shake Angel's hand first. "Lovely to meet you, Mrs. Worthington." She lets her hand go as Angel is slack-jawed at being called that name. The woman grabs up my hand in a nice firm shake. "Nice to meet you too, Mr. Worthington. Now I know I caught you off guard there, not my intention, I assure you."

I nod and ask, "So what do we have going on here? Motivated seller, or someone looking to stick to the wealthy?"

Her smile tells me she has a little secret, and she leans in close and talks in a hushed tone as if anyone else is even around, "Okay, here's the deal on this beauty. There was a mass murder here in the basement a few years ago and the man who inherited this place doesn't want to live here."

"No way!" Angel says as she looks with wide eyes at the woman.

The woman erupts with laughter and claps her hands. "No way, is right. I love to open with a joke."

Okay, this chick's a little looney!

14

ANGEL

The firelight lends a golden hue to all who surround it. Benny's gang, as I've been thinking of the people in his motorcycle club, are a bunch of cool people. Ashley and her husband and Phoenix and her fiancé seem to be the people Benny is closest to.

They came out to my grandmother's with us and five more guys came too. The others preferred to stay behind in the hectic night scene of Sturgis as the rally has gotten underway big time, making our town a circus of sorts.

My grandmother took advantage of us being here to feed her animals in the morning and made an overnight trip to see her sister who lives one town over. So we have the place to ourselves.

"I'M GOING INSIDE to grab a bag of marshmallows," I tell Benny who has his arm hanging loosely around my shoulders as we sit on a large log by the fire.

He gets up, taking my hand and walking with me to the little farmhouse. "You having a good time, Baby?"

I nod. "Yeah. They're a cool bunch. Easy to get along with."

We walk inside and I get the bag of marshmallows off the counter and turn to walk back out. He stops me and pulls me in for a kiss.

It stops my heart and I have to wonder if I'll always react this way to him. He ends the sweet kiss and looks down at me with glistening eyes. "So, the house, Angel. Can you see yourself living there?"

I laugh and shake my head. "That place isn't a thing I've even fantasized about."

"I know that," he says then kisses me again, taking my mind completely off the place I can't even think of as a mere house. He pulls his mouth away and looks at me. "Bet you never fantasized about being with a billionaire either."

I shake my head. "Can't say that I have. But really, Benny, a nice big family should have that place. It has so much to offer."

His grin is contagious and I find myself grinning too as he says, "And we will eventually use it all. Give me a minute or two, Baby." He laughs.

"You know what I mean," I say as I gently hit him in the chest. "It'll be just the two of us rattling around in the monster sized home."

"And right now it's just the four of us in my family rattling around a monster-sized home back in New York. We don't use a quarter of the rooms in that place. Yet we still have it. So thinking only about what you saw today. How do you like it?"

"Okay, I love it, alright. I mean, damn, Baby, what's not to love? The whole room devoted exclusively to that pool table is awesome. The indoor swimming pool is beyond anything I've seen before. There are so many rooms for various entertainment purposes. My God, the thing has its own theater." I have to close my mouth as the whole thing is so overwhelming.

"I can see you fighting yourself over it. It's okay to be kind of freaked out by it all, but take it all in as well. You'll be with a man who makes a lot more money than most. Deal with it, Pumpkin." He kisses me again and I go limp in his arms and have to hold on tightly to him.

When he ends it, I give him the answer he's been waiting for, "Get it. I want it. I do."

He picks me up off the floor and spins me around. "Yes! We're getting our own place!"

Well, he is. It's not like I can contribute shit to it.

HOLDING ME BACK, he smiles as he says, "And that massive eight car garage is pretty spectacular too. You know what I thought about when I saw it?"

"How many motorcycles you can fit in there?" I say with a giggle.

He shakes his head. "No. I thought about you building your own brand of motorcycles in there. Designing them and building them right there. I can hire the help you'd need and you could have your very own business. What do you think about that?"

My head is spinning. I think it might actually be moving in circles between my shoulders. "Benny! No! You can't be serious."

"I am serious. I want to help you make your dreams come true and I'd like to make some of my own come true too. With your help, I want us to design something for me. Something uniquely mine. Then I can drive it around and tell everyone my smart as fuck wife made it for me."

Wife!

"Benny, don't go getting ahead of things. This is going really fast as it is. Wife is a term that has all kinds of legal crap attached to it. You're worth a ton of money. I don't want that part rushed in the least. You have a lot of paperwork to take care of before that's even considered." I pull out of his arms and go to the fridge to grab a bottle of water.

I turn to find him right there and he catches me up in his arms again. "I love you, girl! Making you mine in name too is at the forefront of my mind. I don't know how long I can hold off on that. And there will be no paperwork to do. No pre-nup. What I have is yours."

"Bad idea, Sweetie. Very bad idea." I kiss the tip of his nose. "I'm not going to let you do that. And we can talk about that later. I'm not about to stand here and discuss such things yet."

THE SCREEN DOOR squeaks as Ashley comes inside. "Hey, sorry for interrupting. Can I use the bathroom, Angel? Rod told me to go outside and I can but I really don't want to."

I laugh and point toward the bathroom. "It's over there and please feel free to use it whenever you need to. Tell Phoenix too. And anyone else who needs it."

She nods and leaves us alone again. Benny pins me to the fridge. "When can we discuss such things?"

Then it occurs to me that his family may be the reason he wants to hurry things along. Before they can intervene and stop anything.

"How about after you introduce me to your family?" I say as I watch his reaction.

"Why after?" His eyes narrow. "Why not have things settled before that?"

I press my hand against his chest to push him back some. "I knew it. I knew you were hurrying things along to get this past your family. Benny, you come from a powerful family. You have to know that even if you marry me and knock me up, they can get in between us if they want to."

"No, they can't. I won't let them."

Another thought pops into my head. "Benny, is this some sort of a rebellious thing? I can see the whole motorcycle club thing is. Am I a thing that will not be appreciated or maybe even tolerated? Is that why you're jumping forward with this by leaps and bounds?"

"Don't think about my family. Let me think about them. You just let me handle things. And the answer is, no. I'm not trying to hurry things along for any reason other than I want to start a life with you. I can see so many things for our future. Six kids, three dogs, maybe even a damn cat to keep the mice away." He laughs and tweaks my nose. "Just fucking with you. Come on. You bringing up my family has me needing a drink."

I let him pull me along and grab the marshmallows again. As we go outside I have to think to myself that he isn't kidding about any of it. And I think he's hurrying things along, thinking if it's all said and done then they can do nothing about him marrying a poor girl instead of a rich, East coast debutant like I'm sure he's supposed to do.

And I have no idea if any of this is real or his rebellion!

I watch as Benny turns into Blaze in small increments right in front of my eyes. Step one, take a long drink of whiskey straight from the bottle. Step two, pull a cigarette from the untouched pack he has in his T-shirt pocket.

Step three, light it up and take in a deep drag. Then step four, pull me along with him to the back of the house, pin me to the wall and kiss me while he grinds his cock against me.

The typical things that make you feel like a renegade.

And right on cue he pulls back from me and looks at me. "Angel, you think you could help ease this tension a bit?"

I nod and look into his eyes, finding a lot of angst in them all of a sudden.

He undoes his pants and gives them a push. They go to his ankles, leaving his hard cock pressing against his boxers.

I go to my knees on the ground in front of him as he turns and leans against the side of the house. I can do this for him. I can and will.

I can ease the pain his family causes him for the moment. But it won't make it go away forever.

His moan is soft as I take him into my mouth. He takes a couple of handfuls of my hair and moves my head back and forth the speed he wants me to go.

The pace is fast as he needs to climax to dull the edge of whatever it is talking about his family causes. His words are spoken between clenched teeth, "Fuck, you suck my cock like you were made to do that, Baby. It fits down your throat like a glove. Suck it, Baby! Suck that fat cock!"

I grip his ass in my hands to move faster with the push of his hands. I suck harder as he moans and cusses at random times.

Not sure if it's because he just likes it that damn much or he's mentally cursing his family for whatever his reasons are. All I know is while I have man issues, he has family issues.

We're just a couple of broken people. It doesn't mean we can't be together if that even is a thing his family will permit. It just means I need to be more sensitive to the fact although he might be rich as fuck, he has things that bother him and mold his mind too.

My mouth moves fast over him and then he stiffens and it shoots down my throat. I swallow and find him yanking me up by the hair and slamming his mouth to mine.

His tongue moves in and he kisses me hard as he undoes my pants with one hand and moves it inside my panties until he has two fingers inside me and moves them in and out until I can't take it anymore and cum.

He moves his hand out of my panties and places the two wet fingers in the side of my mouth, joining our juices inside our mouths.

The taste changes and he growls, and the kiss gets dirtier, hungrier, greedier. It sends him into a frenzy for a moment and then it slows.

He pulls away from me and looks at me. His eyes are hard then he blinks and they go back to my Benny. "Fuck! Fuck, I'm sorry, Angel."

I shake my head and take him by the shoulders. "Don't be. You need me too. I can see that now. You need me to be strong for you just like I need you to be strong for me. Maybe we are meant to be together. Maybe we can help each other. You can be you with me. Blaze when you need to be. Benjamin, when you have to be. Benny when you want to be."

"God damn it, I love you, Angel. My Angel who understands me better than I do." His hand wraps around the back of my neck and he pulls my mouth to his again. Only this time, his mouth takes mine in a gentle kiss.

I run my hands over the short sides of his hair up into the long top and press my chest to his. Our hearts pound in unison as our mouths mingle.

With no idea how long this will be allowed to last, I want to make every last second count before that happens.

It might end because his family makes it. Or it might end when he finds this middle man he needs to become. Or it might even end when I find my full strength.

HE EASES the kiss and leans his forehead against mine. "Angel, tell me you will marry me. Please tell me that one day you will become mine in name too."

"I will marry you one day, Benny. I will."

I say the words because he so desperately needs to hear them. I'm not lying to him but the reality is, I have no idea if that will come true or not.

I can't see the future and if hearing what he wants will help him. Then I'll say anything he needs me to.

He buttons up my pants then leans over and pull his up. "Guess we should get back to the party, Baby."

"Guess so. You feel better now?" I ask as he runs his arm around my neck and pulls me close to him.

His lips touch the side of my head. "Yeah, I feel better. You sure do know how to make your man feel better, Baby."

My man.

I have a man.

One to take care of.

Am I really up to this?

HE STOPS JUST before we get back into the firelight and can be seen. He turns me to him and I see the vulnerability in his expression. "Angel, I want to thank you. Thank you for finding me."

I nearly cry as he looks so fragile and innocent.

"You found me, remember," I say and try to hold back the tears.

"That's not what I mean. I slipped away there for a moment. I don't want to be Benjamin or Blaze. I want to be the man I am with you. I want to be Benny. Your Benny. I always want to be him. You found that man in the first place and you just found him again. That's how I know you're the one for me. You make me a better man. So thank you for finding me. I've been lost my entire life." He kisses my cheek and I can't stop a tear from escaping.

He looks at me then wipes the tear away. "Let's try really hard to keep these out of each other's eyes."

"Will do." I put on a smile and sniffle then let him lead me back to his friends.

And know now I have to be careful not to hurt this man as he's as fragile as I am.

15

BLAZE

The last week has flown by as we've been busy with buying the house. But it's now ours and today we're moving in. I made Angel sign all of the papers of ownership too.

She protested, of course. In the end, though, I won, and she's part owner in the place too. I saw the smile on her face when they handed her the keys to the house. She was happy.

I'm waiting here for the furniture company to bring the new mattresses for the enormous bed in the master suite. The house came furnished as we found out there was a death that left the house on the market.

Only it didn't occur here. The widow of a Greek tycoon passed away in one of her other mansions in Spain. The couple never had children and had ten homes around the world. So the sale was easy and the items in it stayed.

I'VE ALREADY HAD Angel's things brought over and she'll be on her way here after she does a bit of work at her uncle's shop.

Cuddles, has settled in nicely and is checking out the enormous yard she now has.

I watch her out of the line of the floor to ceiling windows that runs along the sun porch along the back of the house. My phone rings and startles me as I was taking in the gorgeous scenery.

And I see it's my mother. "Hello, Mom."

"Benjamin, what on Earth have you done?"

"What has Grandfather told you all?"

"Well, that isn't what I'm talking about. He told us you refused to come back for the meeting with that Bain fellow. He said you didn't agree with the firm's decision to represent the man and he told you maybe you should think about leaving the firm. Is that why you bought a home in Sturgis?"

Her question floors me. "How do you know I did that?"

"You used the bank account I opened for you when you turned eighteen. We never took my name off of it and when an exorbitant amount of money leaves, they notify me. So why buy a home all the way over there unless you're contemplating leaving the family business?"

"I have a use for a home here. I've met someone, Mom." I wait to see how she's going to react.

The wait is excruciating as she's dead silent. Then she clears her throat and says, "Benjamin there aren't a lot of eligible woman of the stature you are to marry hanging around in a motorcycle town like Sturgis is."

My hand balls into a fist and I slam it against my leg. "I should be able to marry who I want. Who I love. Her financial status shouldn't come into it."

"Tell me you haven't jumped the gun and asked this woman to marry you yet?"

· · ·

"It's complicated now. One day we'll be married. And I put her name on the paperwork for the house. She's an owner in it with me."

Mom makes a deep sigh then says, "So she does have money. Why didn't you just say that?"

"No, she doesn't have money or come from money. I just wanted to make sure she knew this place is hers as much as it's mine. I wanted her name on it too." I look out the window and watch Cuddles chase a bird who dared to land on her lawn.

"That was an unwise decision. I don't know why you'd do that. If she didn't pay at least some on it, why would her name get to be on it?"

"Because that's the way I wanted it. I'll go back to New York sometime soon to make sure I get what I have coming to me from the firm. Then I will resign and start my own. Two-thirds of the clients are ones I brought in. They'll go with me."

"Benjamin, you need to rethink things. So about this woman. You aren't married and even though you have a home together now doesn't mean you have to marry her. You're meant for more, Son. And what will you do if your grandfather does cut you off financially?"

"It might stifle more income but it won't break me by any means. I've made investments on my own. I have several accounts only I know about. He can't stop me from making money on my own." I get up and pace as this conversation is making my insides hurt.

"Darling, I just don't want to see you squander away your legacy. You are a Worthington for God's sakes. Certain things go along with that. Things like marrying within your class. Staying with the family business is also a thing that should be a top priority to you. Mingling with trashy women is one thing, trying to make one your wife is quite another."

"She isn't trashy, Mother. Angel is about to hold a Master's Degree in Engineering. She's the smartest woman I know."

"Does she ride a motorcycle, Benjamin?"

I HESITATE to answer because my mother has an idea of how a lady acts. Ladies do not ride motorcycles in her opinion. "She does. So what?"

The sound of my mother sighing, as she falls back onto what sounds like pillows on her bed I bet, I can hear over the phone then she says, "Oh, Son! Why a thing like that? Next, you'll be telling me she drives a truck or some horrible thing like that. Lord, please do not tell me she wears tight leather pants and boots too."

She does, and she looks hot as hell in them!

"Mom, don't worry about what the woman wears. She's fantastic and funny, smart and she makes your son happy. I'm happier than I've ever been. Can't that be enough?"

The doorbell rings and I make my way to let in what surely must be the furniture delivery guys. I can't wait to get those new mattresses on and start breaking in the new house.

"BENJAMIN, come home so we can talk. Bring the girl if you want. Let her see what's expected out of her. I bet she won't be so keen on marrying you when she sees how she's expected to dress and behave."

"Mom, I have to go. I have work to do. Love you bunches."

"What? Love you bunches? Who talks like that, Benjamin? The trailer trash girl? Son, please…"

"Sorry, got to go. Bye Mom." I end the call and open the door. "Hi, come on in and follow me upstairs, guys."

Two burley men follow me up the staircase with the

mattress. The one right behind me seems to be marveling at the house. He lets out a long whistle. "Boy, I bet this set you back a bundle."

"You'd win that bet." I open the bedroom door. "In here, guys."

"Gee, this room is bigger than my whole damn house," he says as they prop the mattress against the wall. He points to the mattresses that are still on the bed. "What you want us to do with those?"

"Take them where ever you want." I walk over to the bed and look the clean and most likely barely used thing over. "It looks to be in perfect condition. I just wanted brand new ones. You can have these if you want."

The guys come over and both sit on the mattress. "It's very comfortable. Sure, we can take this out of here for you."

I give them a nod. "I'll leave you to it then. I have to get some things going in the kitchen before the old ball and chain gets home from work."

The local meat market had a couple of steaks I found to my liking earlier today and they had a couple of lobsters that had been flown in by helicopter from Maine. I plan on making my sweet lady a feast for our first night in the new house.

I want to get a bottle of red wine out and open so I can give her a glass of it when she gets here. It's funny that my mother said something about Angel driving a truck because I just ordered her one online this morning. It's going to be delivered here next week as a surprise.

The delivery guys come down the stairs with the old mattress and go out the front door just as Cuddles starts to scratch at the back door, wanting in.

I go over and open the door for her and she zips inside jumping up and down so I get her a treat from the cookie jar we brought from Angel's house. "Who's a good girl?" I pick her up and give her the little dog biscuit.

The men come back through with the other mattress and the little fur ball changes into Cuddles right in my arms. "Cuddles, what the fuck?"

She wiggles and almost gets away from me as she lunges to get at the men. They get up the stairs and she is still fighting me. I take her to the laundry room that's off the kitchen and put her in there and close her up.

She is a bit on the mean side where strangers are concerned. I thought Angel was being a bit overdramatic about that.

They guys come back down and I go to the door with them. "That's it then, guys?"

"Yeah, it's all ready for you," the guy says.

I hand him a couple of twenties. "Give one to your buddy."

"Will do," he says and they leave just as I see Angel pulling in on her bike.

She climbs off and comes to me her arms open as she gets to me. "I need a hug, Benny."

Wrapping her in my arms, I hug her tight. "Why the needed hug, Babydoll?"

SHE TAKES IN A DEEP BREATH. "I handed my house keys over to my landlady after I left work. It was the last part of my independence and I feel a little shaky."

I lift her up and carry her inside. "No reason to feel shaky. This is your home, Baby."

Her head rests against my chest as her hand moves over it. "This feels like a dream. My whole house and yard could fit in the living room alone."

"Now you get to see how the other half lives, Pumpkin. Speaking of that. I'm going to need to go to New York sometime to deal with some business. I'll hire a private jet to take us out there. I won't make you stay with my family in their place. We'll get a room at the Four Seasons. It'll be cool. I'll take you sightseeing and make you an appointment at a fancy salon to get your hair and nails done."

She looks at me with drooping eyes. "You don't like my hair?"

"Of course, I love your hair. It's not that. It's just that I want to pamper you. Show you the finest things I can." I kiss her cheek and she smiles a little.

"Oh. And I'll get to meet your family?" She looks so hopeful.

"You do. But I'd not get my hopes up about them. They're snobby. Not at all down to Earth like you are." I place her on her feet in the kitchen and pour us a couple of glasses of wine.

She takes hers and I take her hand, leading her to the outside patio so we can watch the sunset together. Then I hear Cuddles barking and Angel looks oddly at me. "Where's the dog?"

I TURN BACK and go let her out of the laundry room with a chuckle. "Hey there, killer. I had to put her in there so she wouldn't kill the delivery men. I thought you were kidding about her being aggressive to strangers."

She shakes her head. "No, I was telling the truth. That's why her liking you surprised me so much. So when will this trip to the fancy town of New York occur?"

"When do you want to go?" I ask as I take her hand again and lead her outside.

"Whenever, I guess. Maybe if you send me to a fancy salon and buy me some clothes your family will deem appropriate, you can transform me into the right girl for you," she says as I sit down and pull her down to sit on my lap.

I can't tell her that no amount of transformation will help.

My family wants paperwork. Like a well-bred animal, the paper is what it's all about.

"I'm not about transforming you into someone you don't want to be. But if it would make you feel better if you dressed to fit in, I suppose I can help you make that transformation. I'll make sure you feel very comfortable before I take you to them." I pull her braid over her shoulder and play with it.

She leans in and kisses me. "This is nice. The view is amazing. Your lap feels like home already." She laughs, and it makes my heart jump.

"Your ass in my lap feels like home." I kiss her and she places her glass on the table and wraps her arms around me, deepening our kiss.

My cock springs to life as our tongues twirl around together. When our lips part we both are breathing heavily. She whispers, "That was our first kiss in our place, Benny."

"And after dinner, I'm going to devour you for the first time on our brand new bed in our bedroom, Angel." I tickle her ribs a little, sending her into a fit of laughter.

"Stop!" she screams.

I stop and gaze at her with the sunset's oranges and pinks filling the sky behind her. "You're beautiful, my Angel."

She strokes my beard. "You're pretty too." Her smile is bright and her eyes tell me she's happy.

Happier than I think she knew she could be. And I have barely begun to show her all I can bring to her life.

"I bought steaks and lobsters for dinner. Would you care to accompany me to the kitchen and help me prepare our first dinner in our first home together?"

Her hand travels over my shoulder and up my neck, sending

sparks all through me. "I would. The sun's just about to drop out of the sky."

I turn her in my arms and she lays her head back on me as we watch the sun leave the sky on our first night home. Our first real home.

I feel like she and I have been together forever. She and I seem to have an instant history. It's odd but a great odd.

She climbs off my lap and holds out her hand to me. I take it and run my arm around her. "So I need you to throw the lobsters into the boiling water. That shit freaks me out," I tell her.

"You bought live ones? Oh, Benny, I can't kill them either."

Cuddles, runs along behind us, coming inside like she owns the place. I laugh. "Maybe Cuddles could toss them into the boiling water. I'm sure the killer in her wouldn't even flinch."

And now it looks like we're going to need an aquarium for our new pet lobsters!

16

ANGEL

"Come on, they're all leaving in the morning," Benny calls out to me from the bedroom as I'm braiding my hair in the bathroom mirror. "This will be our last night out."

I like his friends but hanging out in a noisy bar just isn't my idea of fun. But for Benny, I'll do it for tonight, anyway. Once they all leave and it's down to just he and I. Then we can start to settle into our own routine. And bars have no place in it.

As I walk out, he holds up a little box. "Look what I found when I was in town this afternoon while you were working."

"What did you find?" I ask as he comes toward me, taking the lid off the box.

I see a set of earrings. In the shape of motorcycles. Very trendy and not my style at all. But he bought them, so I'll wear them. He pulls one out of the box and puts it on me.

He kisses my neck just behind my ear. "They're cute on you. I knew they would be." He puts the other one on and kisses the other side and now I think he's ready for us to leave.

"Thank you, Benny. I'd never have bought these for myself." It's not a lie.

. . .

He laughs and pulls me along with him. "I know they're a little whimsical for you. But the old woman who was selling them said she'd made the trip all the way from Kansas to sell her handcrafted jewelry at the rally so I had to buy something."

I kiss his cheek as we head down the stairs. "Sweet to your very core, aren't you?"

He shakes his head. "I hope you still love me after you see me in New York."

"How bad could you be?" I ask, knowing I had a real attitude when we first met and he managed to tame this tiger. He has to use that charisma on others as well.

"I can be ruthless when I have to and chances are with my family, I'll have to." He puts my helmet on and holds my hand so I can get on the back of his bike, behind him.

"You sound a little scary, Benny." I hold tight to him.

"Baby, you don't even know." He starts up the bike and off we go to the large biker bar his friends are at.

The scene is pure chaos as we pull up to the jam-packed bar. Music is so loud you can hear it before you even enter the parking lot. He pulls to a stop in the line where his fellow bikers are parked.

"Wow, this is nuts," I say as he leads me inside.

"You never go to these things do you?" he asks.

I shake my head. "Not my thing."

"We don't have to stay a real long time. Only until two or so."

Mentally, I grimace. Staying until two in the morning sounds like torture. Once we get inside and the first members of his gang sees him, they hand him a bottle of Jack Daniels and Benny takes a swig then hands it to me.

I shake my head and Benny nods his and holds the bottle to my lips. "It'll loosen you up."

It'll have me puking before the night's over is what it'll do. But I take the drink and cross my fingers I won't make a fool out of myself.

Drinking the hard stuff has never agreed with me. So when Ashley comes up to me and hands me a beer, I take it. Grateful to have something to sip on that's a lot weaker than the liquor.

She shouts into my ear because the music is so loud she has to, "I like your earrings." She moves her long blonde hair back behind her ear to show me she has a matching set. "Rod and Blaze got swindled by the same old woman today."

I laugh and know I'm going to miss this woman when they leave to go back to their normal lives. Whatever that is.

IT OCCURS to me that it's been two weeks and I haven't gotten to know anything about any of his friends. I really am antisocial.

Benny goes into Blaze mode around his fellow bikers and it's always kind of odd to me. The cigarettes get lit up and if a joint is passed around, he does partake.

He knows better than to even try to push that on me. I don't smoke at all. Never have and never will.

Some hard song comes on and it has the whole bar full of people revving up their already loud noise. Benny turns back to me and pulls me into his arms, lifting my feet off the floor as he swings me around a little to the music.

I guess to most this would be amazing fun. But all I can think about is how loud it all is, how crowded the place is, and how the hell we'd get out if a fire broke out in here.

Yeah, I know. I'm a weirdo.

Once the song ends, he places my feet on the floor and proceeds to drag me behind him through the crowd and the next thing I know we're in a ring of his friends again and they're all yelling in each other's ears about shit I can't hear and wouldn't understand if I could.

I FEEL like a foreigner in my own home town. It's kind of awful.

I feel a tug on my arm and find Phoenix and Ashley. Phoenix shouts, "We're going on a bathroom run, wanna come?"

Anything sounds better than this. I nod and tug at Benny's hand and shout into his ear when he leans back, "I'm going to the bathroom with Ashley and Phoenix. I'll be back. Be good."

He laughs and pulls me in front of him and gives me a quick kiss. "I will."

As I walk away, he lands a sharp slap on my ass and gives me a wink to which I wink back. He makes my heart melt with just one look. I'm so smitten.

The women's restroom isn't much of a reprieve from the loudness but it is a little less deafening than in the main area. I lean against the wall as we wait in the line.

"SO YOU GUYS are heading out in the morning. I have to admit I'm going to miss you two." I nod as some woman wearing a ripped up shirt walks past me and seems kind of pissed.

But who wouldn't if someone ripped their shirt nearly off.

Ashely laughs as she sees my face as I look the woman over as she leaves. "Rough crowd out there."

I nod. "I'd say so."

Phoenix pulls out a pack of cigarettes and Ashley waves her off when she offers and so do I. She gets one for herself and lights it up. I try hard not to cough and act like a baby about the smoke.

"We're going to miss you too, Angel. You're a real trip. Your humor will be missed," Phoenix tells me. "But we'll see you in Vegas for our wedding next week, right?"

"Your wedding?" I ask as I have no idea what she's talking about.

Ashley looks a little surprised as she asks, "Blaze didn't tell you?"

"No." I look at Phoenix. "You and Paco are tying the knot then?"

She nods. "Yeah. Blaze is paying for us to stay there for the whole week. I really can't imagine why he hasn't told you. He said he was coming."

I shrug my shoulders. "Maybe he's not taking me." Anger starts to flow through me that he'd not invite me to the thing.

Ashely laughs. "I'm sure he's taking you, Angel. The guy goes nowhere without you after all."

"He must've forgotten you weren't there that day we told everyone, and he said he'd be there. That's most likely it. Just mention it and see what he says about it," Phoenix suggests.

THE URGE TO bite my nails is awful. Why didn't he tell me? Is he really planning on going without me?

The line moves and I can see we're finally next in line to get to use the handful of toilets. I tap my foot and both women look down at it. Ashley looks up at me. "Are you mad?"

"Nope." I cross my arms in front of me. "Just really have to pee."

So what if it's a lie?

After I get into the stall, I try hard to calm back down. I don't know why I'm letting this go all over me but it is.

Quickly, I take care of the business I came in here for and find the other two washing their hands and I do the same. In the mirror, I see my cheeks are flushed and I really need to try to calm down.

The loud noise and heat with the crowd does little to help as I follow them out and back to Benny. I'm taller than either of them so I can see over their heads as we get closer to where we left our men and I see a tall, heavyset, blonde woman pulling on Benny's arm.

I suppose trying to get him to dance with her. I stop as he pulls out his pack of cigarettes and lets her take one from the pack then he lights it for her. She blows the smoke off to one side then leans in to say something else to him.

I barely notice Ashley and Phoenix looking back at me as I move faster to tell the woman to get away from my man. They part so I can get by them and I yank the skanky chick's arm as soon as I can reach her.

She looks me up and down with a half-smile on her red lips. "What?"

"He's taken. Get lost," I shout in her ear.

She looks back at me just as Benny turns around and his eyes get really big as she says, "Look, Bitch, he ain't got no ring on his finger so he's up for grabs."

I look back to see Ashely and Phoenix with their jaws dropped and make a fist with my right hand and turn back to the dumb ass and smack her so fucking hard her head snaps back.

Her cigarette flies through the air and her ass drops like a rock. Ashley and Phoenix move to either side of me and pull me along as Ashley shouts, "Time to move our party elsewhere, guys."

The whole pack of Benny's friends just moves a good ways over, leaving the fat chick lying on the floor. Benny takes my hand and pulls me away until he finds some place a little less loud.

"Why'd you do that, Baby?" he asks as he takes my right hand and looks over my red knuckles.

"A couple of reasons. First, she was touching my man. Second she used the word bitch and I don't appreciate that."

He kisses my knuckles and then me. "You're something else, Rocky. One punch and she was out."

"Why didn't you tell her to fuck off instead of giving her a fucking cigarette and a light?" I ask as I narrow my eyes at him.

"She'd been bugging me and wouldn't let up. I gave it to her thinking she'd go away," he says, and he looks sincere.

"You give a bitch a cigarette and a light in this place, she'll think you want her. Do you want her, Blaze?" I stare him down.

"What the fuck? No, Angel. What the fuck's wrong with you?" He looks genuinely confused.

"Why didn't you tell me about Phoenix and Paco's Vegas wedding you're going to in a week?" I cross my arms in front of me and tap my foot.

His eyebrows go way up. "That? That's what has you so fired up? Fuck, Baby. I forgot. With all we've been doing, I really just forgot. Why would that make you so mad?"

"Were you planning on taking me with you? Or just leaving and telling me nothing?"

He shakes his head. "I'm not him, Angel. I'm not Gage. I'm not leaving you."

The fact he knows what's-his-ass's name has me puzzled because I never say it. "Who told you his name?"

Suddenly he looks worried. "I've been sworn to secrecy. It doesn't really matter, anyway. Come on, Baby. This is silly…"

I cock my head to one side. "What's so silly about me being mad that you've discussed my private business with someone in this town? Who was it?"

He shakes his head again. "No, now, I made a promise and I'm going to keep it. And you need to stop being crazy."

I try to walk away but he catches my arm so I turn back and say, "Fine. But when we get home, I'm going to use the belt to get it out of you. I don't like people talking about my personal shit. Not ever!"

His grip on my arms tightens. "What did you say to me? You're going to use the belt on me? To get something out of me? Fuck that shit!"

"You're hurting my arm," I say as I look at the way he's holding it so tight.

"And apparently you think you're going to try to hurt me later. So." He glares at me and I glare right back.

"Tell me who it was, Blaze."

"Don't you fucking call me Blaze! You and I need to go somewhere a little more private, Angel." He tugs me along with him and takes me outside and around the side of the building where he pushes me up against the wall.

"Stop!" I shout at him.

His hand goes over my mouth, making me be quiet. "Listen to me, young lady, you will never lay a hand on me in anger. Nor I, you. The belt, the whip, and our hands are not to be used in anger. Got me?"

I nod and he moves his hand from my mouth. "Blaze..."

"Why are you calling me that?" He takes me by the shoulders.

"Because that's who you're being right now. I don't think you forgot to tell me about going to Vegas." I look him in the eyes as he darts them back and forth.

"I did forget. I asked you to go to New York with me, for God's sakes. Why on Earth would I take you there and not to Vegas, Baby? You're freaking out for no reason." He lets me go but pulls me into a hug and holds me tight. "What's really wrong, Baby?"

"I don't know," I confess. "This can't last. It's all too good to be true. And I know that no matter how hard you try, your family is going to fight this."

He lets me go and takes a step back. "Angel, I'll fight them over you."

"You shouldn't have to," I say and the tears start falling. "You should just do what's expected of you. Be with a woman in your league. You're so far out of mine, it's not funny."

"Don't talk like that. You're a brilliant woman and you're on the cusp of your own greatness. Have a little faith in yourself and know you will become someone who's amazing." He looks over my shoulder and I hear footsteps moving over the gravel in quick steps. "Who's this mother fucker and why does he look like that?"

I turn around and nearly fall down. "Gage!"

To be continued...

THE BILLIONAIRE TAKES CHARGE OF HIS ANGEL

Book 3

17

BLAZE

"Gage?" I ask as I watch a strange man scoop my Angel up in his arms.

And she's letting him!

"Angel, I've missed you. I've been looking everywhere for you," he says as he holds her tight. Then he lets her go and walks up to me with a few quick steps.

I'm shocked as he knocks me in the chest, shoving me back and I hit the wall behind me. "Hey, mother fucker," I shout at him and draw my fist back.

Angel is suddenly between us. Her back is to me and her hand is on the other guy's chest. "Gage, what are you doing?"

"I saw how he handled you." He looks at me. "What makes you think you can be so rough with her?"

I'm at a complete loss for words right now. This can't be real. This asshole ran off on her and she's not calling him out on it.

"He wasn't being rough with me," she says as I watch her hand run over his chest. "He and I were having a little argument. He wasn't hurting me."

His demeanor changes rapidly and he takes her hand, the

one she's been running over his chest for reasons I can't explain. "Angel, we need to talk."

"The fucking hell you do," I let him know. "You left her. Without another word from you in the last couple of years. You broke her, you asshole. You don't get to talk to her now." I run my hands over her shoulders. "Tell him, Baby."

She looks back at me over her shoulder. "Benny, I'd like to talk to him. To get some closure after all this time. Please let me."

"Let you?" the guy asks. "Angel, he doesn't have to let you talk to me. I'm the man you love. How could you have forgotten that?"

Her voice is weak as she says, "Gage, I haven't forgotten anything. But you have to understand that I've moved on. Benny and I live together. We love each other. So I won't be talking to you unless he approves of that. I care too much about him not to have his approval."

He pulls the hand he's been holding to his lips and kisses her palm and I about come unglued. "No you don't! You, son of a bitch!" I try to reach around Angel to yank her hand away from him.

She presses her back against me and pulls her hand away on her own. "Gage, you don't get to do that. You can't show up here and think you and I still have anything. You left. You never called. I moved on because you left me alone."

"That's what I want to talk about, Angel. I have my reasons why I haven't tried to contact you. Just come and talk to me about it all. Once you know everything, I think you'll feel differently about us." He looks at her with sad, puppy dog eyes and I want to kick his ass.

The way she's looking at me with slightly drooping eyes makes my heart ache. "Benny, I'd like to talk to him."

I don't want to let her do this.

"Angel, I…"

"Please, Benny. There's so much I want to know." She looks so hard at me it's as if she's looking into my brain for some compassion.

"I don't want you to be alone with him. You have to understand," I say as I run my hands up and down her arms.

"I do," she says. "But I really need this."

It takes me forever to decide what to do. I look at the prick who's decided to show up at the most inconvenient time. "Where do you plan on talking to her at?"

WITH A NOD, he gestures to a tall red truck that's parked behind him. "In my truck. We won't leave the parking lot. Unless she decides to come with me."

Angel's eyes go wide. "You want me to go with you, Gage? You want me back?"

He nods. "Baby, I've been driving for hours to get to you. It's all I could think about since… Well, I'll tell you all about it. But I do want you back."

"No, I can't let you talk to her." I shake my head. "I can't. I won't! You just stood here and said you want to take my girl. I can't allow that." I stop talking as Angel puts her hand on my chest. Tears stream down her pink cheeks.

It breaks my heart and I run my thumbs over them to wipe the tears away. "I won't leave with him. I love you, Benny. I just want to know why he did that to me. That's all. I promise you that. I love you. My heart is yours."

"Angel, he doesn't deserve your time. He left, and it took away a big part of you. A part you're just now beginning to get back. If you fall for his shit, it will end us and you'll go back to being that broken girl. Don't do that to us." I stroke her cheek as I nearly beg her not to do it. "Don't do that to yourself."

She looks so torn and I hate that. I want her to stand up to him. Be defiant, and not even want to hear whatever it is he has to say to her.

She and I look at each other for the longest time, our minds connecting in a way mine can do with no others. I feel confident she's going to do the right thing for us.

Then his voice breaks our connection as he says, "The reason I left was to see the world. Angel had college to worry about. She had a brilliant career ahead of her. I didn't want my yearning to see the world put her career on hold."

Without looking at him as I try to keep her eyes trained on mine, I say, "How generous of you."

"Look, I know it's hard to understand," he continues. "I lived in a tiny town my whole life. When I got out of high school, I bought a motorcycle and made my way to Sturgis to spread my wings like I'd wanted to do since I was a little kid. I met Angel, and it stopped my growing process."

"I met Angel, and it began mine," I say as I run my hand down her long braid.

He shifts his weight to his other foot and groans. "Look, this is fucking hard for me to take, watching your hands move over my true love like that."

Angel's eyes narrow and she spins around and snaps at him, "Your true love? Gage, how can those words even come out of your mouth?"

Get him, girl!

Finally, the anger that should've come from her from the start.

"Look, Gage, I'm not going to let you get by with talking in a way that's not true. I'm not your true love," she says.

He interrupts her. "Yes, you are."

She shakes her head. "Stop that! No one leaves their true love and never even calls to see if they're alive."

"Funny you should say that." He frowns at her. "Why is it you never attempted to call me? Not once, from my understanding."

"You left me. Why would I call? To beg you to stop following your odd dream of seeing the world? I'm not selfish like that." I can feel her beginning to tremble.

I wrap my arms around her from behind and kiss her cheek. "It's okay, Baby."

Her hand moves over my cheek and her body stops shaking. The man who left her looks at me with an expression that begs me to let her go. But I won't.

He gestures to us. "This is hard to watch. Please let her go. Stop holding her, at the very least. It's hard not to come at you and rip your fucking head off with you all over her like that."

She looks at me. "I can see what he's saying. Let me go, Benny."

"No." I'm not letting her go just because this ass-wipe wants me to. I look him in his dark eyes. "Be uncomfortable, be very uncomfortable."

HE LOOKS RIGHT BACK at me and I have to give it to the man, he is persistent over a woman he left alone for two years. "Fine, hold her, but you need to know she and I had a special bond. I thought it was strong enough to allow me to pursue my lifelong dream and be able to come back and pick up where we left off. We hadn't broken up. I was merely going on a trip."

"Gage, you took everything you owned with you," she says with a despondent tone in her voice.

"One bag, Angel. Everything I owned filled up one bag. You know I hadn't accumulated much of anything while we were together. You and I moved into that little house and the things we got, the furniture, the bed, the dog, those stayed there with you and our home. I only took my clothes and toiletries." He looks at her with hurt in his eyes. "So how can you say I took everything when I left you with what we had gotten together?"

"Every last item of clothing, Gage? You needed the damn bar of soap that you used? Every bottle of your cologne, you needed? There wasn't a thing left of you. Do you know how long I went without washing your pillow? Nearly a year because it still had a trace of you on it." Her body begins to shake again and I hold her tighter.

With all she's saying, I know she did love this man. Maybe not with the same kind of thing we have, but she did love him. And by her actions, she still might have some of that love stored deep inside her.

"I'M REALLY sorry you thought I was leaving forever. I wasn't. How could you think I was walking out that door without a tear in my eye if I was leaving you?" He shakes his head and looks confused. "Angel, I loved you. With everything in me, I loved you. I left that day to go on a trip and then come back home. I thought you understood that. I'm very sorry you didn't. And now it makes sense why you never came looking for me. Not even a phone call to see if I was alive."

"I don't understand, Gage. Not at all. That day you left, you had just told me about your plan of traveling the world. I had just found out how you'd been keeping money squirreled away for three years. You'd been doing that without telling me a thing all that time. Never did you mention your dream of traveling or the fact you were putting money away to do that." She looks at him and waits for his reason.

He looks back at her and smiles. "How many times did you tell me I was a bad communicator, Baby?"

. . .

I'm stunned that he can stand there and smile about a thing that caused her so much pain. "Dude, that's no excuse for what you did to her," I tell him. "You turned her into a shell of what she was. I've only seen a few of the tears she cried over your no good ass. I can't imagine the number she shed before I came along. Whatever you were thinking was going to happen by you coming back here and picking up where you left off, is not going to happen."

He levels his eyes on me and his lips form a thin line as I'm sure he's biting back a string of curse words he'd love to hurl at me.

"Gage, he's right," she says. "Lack of communication may be to blame here. But that's a thin excuse for two years of no communication."

"Are you willing to accept your part in this, Angel? You also stopped communicating," he says.

She nods. "I can accept that. I should've called, I suppose. I was hurt, though. I can look back now and see I should've called if only to get the closure I desperately needed. So, yes, I am partly responsible but a very small part."

"And can you admit that your school and work took you away from time you could've spent with me?" he asks as he looks at her in the same way a parent asks a child if they understand what they did wrong.

"Dude, we're talking work and school. You can't expect her to feel bad about taking time away from your precious ass to further herself. What a fucking prick you are, man." I let Angel go because now I'm shaking with anger. "If you think I'm going to stand here and let you talk shit to my woman, you're sadly mistaken. I see right through your very selfish ass."

"I'm not selfish. Tell him, Angel," he says as he glares at me.

She doesn't say a word as she takes me by the arm and looks

at me. "It's okay. No need to get mad about anything. His words can't hurt me anymore."

He cocks his head. "What does that mean?"

She locks her eyes on him. "It means you can't hurt me anymore, Gage. You used to try to make me feel bad because I had to study instead of playing video games with you. You told me I was more in love with my books than you. It made me feel bad. But not so damn bad that I'd stop learning and played games with you."

"A person needs attention, Baby. I tried to explain that to you on many occasions."

"Interesting that you could take the time to let me know how I wasn't paying enough attention to you, but never the time to tell me you had a dream of traveling the world and was hiding money to make that happen for you." She crosses her arms in front of her. "And part of the reason I had to work so much on top of going to school was because I had to pay for the majority of things because you never seemed to have any money. Only you did have money. Lots of it, if you managed to put away enough to travel the fucking world!"

Her ire is up and now I think this asshole is about to get ripped a new one!

I watch from just behind her as he narrows his eyes at her and says, "You worked because you wanted to be there to watch the work the mechanics did on the bikes. And you know that's why you were there so much. Since you were bringing in so much money, why not let you pay the bills so I could put my hard-earned money up so I could one day have my dream?"

SHE THROWS her hands into the air. "And we're back to your dream. The one you never talked about. This is getting to be a circle and I'm kind of sick of this circle shit. You know what,

Gage, this is over. I don't want to talk to you about anything. This is more than enough closure for me."

She turns back to me and takes my hand and we start to walk back inside.

His voice is low as he says, "I was in a wreck the day I left. I'd been on the road for three hours when something happened. I can't remember what because I was injured so badly that I was in a coma in a hospital in Sioux Falls where I was Halo-flighted to, apparently. I can't recall any of that. I just know I woke up three months ago and had to be retaught how to walk and talk. The only thing I could remember was you."

This is not good news for me...

18

ANGEL

My head is spinning with what Gage has just told me. Letting go of Benny's hand, I run back to Gage. I look into his dark eyes and see the pain behind them.

"Gage, I'm so..."

His mouth on mine stops my words as he grabs me up and kisses me hard. Without thinking, my arms go around his neck and I hold him and kiss him back.

My heart is pounding and my head is spinning. The kiss ends and still he holds me tight in his arms. They used to be so strong and now I can feel some weakness in them.

"You don't have to say it, Love. We can move on and put that behind us," he says with a husky whisper.

I run my hands through his shoulder length, dark waves I used to love to mess with so much. Suddenly I remember Benny and pull myself out of Gage's arms. "I, uh, shit! I shouldn't have done that." I turn back to see so much hurt on Benny's face. I take a few steps back toward him.

I stop as he holds up his hand. "Don't."

With no idea of what to do, I stand still. "Benny…"

He shakes his head and I see his eyes glistening with unshed tears. "Angel, I just saw the worst thing. Worse than I ever imagined. You still love him."

I shake my head. "No. No, it's just that I had no idea he'd been hurt. It hit me like a brick. My mind went blank."

I try to explain something I don't understand myself then I feel Gage's arm run over my shoulders. "You do love me, Angel."

"Don't, Gage!" I shout and move his arm off me. "Don't make me be mean to you. I'm with Benny now. End of story. I'm sorry you were hurt. I really am. But the fact is I love Benny more than I ever loved you in the three years we were together. I love him more than I ever loved you from the first night he and I spent together."

"But the kiss," Gage says as he looks at me with tear-filled eyes. "Angel, you felt something. I know you did."

I shake my head and find I'm right in between them both. Both men looking so rugged and strong on one hand and weak as kittens on the other.

Benny's expression is killing me. "You did feel something. I saw it in your eyes when you opened them. I saw it in how you ran your arms around him."

Then it all hits me that everything I believed was wrong. The heartbreak was for all the wrong reasons. And I should've been there for Gage.

My legs go weak and I find myself slowly moving to the ground and sitting on it. Then I lay my head in my hands and cry. "What have I done?"

For the longest time, no one says a word. Then I hear Benny say, "Look, man. I'm sorry for your accident. I really am. And I promise not to interfere with her decision. But the fact is, she and I are in love. She and I have made plans together. So for tonight, I'm taking her home. To our home."

"I don't have a place to stay. I came here thinking she still had our house," Gage says. "I'd planned on staying with her."

"She let that rental go when she and I moved into our place. Since the circumstances are so weird, I'll set you up in the hotel I was staying in. Tomorrow maybe she'll feel up to talking to you about things. She and I have some talking to do as well. But right now, she's breaking down and I need to get her home where she feels safe. Agreed?" Benny asks him.

I feel like a spectator in this whole thing. One who is watching from very far away. This has to be a dream. This can't be real.

"Yeah, I can see she's not going to be able to talk tonight. Thanks for the motel room. I really appreciate it, man." I hear Gage say.

Then I'm scooped up and rest my head on a chest. A wide chest. A strong chest. Benny's chest. I run my arms around him and bury my face in it. I can't stand to look at either of them right now. It's too hard.

I can hear the sound of gravel crunching under both of their boots and know Gage is walking right next to Benny. There's the sound of a car door opening then Gage says, "I'll follow you to the motel."

"Okay," Benny says as he carries me away to his bike.

"I'm sorry, Benny. I really am."

"Shh. Don't apologize, Baby. We'll work this all out. You just try to calm down." He puts me on the bike and has me in front as he climbs on behind me. "We'll ride like this so my arms can hold you in. You lean back on me, my Angel."

. . .

I DO as he says and feel so damn weak. Weaker than I've ever been. It's even worse than the day Gage left me.

Why is that? Why is this making me so damn weak?

I struggle to stop crying but I can't seem to get it under control. It's not horrible sobs just constant tears. I feel as if I'm kind of coming unglued. I suppose this is what some call falling apart at the seams.

I'm just a wreck. My mind isn't working. My body just wants to shut down. I just want to shut down.

It seems I have decisions to make and I have no idea what the right thing to do is. It used to be black and white. Gage left me and I was free to move on. And I would be a fool to take him back.

Only thing is, now I know he was hurt and needed me and I was too stubborn to pick up the phone and make a call to make sure he was alive. I wonder why his family never called me to tell me.

Or was his family even aware of his accident? How long was it before they were made aware? If ever. And what must they think about me?

I bet they hate me.

In the three years Gage and I were together, not once did he take me to meet any of them. They never visited us.

They did live very far away, in Texas. It made sense at the time that we never had the money to go and they never had the time to come up. But they knew we were together and they should've called me when they found out he was hurt.

We pull into the motel parking lot and Benny gets off and puts his arm around my waist as I lean into his side. "I think I should leave you in his truck while I check him in. You're kind of a mess right now and I don't want the clerk to think you're wasted or anything like that and call the cops."

I nod in agreement. And wipe my eyes and make a big sniffle. Gage gets out of his truck and hands me a bunch of napkins from McDonald's. "Here, Angel. Use these to blow your nose and dry your tears. I hate to see you like this."

I take the handful of napkins and give him a nod then ask, "Gage, why didn't your family call me when they found out you were in an accident?"

"I'm not sure. I just know what they told me when I woke up. They were waiting to see if you would call. The paramedics found my cell phone and had brought it in with me. The nurses had kept it charged up in case anyone called. Mom took it over when my family got to me." He looks away for a second then back at me. "They thought maybe you and I had broken up. I hadn't told them a thing about my trip. So they didn't call you. And once I woke up and asked for you, they told me to forget about you like you had forgotten about me."

"Oh, I see."

BENNY SQUEEZES me a little and kisses the side of my head. "I think she should stay out here while I get you checked in."

"Yeah, she's kind of a wreck. Put her in the truck."

I'm picked up and placed in the driver's side. Gage laughs a little then says, "Don't drive off, Angel."

I make a grunt and blow my nose. "I can't even see right now to run away."

"Good," Benny says then closes the door.

I can see well enough to watch the two men in my life walk away, side by side. I think about how ironic this all is and how much I wish it wasn't happening at all.

Just when life gets good and somewhat easy, God has to toss a monkey wrench into things and make it all fucked up. He must have quite the sense of humor.

I run my hands over the steering wheel and for a second, I

do think about running away from this. Just putting the thing in drive and peeling off and driving until I can't anymore. Then maybe take a bus to Canada and change my name and become a nun.

Nuns have to have easier lives than normal people. No relationships at all to worry over. No kids to worry about. No men to worry about. All they worry about is being good, staying sin free, and talking to God a bunch.

Yeah, those broads got it made.

I see the guys coming back out and see Gage taking Benny's bike and walking it to park it in front of one of the motel rooms. Benny walks toward me and opens the driver's side door.

"Scoot, Pumpkin," he says. I do as he's said to. "We're taking this. The bike ride is a bit far for you when you're in such a bad condition. I'll bring his truck back to him in the morning and pick up my bike."

"Okay," I say and blow my nose again.

"If you're up to it by then. I'll let him follow me out to the house where we can all talk and figure things out. But I won't allow that until you're up to it. I told him I'll keep the room for him until things are figured out." He lays his arm out along the back of the seat as he looks back and backs out of the parking space.

I lean into his side and rest my head on his shoulder. "Thank you."

He pulls me in close and wraps his arm around me, making me feel safe and loved.

The decision should be so easy. And maybe in the morning after a good night's sleep and a whole pot of coffee, I will be able to make the decision easily. I hope so, anyway.

"I'll sleep in the room next to ours so you can think, Angel," he says out of nowhere.

I sit up and look at him. "No! No, Benny!"

"I think you should be alone to think." He looks straight ahead without looking over at me.

"No, Benny. Or is it I because you're mad at me?" I ask as I wipe my eyes.

"I'm not mad." He glances at me sideways. "I'm probably just as confused as you are. I mean, here we both thought this guy was just a really big asshole and come to find out he was in a coma all this time. There's a lot for you to think about. I know that. And I saw how you reacted to him. You did love him at one time."

I lean back and drop my head onto the back of the seat. "Please don't leave me alone, Benny. I'll just go in circles in my mind. I need you, Baby."

His eyes flash as he turns his head to look at me. "If it will make you feel better, then I won't leave you alone. But if you need space all you have to do is ask me for it. I want you to know I understand this is not a normal situation."

Leaning into him, I run my fingertips over his upper thigh. "Benny, I love you. Although this situation is not normal, my love for you will overcome anything I feel for Gage. I know it will."

"Hope so." He kisses my forehead and I feel something in the light kiss.

Something that tells me that he's guarding his heart in case I do pick Gage instead of him.

"You're a very good man, Benjamin Worthington," I tell him and stroke his chest.

The muscles ripple underneath his tight black T-shirt as my fingers run over them. He takes my hand off his chest and kisses it. "I'm not, Angel. You bring this man out in me. If you knew how badly I want to still rip the guy's head off, you'd think differently."

"Why do you still want to rip his head off? He didn't leave me like I thought," I ask.

"Because he kissed you and wants to steal you away from me."

I nod. "Yeah, that would make me kind of want to rip someone's head off too. You know, Benny, you have more patience and tolerance than I do."

"I know," he says then we both laugh.

I play with his beard. "Promise me you won't hurt him, though. I already feel pretty terrible that he was hurt, and I wasn't around to help him."

He pulls into our drive and looks over at me as he parks the truck. "You know I won't hurt him. Unless he really pisses me off, then I will."

"Well, of course, if he really pisses you off. I'm going to need you two to play nice while we all figure things out." He gets out of the truck and I scoot over. Then he picks me up and carries me. "I can walk, you know."

"I know that. I want to carry you." He kisses the tip of my nose.

Laying my head on his chest, he carries me inside where Cuddles greets us at the door. "So, this was his dog, huh?"

"He got her from the pound when she was a puppy."

The dog jumps around his feet, threatening to trip him up but somehow he evades her efforts. "You know something he said keeps running through my mind."

He takes the stairs up to our bedroom as I ask, "What's that?"

"He said his cell phone was there, in the hospital, turned on, right?"

I nod as he gets to our room and pushes the door open. Cuddles runs in ahead of us and goes straight to the little doggy bed Benny picked out for her. Our bed is too high off the ground for her to jump up on.

"I think he said that. The truth is my head is more than a bit foggy." He lies me on the bed and starts to undress me.

His fingers run over my stomach as he unbuttons my pants. "If he had his phone, and he said all he could think about was you when he woke up then why didn't he call you?"

"Maybe because his family still had the phone and I think he said he forgot how to talk too."

He takes my boots off then pulls my pants all the way off. I sit up and pull my little top off and unclasp my bra and take it off too. Benny nods as he looks as if he's thinking hard.

He strips my panties off then begins the process of pulling off his own clothes. "But when he could speak again, what stopped him then? Do you have the same cell number as you did when he left?"

"Yeah. And my work number was on his phone as well. And now I do wonder why he didn't call. Especially before he set out to come to Sturgis to find me. He could've made a phone call and done that. But maybe he has some brain damage now. I couldn't really tell, but I wasn't all there, to be honest."

He lies next to me and pulls me to lie on his chest. Soft lips touch the top of my head. "Sleep, my Angel. Tomorrow we'll get our answers."

And now I can't do anything but lie here wide awake and think about why he didn't just call.

Something doesn't seem right about this...

19

BLAZE

My night was pretty sleepless as Angie tossed and turned most of it. But she's sleeping peacefully now that the sun's come up. I was woken up by my cell phone springing to life at six this morning, a half hour ago.

I had put the phone on silent but the light from the screen woke me and I found my father's name on it. I didn't answer it, of course, as I have a lot on me as it is without adding their drama to it.

Climbing out of bed, I want to get the coffee started so it'll be ready when she wakes up. She always does better with a little coffee to help start her day. And I think this day is going to be pretty eventful.

I pull on my underwear and head out of the room to go to the kitchen, scratching my beard as I go. I feel like something the cat drug in.

Cuddles follows me and jumps around all happy and I wonder how she'll feel about seeing her old master, Gage. She'll probably split a seam I bet.

Just as we hit the last stair, she bolts toward the front door, yapping her little ass off. I follow her and see a black town car parked in our drive.

Now who could this be?

QUICKLY I GO BACK UPSTAIRS and throw on a pair of jeans and pull a T-shirt over my head and head back down to find out who in the hell thinks it's okay to pull up in my drive so damn early in the morning.

I throw the door open and Cuddles runs out to the car barking like a mad dog. As I thought, even though she's tiny, no one wants a piece of that action. The window in the back goes down and my father's head pops out of it.

Fuck!

"I wouldn't get out if I were you. We think she has rabies," I shout.

The way his eyes go all wide makes me laugh. "Really, Son?"

I walk out in my bare feet and pick up the frantic poodle mix and hold her under my arm. "You're safe now."

My father's driver gets out and opens the door for him. My mother slips out of the car behind my father and I walk toward the house. With the dog trying desperately to gain its freedom and kill my parents.

If she could do any real damage, I might just let her go.

But since she can't, I hold onto her until we get inside the house. "Let me just put Killer here out in the back."

I walk away as my parents look all around the great room and try not to look impressed. That would be too boorish of them as my grandfather would say.

When I come back, I see they've sat down on the giant leather sofa and seem to be a bit confused by everything. "You keep a dog in the house, Benjamin?" my father asks me.

I nod. "You guys want to follow me to the kitchen. I need to get some coffee going and maybe a pitcher of margaritas."

They get up and follow me as Mother says, "Surely, you jest."

I shrug my shoulders. It seems like a little alcohol might be in order this morning which is starting way too early and way too awful. Not that it was going to be an awesome day, anyway with Gage in the plans for the day.

Gesturing to the barstools by the island in the kitchen, I say, "Take a load off. That must've been some ride. I'm sure you two are beat. I can set you up in one of our many guest rooms if you guys need a nap."

My father looks at me as if I'm insane. "Benjamin, you must know we took our jet to the small airport just outside of town and had a car waiting there for us."

"And you brought your own driver from home? You didn't think James might like the day off since you're away from New York?" I ask as I pour some water into the back of the old style coffee maker Angel insisted on.

My mother shakes her head, making her blonde bob haircut bounce around her neck, that's strung with pearls. Always the picture of the perfect wife and mother, she is. Much like June Cleaver. I guess she's her role model.

"What are you doing there, Benjamin? When is it you learned to cook, Son?"

"I took a cooking class in college," I say with a smile as Harvard offers no cooking classes in its legal schooling.

My father frowns. "Seems you've become quite the jokester this year. I don't see the need for humor myself. It gets in the way of real things. Life, work, respect. Of which you are rapidly losing mine by the way."

"Am I now?" I spoon in the fresh coffee grounds Angel loves

and look at my father. "I'm losing some for you and especially my grandfather. Representing that horrible man. Bain isn't a thing I thought you approved of either. Nor my brother for that matter. But when Grandfather speaks, you two cower. I'm done cowering. I won't work for a firm that takes that man's back."

Mom chimes in, which is not at all like her, "Mr. Bain has every right to charge the price he sees fit without the government telling him what he has to do. This is a country with a free enterprise system. If we let them do this to him, then it sets a precedent where they can do it to others as well. Setting the prices, they see fit without the knowledge of what it costs to produce things."

I shake my head and look at my mother. "You're right in the regards of the government and their interference in most things. Bain holds the keys to the only drug known to extend the lives of people with AID's, though. He's jacked up the price the original producer found they could sell the product for and still make a profit."

My father clears his throat. "But our client, Mr. Bain, has a product which is high in demand. He's justified in raising the price. Others in areas of in-demand products do the same thing."

"BUT, Father, those are things people want. Their lives don't depend on them being able to get it. People should be able to affordably obtain what's necessary to live. I shouldn't even have to argue about this with you. In the beginning, you were on the right side. What the hell happened?" I ask and then I see Angel stumbling to the top of the stairs, rubbing her eyes.

"Is Gage here already?" she asks in a mumbled voice.

"Shit," I hiss and run to her as she's wearing only a robe and her hair's a mess.

She didn't even bother to do a thing. She's must've woken up and thought I was down here arguing with her old boyfriend.

"Angel, my parents are here."

She stops on the third from the top stair and spins around. "I'll be right back. I have to change my clothes."

I'm thankful the position my parents are sitting in didn't let them see her. Neither of them ever leave their bedroom without looking a thousand percent ready for the day.

And then their eyes level on me. "What was she wearing, Benjamin?" my mother asks.

"A robe. We're very informal here. This is the country. There are usually no unexpected visitors here. So we don't usually get dressed for the day until after we've had coffee and breakfast." I pour Angel a large cup of coffee and put some cream from the fridge in it. "I'm going to run this up to her. Be right back. Make yourselves some if you'd like. Everything's right here in the kitchen."

I haul ass to our room and find her frantically brushing her teeth and hair at the same time. She spits out a glob of toothpaste as she sees me come in. "What the hell, Benny?"

"They just showed up. It's about work," I say as I sit the coffee on the vanity top.

"It's about me too," she says then rinses her mouth out with mouthwash.

I shake my head. "No, I think it's just work, Baby. I don't want you to stress about it. Not one bit. You have enough to worry about without that. And so do I."

I look around and find a hair clip I bought her a few days ago that isn't expensive but it looks like it is. Quickly, I braid her hair and clip the end with the clip.

She looks at it in the mirror. "That looks nice. Please pick me out something to wear they'll approve of, Benny."

Hurrying to the closet, I pick out a simple beige dress she

has. I've yet to take her shopping and now I'm regretting it. Some white flats I find and take them to her. "Didn't I see a strand of pearls in your jewelry box?"

She nods and I rush to get them and place them around her neck.

Perfect!

She looks very normal. Very bland, but my parents like people that way.

Running my arm around her shoulders, I take her out to meet my parents. The words, 'don't be nervous,' keep running through my brain as we go down the stairs.

She takes in a deep breath as we hit the last one and looks at me, then gives me a wink. Somehow she managed to get just enough makeup on to look radiant.

We round the corner to the kitchen and she beams at my parents who look at her with a mix of astonishment and wonder. Angel steps forward, her hand extended. "Hello, I'm Angel Jennings. Benny's told me so much about you both. It's such a pleasure to meet the people who made this magnificent man the person he is."

My father and mother get up off the bar stools. Father shakes her hand first. She shocks the hell out him and me both as she pulls him into a hug. Then does the same thing with my mother.

"Well, oh my," Mom says as Angel gives her a pat on the back too.

Angel steps back and comes to my side. I run my arm around her shoulders again as she says, "I know people of your stature aren't big on hugs, but in middle America we're huge on them. Please take a seat. No reason for you to be standing. We're very informal way out here in the country."

ANGEL LOOKS BACK at me and runs her hand over my beard,

straightening it some. "Thanks," I say then look back at my parents who are looking at us with slack jaws.

"Um," my father says. "Well, I don't know what to say. It's a pleasure to meet you, Angel. Is that your real name or a nickname of sorts?"

She smiles and moves away from me to go to the fridge. "It's my real name. Care for a juice of some sort? We have every kind there is."

Mother runs her hands over her pearls and stares at the ones Angel has on. "I'll take an apple juice, Dear. Mr. Worthington will take a prune. Did our son buy you those pearls?"

Angel grabs two juice glasses from the cabinet and looks over her shoulder at my mother. "No, these were my great-grandmother's. They were handed down to me. I love wearing them. They remind me where it is I come from."

"Where do you come from, dear?" Mom asks as I hold my breath as the answer will not make her happy.

Angel takes the juices from the fridge and fills the glasses. "I come from a family of hard workers. My great-grandfather was a railroad engineer way back in the day. He made a nice living, but it took him a lot of hours to make that kind of money that made them only middle class. I'm proud to say that I'm the very first person in my family to get a Master's degree. Some have Associate's and a few have their Bachelor's but I'm only months away from gaining the highest degree that anyone in my family has achieved."

My father gives her a genuine smile as she places their drinks in front of them. "That's quite an accomplishment. And what is your degree in?"

"Engineering. I want to build motorcycles," she says with a huge smile.

My mother nearly chokes on her juice. "Why those things? Not very lady like, I must say."

. . .

ANGEL LAUGHS LIGHTLY. "Not one bit. You're right about that. But they're not about ladies or gentlemen. They aren't about boys or girls. They aren't about men or women. Motorcycles are about experiencing the freedom of the road. The wind, the sun, and the moon, the elements in their rawest forms. That's what they're about. I want to make a machine that's easier for people of lighter weights to handle. To feel the road beneath their tires better and feel more confident in their ability to handle such a powerful machine."

My father looks at me with his eyebrows way up high. "My, she's an impressive young thing, isn't she?"

My heart stops as they're reacting to her so much better than I thought they would. "She is quite impressive."

Angel takes an apron out of the drawer. "I'm not all that. Now, if you'll help me, Benny, we can whip up some omelets for breakfast."

I go to help her then say, "Father, we'd like to invite James in to eat."

"Someone's outside?" Angel asks.

I nod. "Their driver. He came with them from New York."

She shakes her head. "Get the eggs out and start the sausage and bacon mixture we made up yesterday morning heating up. I'll run and get him."

"OH, IT'S NOT NECESSARY," my father says. "I'm sure he'll turn you down."

She stops and spins around. "Why's that?"

Mother rolls her eyes. "Staff doesn't eat with us, Dear."

"At my house they do," Angel says and takes off to retrieve the driver my parents have had for the last twenty years.

Once she's all the way out of the house and I hear the door shut, I ask, against my better judgment, "So, what do you think?"

They look at each other as if mentally communicating. Then they look back at me as my father answers, "She's wonderful. She'll need to be schooled in the proper ways of etiquette and the rules of our social status, such as staff and things like that. Do you suppose you could teach her those things, Benjamin? Also, she'll have to stop calling you by that nickname. Oh, what your grandfather would do to her if he ever heard that name come out of her mouth. I fear for the girl, you know?"

"You know, I was afraid for her too. But she just absolutely blew me away just now. I think she'll deal with Grandfather just fine. I won't be teaching her a thing. She's teaching me."

I'm one step closer to becoming the man I'm meant to be, thanks to finding my Angel.

20

ANGEL

With the arrival of Benny's parents, it's knocked my business with Gage back awhile. I didn't want to seem rude, so it took some doing to be able to get out of the house on our own.

Thankfully, Benny's parents needed a nap after the huge breakfast we made and we told them we had to go buy some things so we could have a nice dinner. They commented on the fish tank in the kitchen with the two live lobsters and asked about having those.

Benny told them we could never eat Fred and Ethyl. He wants to make them his specialty, spaghetti and meatballs.

ALONE IN GAGE'S TRUCK, I find myself so drawn to Benny that it's kind of freaky. I lean into him as I sit next to him and he drives us into town. "I think your parents are nowhere near as stuffy as you described them."

"They really are. But they're different around you. I can't explain it. You bring out something in people, Angel. You're a rare find, my lady."

"I think you are." I put my head on his shoulder and run my hand over his leg. "I want you so damn bad right now for some reason, Benny."

"Shut up!" he says as he pulls his shades down to look at me. "Are you being serious?"

I nod and bite my lip. "Want to pull over before we have to deal with Gage?"

"You're fucking with me, aren't you?" He shakes his head and laughs. "This is your old boyfriend's truck and you want me to fuck you in it?"

"Now I get why it's making me so hot for you. Yes, that's exactly what I want." I run my hand over his jean covered cock, and he looks at me again.

"You're a bad girl, Angel."

"Seems so." I unbutton his jeans and pull the zipper down nice and slow then put my hand inside them to feel his skin under my palm. "Um, maybe my mouth will help you pull over and make me scream for mercy."

I lean over and my pearl necklace touches the tip of his dick and he groans, "Fuck, Angel."

"I haven't even touched you with my lips yet," I say with a giggle.

He pushes my head down. "Stop talking and suck it, Baby."

I do as I'm told and find his cock hard as a rock as I take it all in. Up and down I go as he keeps driving. His groans fill the cab of the truck. "I can't wait for that truck I bought you to come in," he whispers.

I stop and pull my head up. "You bought me a truck?"

He pushes my head back down. "Get back to work, Wench. Yeah, I bought you a badass truck. And now that I realize how much better it'll be cruising in it from time to time, you better believe you and I will be taking in the sights. Like the sight of the back of our pretty little head bobbing up and down in my lap as I drive down the road."

I stifle a laugh because this isn't the time for laughing. I hear the sound of a bunch of bikes roaring past us. So I pull my head up just a little. "Are we in town?"

"Yeah, we are. You might want to speed this up a bit."

I suck harder as I reach in and take his balls in my hand and massage them. He stops at a stop light, I suppose, and runs his hand over the back of my head. "Yes, Baby! God damn it! Get ready! Fuck!"

He blasts down my throat and I drink it all down then sit up and wipe my mouth with the back of my hand and look out the tinted windows at the people in the car right next to us.

"Did you get us tinted windows on the truck too?"

He nods and pulls me to him and kisses me hard. "That was awesome, Baby. Thank you."

"Go park behind the dollar store, so you can show me how thankful you really are." I hold his cock in my hand and move it up and down to get him ready again.

He smiles and goes where I told him to down a back alleyway and he pulls to a stop then tosses me on my back on the long bench seat. He pushes my dress up then starts to rip my panties off.

I stop him. "I'll need to keep these intact, Benny."

"Oh yeah," he says with a grin.

He moves them to the side and moves his body over mine and slams his hard cock into me. "Yes!" I hiss.

He slams into me over and over as he looks into my eyes. "You like me fucking you in his truck, don't you, you bad girl?"

I bite my lip and buck up to meet his hard thrusts. "I do. Show me who I belong to."

. . .

HE LEANS DOWN and bites my neck then sucks it hard. His teeth graze over my neck up to my ear. "You tell me who you belong to."

My hands move up underneath his white T-shirt that's so sheer you can see his ripped abs through it. I can feel them moving against my stomach. "You, Benny. I belong to you."

My heart's pounding and I can barely breathe as he slams into me hard. His breath is hot on my neck as he nips and sucks it, leaving his mark on me. He moves faster.

He pulls back one of my legs and goes in deeper, making me stretch in a new place and I moan. "Don't come until I tell you to, Baby."

My stomach tenses as now I know I can't let go. "What'll you do to me if I don't mind you?"

"String your ass up and whip you until you're soaking wet."

I moan and arch up to him. "I just might like that. Better come up with something different."

He laughs a little then says, "Okay then. I'll spank your ass so hard you won't be able to sit down for a week."

"Oh, Benny, you should do that, anyway." I wrap my legs around his waist.

"Damn, Baby. Just don't come until I tell you to. Shit, you're too hard to threaten."

He pulls my braid, making the other side of my neck stretch out long then he bites me hard and I scream with the most delightful pain. "Benny!"

My body starts to shake with the need to let it fall apart but I hold on as he plunges into me. He starts moving with short strokes as his dick starts to jerk then he groans out the words, "You can come now."

We let out horrible sounds as our bodies pulse and squeeze the others. He lies on top of me as we pant and try to catch our breath. Then he pushes his body up a little and looks around.

"What?" I ask as he looks a little worried.

"We need to clean you up or you'll get jizz all over his seat."

I POINT at the glove compartment. "That's most likely filled with assorted condiments and napkins."

"You know him so well," he says with a frown.

He opens the glove compartment, and it's filled with exactly what I said it would be. Getting a handful of them, he hands them to me then gets off me. I sniff the air. "God, it smells like sex in here. This was a terrible idea, Benny. You shouldn't have let me talk you into this."

I sit up and clean myself up and look in the glove compartment for some kind of bag to put the used things in. I find a small thing of perfume and spray it around then put it back.

Benny cocks his head at me. "Angel, why would he have perfume in here?"

With a shrug of my shoulders, I answer, "Don't really know."

Then I put it back inside and when a few packets of ketchup fall out, I see a picture. I pull it out and see Gage with his arm around a girl I went to school with.

I hold it up and look at Benny. "See the shirt this chick is wearing?"

He nods. "That's mine. That's my shirt she has on. I asked him if he'd seen it anywhere when I found it missing. He told me I probably lost it in the wash. But there she is wearing it."

"So that was before he left?" he asks as he takes the picture out of my shaking hand.

"I lost that shirt two days before he left me. And I never put two and two together because I had no idea he even knew her. Her name is Sandy. She went away to college supposedly. And it was around the same time he left." I take the picture and put it back where I found it. "Can you take me to Bell's Diner so I can ask someone there some questions?"

He nods and we take off. My mind is moving very fast as we go and when we pull up to the diner I see the person's car there who I need to talk to. "You want me to go with you?"

I shake my head. "This will only take a minute."

I climb out of the passenger side and go in to find Sandy's best friend. Patty and Sandy were inseparable until Sandy moved away to go to college.

Patty looks up when I walk in. "Hi, Angel. I haven't seen you in forever."

"I know. I stay to myself a lot. Too much, I think. Anyway, about Sandy. When's the last time you talked to her?" I put my hand on my hip and tap my foot as I wait for her answer.

"You seem a little pissed, Angel. What's up?"

"When did you last talk to her?" I ask again.

She sighs and says, "A few days ago. She's moving back. She and her boyfriend broke up, and she's coming home. She said she didn't sign up to be taking care of a man for the rest of his life. Her boyfriend had a terrible accident. The guy was in a coma for almost two years. He's on disability now and she says he only plays his games all day and expects her to wait on him hand and foot even though the doctors told him he needs to exercise and stuff to get back to his old self."

"Do you happen to know how long they've been together?" I ask.

"Well, they met here a little over two years ago. The tragic thing is they left to move to Texas where his family is from. The day they took off, he was on his motorcycle and she was in her car with all of their things packed up in it. The guy had a terrible accident on his motorcycle and ended up in a coma. He came out of it a few months ago."

I shake my head and hold up my hand. "Is his name Gage?"

"Yeah, you know him?" she asks.

I nod. "I really shouldn't have been such a homebody. Work and school were my entire life and Gage, of course. He and I lived together until he took off. He told me he was going to travel all over the world. And guess who just came back into town last night to find me. I wondered why he didn't have my phone numbers anymore. But of course he had to delete them, didn't he?"

Her eyes go big. "I swear she had no idea he was with anyone. I swear that to you, Angel. Please don't start anything with her when she gets back. She's had it so rough with him being in that coma and all she went through to be able to stay in Sioux Falls with him."

"I won't start anything with her. Thanks for the information, Patty." I turn around and leave.

As I climb back into the truck, I see Benny frowning at me. "Are you going to tell me what the hell is going on?"

"Seems, Gage is a lying piece of shit."

"He never had an accident?" he asks.

"No, he had that. He was in a coma and all that. But he left with another girl. Not to travel the world. The reason he didn't have my numbers is because he deleted them, I'm sure." I sit next to the door and find myself shaking with anger.

"Baby, come here," he says as he holds out his arms.

I turn to him and ask, "Why, Benny? Why would he do that to me then and why would he come back now and try to fuck up my life again?"

He reaches out and pulls me to him. "Baby, there are so many selfish people in this world. I have no idea why he'd do all this. I can tell you that I'm fucking happy as shit that he's an asshole, though."

I have to laugh. "You would."

"So let's go give him his damn truck and get my bike and you can tell him to fuck off forever. I can punch him if you want." He kisses my cheek. "Only if you want me to."

"I do, but don't. He was in a coma and I don't know what all he had wrong with him so we'll have to leave the physical stuff out." I lean my head on his shoulder. "Thanks, though."

I feel good and bad, it's odd. It's a relief that he's no longer a real issue in my relationship with Benny, but he's still a man I loved once and he lied to me.

We pull up to the motel and I find Gage coming out as soon as we stop in front of his little motel room.

"Should I give him one more night here or what, Angel?" Benny asks me.

"I really think you've already done more than enough for the ass."

He opens the door and gets out then helps me down. The perfume wafts out as we get out and I see Gage's eyes go kind of big but he quickly loses the 'oh shit' expression.

"Hi, Angel. You look great. Kind of like a pretty school teacher. Not like yourself much at all. But still pretty," he says. He holds his arms out. "Can I have a hug?"

Benny laughs. And goes to his bike and gets on it. Gage's eyes follow him and he looks a little confused.

I cross my arms and give him a nod. "You can have a hug if you really want to come that close to me. I wouldn't advise it, though."

He takes a few steps back. "And why is that, Angel?"

"I found a photo of you and Sandy."

He looks right into my eyes and says, "Who?"

"You know the thing that makes me the maddest is that you would see a real relationship end just to have me take care of your ass for the rest of your fucking useless life." I take a step toward him and he takes another back.

"Angel, what are you talking about?"

"I know Sandy, sweetheart. I went to school with her. I know her best friend, Patty too. And you'll be happy to know that Sandy will be back in town soon. Try your hand at that again. The poor girl apparently was there for you at the hospital."

"Is that what she said? That girl's a sociopath. A freaking liar, Angel." He stands his ground as he goes on, "She told me her name was Melissa. I left town because of her. She was threatening to tell you that she and I had been messing around. She liked me. Wanted me. But I was faithful to you and she hated it."

His words, though most likely bullshit, do remind me of another boy in school saying something very similar.

I look at Benny. "This may be a little bit true, Benny. What should I do?"

"Fuck!" he says. "You're too smart to fall for this bullshit, Angel."

GAGE TAKES me by the arm and I look at him. "I did hide some stuff from you but it was for your own protection. She threatened to kill you. I left to get away from her. When I woke up at the hospital, she was there. Angel, I think she might have been trying to run me down or something. I think that's why I wrecked. I came here to get your help because my parents left me with her. They believed all her lies and with my memory loss I kind of did too. She had that picture of us with my arm around her and all. But I don't remember her. I only remember you."

Well, what the fuck do I do now?

21

BLAZE

It's times like these that I wish I had a portable lie detector test!

Angel looks at me with an expression that asks me what she should do. I want to say, 'tell him to fuck off, anyway,' but I don't say that. "Fuck!" I look at Gage and see real sadness and worry in his dark eyes. "Get in your truck and follow us home. I don't know how my parents are going to react to this shit. Get on, Angel."

She hurries over and climbs on back of my bike as she says, "I'm sorry, Baby. This is getting to be a real cluster-fuck, isn't it?"

Sarcasm is heavily laced with my words as I say, "You think?"

She smacks me in the arm. "If it's getting to be too much for you, I can..."

I START up the bike and drown out her next words. I know what they are, 'can leave.' I shake my head and drive away as she hangs onto me.

My mind is numb as I try not to think about how my parents

are going to act when we bring home this man with his peculiar story and the fact he wants to take my girl away from me.

It's hard to keep my thoughts positive in nature. And when I pull into my drive and see another long black car there, I shudder.

Grandfather!

When I stop, Angel asks, "Who do you think is here now?"

"By the chill that ran down my spine when I saw the car, I'd say it's my grandfather. So this should be one fucking awesome day."

I get off and hold out my hand to help her. Once she's off, I pull her into my arms. "Need a hug, Baby?" she whispers.

"I need a hell of a lot more than just this hug, but I'll take what I can get for now. This is going to have to be handled delicately. Let me do the talking, Princess." I let her out of the hug and take her hand, leading her up the sidewalk as Gage hops out of his truck.

He looks in awe as he looks up at the huge, log cabin style mansion. "Fuck me, Angel. I know you'll never leave this guy!"

I smile and hope he's right. "I hope she won't, Gage."

Angel makes a nervous laugh which is so unlike her. "Let's not talk about that. Benny's parents are here and someone else too. He thinks it's his grandfather. They're from New York and filthy rich so don't be offended if they come off snobby, as they can't help it."

I stop and look at her. "When did you get so damn understanding, Angel?"

"I've always been that way. I get it. There's more than one way to live life. They can't help where they come from just like the rest of us can't," she says as she starts walking again. "And the truth is, I can't wait to meet your grandfather. I'm sure he's nothing like you've told me he is. Your parents sure weren't as bad as you said they were. Your father is adorable and your mother is so June Cleaver."

I get a lopsided grin because she thinks of my mother just like I do. We're so much on the same wavelength, it's cute.

In no time at all, I see us becoming that couple who can finish each other's sentences. Order food for the other and pick out the perfect presents for one another.

I take in a deep breath before I open the door.

"Okay, you two, just keep it low key. Don't get into any of this story with these people. They'll only judge you very harshly. It's what they do."

Angel looks at Gage, who's walking on the other side of her, and says, "Don't let him freak you out, Gage."

He gives her a nod and we head inside. No one is in the great room where I thought I'd find them. "Mother, Father," I call out.

Then I hear some playful yapping coming from out back and look at Angel. She looks back at me with fear in her eyes. "Oh, no! You don't think they went out there, do you? Cuddles will rip them up."

GAGE'S EYES go all bright. "Cuddles is out there?"

He starts to haul ass toward the sound and Angel shouts out at him, "Gage, wait for us or you'll get lost. This place is enormous."

"I found a map!" I hear him call out.

I forgot the floor plans are still on that table by the stairs.

She giggles and leans her head on my shoulder as I run my arm over her shoulders and she says, "He found a map. That sounds so funny."

We walk to the patio doors and get there just in time to see him open them. My jaw drops as I see my grandfather petting the dog. My parents are outside too and the dog seems comfortable with them.

"Cuddles," Gage shouts.

THE DOG STOPS WAGGING her tail and turns away from my grandfather. Her expression goes to one of confusion for only a moment then she makes a b-line for Gage, who's holding out his arms. She flies into them and he hugs her as she licks his face and makes odd yips.

Angel sighs, "She missed him."

"It looks like I've lost her," I say, quietly.

Angel whispers, "She used to scratch at the door and go outside to look for him when he left. That's when she started sleeping in the bed with me. It was like she was waiting for him to come back. But he never did."

She's just watching him and their dog and I feel left out. And then my time to feel sorry for myself is over as my grandfather says, "Now who do we have here? The prodigal grandson has been found."

They come back inside as Gage goes out to play with the dog. They all introduce themselves as they pass each other and I offer no explanation to who the man is.

My grandfather cannot stop looking at Angel. She smiles at him and extends her hand. "Hi, Mr. Worthington, I'm Angel Jennings."

He takes her hand and I try to keep a hold of her shoulders so she doesn't hug him like she did to my parents but I can't as she slips away somehow.

Her arms go around him as his eyes go wide and my father chuckles then he says, "She's a hugger, Father."

"I can see that," Grandfather says as he lets her hug him then looks her up and down when she lets him go. "My, you are a nice-looking young woman. What do you see in the hippy, here?"

She laughs and comes back to me, taking my hand. "You mean this rascal? There's so much to see in him. He's sweet, kind, sincere, loveable. I could go on and on."

I have to grin and pull her into my arms and kiss her cheek. Another thing that has my grandfather's eyes popping. "Sweet? Benjamin?" He shakes his head.

"Come, let's sit in the great room and visit," Angel says as she pulls me along with her to the large room at the front of the house. She takes my grandfather's hand with her other one and pulls him along too. "I'm so glad you could make time to come visit us. I've been dying to meet you, sir. It's such an honor to have a man of your great accomplishment in our home. You've built such a wonderful legacy for your family. You see, I want to learn as much as I can from you, if you'll indulge me, that is."

She makes us sit on either side of her as she pulls us down on the large leather sofa. My grandfather asks, "And why do you want to learn from me?"

"You see, I'm about to hold a Master's Degree in Engineering and want to build motorcycles. I'd like to have my own company and would love to learn how you managed to do such a remarkable job building yours," she says as she leans back and I run my arm around her shoulders and have to kiss her cheek.

"An engineer. I see. That's something to be proud of, young lady. You have very high expectations." Grandfather sits back and smiles.

Wow, a real smile!

Angel laughs a little then says, "I see no reason to have anything less than the highest expectations when you're talking about the most important thing in your life. It's the most important thing, providing your family with a firm foundation to build upon. Don't you think so?"

. . .

He blinks at her a few times then looks at me. "Don't let this one go, Benjamin."

"I have no plans to, Grandfather." I look at her and want to smother her with kisses.

Angel snaps her fingers. "You know what would be fun?"

I shake my head. "What, Baby?"

"If we had us a big old bar-b-que." She looks at my parents. "You all will be spending at least one night with us, won't you?"

"Well, I...," Mom says then looks at my father. "It wasn't a thing we'd planned on."

My grandfather continues to floor me as he says, "If you invite us to, then we will. It would be rude not to accept the invitation."

"Fabulous!" Angel claps her hands. "I'll invite my grandmother. My parents live in California or I'd have them over to meet you all too. And I'll hire a really great chef to make our dinner. He'll be so over the top excited to cook for you all. He has his own restaurant in town and is famous for his steaks."

I've never been more certain about anything in my entire life. This woman is the one for me!

Then Gage walks in with the floor plan of the house in his hand.

"Hey, Angel, I overheard you talking about having a party. Am I invited too?"

My grandfather looks at the man then back at Angel. "Who might this young man be to you, my darling girl?"

My eyes go wide. My grandfather does not use such words.

Angel answers, "Oh, he's my old boyfriend. The story is crazy, and I'd bore you with the details. But he has a problem and we want to try to help him with it."

"Plus, I love her and want her back," Gage says.

"Dude!" I shout. "Not cool!"

"Well, I do," he says, a lot quieter.

Angel pats my grandfather's leg. "Don't worry. I love Benny with all my heart."

"That's good to hear, Angel," he says then looks at Gage again. "Well tell us your big problem, Gage."

GAGE SITS ON THE FLOOR, Indian style and starts telling his story. I'm kind of shocked and can tell he does have residual effects from his brain injury as a few words he says oddly and his eyes blink rapidly about every twenty minutes.

Angel grips my hand as Gage tells us that this young woman named Melissa came on to him one day as he ate lunch at Bell's Diner. She even came to their house once, telling him Angel said she could borrow some clothes. She put on some and said she needed to take a picture to send to Angel's phone to see if it was okay to borrow them.

It seems she tricked him into getting into the shot with her and somehow got him to put his arm around her and then she used the picture to blackmail him.

He wasn't about to give in until she threatened to kill Angel if he didn't leave her. That was when he came up with the story about wanting to travel the world. Only he was going to go to Texas and stay with his family until he could figure out what to do about the crazy chick.

But he was in the motorcycle accident only hours after leaving town and when he finally woke up, the crazy Melissa was there. Only she was telling him they had a strong love and he and she were leaving Sturgis together.

She told him she was right behind him in her car and saw the accident that was caused by some debris on the road. She stayed by his side and made even his family believe her story.

Sioux Falls is where she got a job and rented an apartment and he moved in with her when they let him out of the hospital. Little by little his memory started returning and Angel was the only person he remembered loving. And he knew he'd never leave her and had never really had anything to do with Melissa.

As he ends his story, I look around to see my parents and grandfather captivated and cannot believe it. Angel holds my hand tight and looks at me. "Benny, what should we do?"

I SHAKE my head and find myself further surprised as my grandfather says, "We have to get this woman to admit what she did." He looks at Gage. "And, I'm sure you do love Angel, but she had no choice but to move on and you have to accept that. I'm sure you two can remain lifelong friends. But nothing more than that."

Gage frowns then says, "You're right. I know you are." He looks at Angel. "The truth is, I never made you glow the way you do with him. You never looked at me like you look at him. Your eyes light up and your voice even changes when you talk to or about him. So, I'll take your friendship if you'll give it."

Angel looks at me and smiles as she asks, "Would that be alright, Benny? Can I be his friend?"

I look at her a long time then at him. "Can you keep your hands off her?"

His lips quirk up into a half-smile. "I think she'll make sure I do."

I run my hand over the top of her thigh. "She damn well better." With my cursing, I cut my eyes to be ready for my grandfather to tell me how it's not allowed but am stunned when he smiles and sits back.

Angel hops up and pulls me with her. "We have a few calls to make to get things ready. You are all feel free to look around the place."

SHE KEEPS GOING until we're at the door to our bedroom where she takes me inside and closes the door then turns back and pushes me against it. Her mouth is hot on mine.

I run my hands down and cup her ass in them, picking her up. She wraps her legs around me and I walk over to the bed with her. Pulling my mouth away, I toss her onto our bed.

She's panting as she looks up at me. "Strip."

I do as she's said to, then push her dress up and this time I rip those white lace panties right off. I flip her over and yank her back to me then slap her ass, nice and hard.

She moans out, "Oh, do it again, Benny."

I do it again and slam my hard cock into her soaking wet depths. "You're so fucking perfect, Baby. So fucking perfect."

"No, you are," she says. "Baby give me five more. I want to see your hand print on my ass when we're done."

"You are one naughty girl, Angel."

"That I am."

22

ANGEL

After some much-needed Benny and Angel time, I managed to make the phone calls needed to get this party going and expect my grandmother to arrive any minute.

Freddy's already brought a small staff with him and is in the kitchen preparing dinner. It feels so odd being the hostess of such a shindig. I never saw myself in this role. Not ever!

I also never saw myself sitting around with both my current boyfriend and my former either.

The doorbell rings and I get up to answer it, sure that it's my grandmother. Without looking through the peephole, I open the door and there stands a version of Sandy Whitehead. Or Melissa, as Gage knows her.

"Sandy?" I ask as I look at the girl who'd been blonde but now is a brunette with dark brown eyes and pale skin.

"No, I'm Melissa and I'm here to get my fiancé."

"You're Sandy Whitehead. We went to school together. You were a couple of grades ahead of me but I do know you, Sandy." I look her dead in the eyes and I can see she's got a lot of anger.

"My name is Melissa Cross. I'm only twenty-five so I don't see how you think you know me." She looks me right back in the eyes and I have to say this little nut job takes her crazy very seriously.

So I try something a little sneaky. "How's Patty doing?"

"I just left her, she's fine," she says and her mouth does a little twitchy thing to one side but she quickly regains her composure. "Where's Gage? I see his truck out there and I was told he followed you and some other man on a motorcycle out of town. My source followed you all and told me he'd be here. Now where is he?"

Benny comes up behind me and runs his arm around my shoulders. "Hey, Baby, what's taking so long here?"

"This woman says she's Gage's fiancé. Melissa Cross here, I know her as Sandy Whitehead, but she insists I'm wrong, and wants to see Gage. What do you think about that, Benny?"

He shakes his head. "I'm afraid, Gage, is our very dear friend, and he's told us a little different story and you aren't a fiancé in any of it. So, we're going to have to ask you to leave. If he wants to talk to you, I'm sure he knows how to contact you."

"Well, he doesn't know my address. Tell him I'm living at 313 Alpaca Drive. And tell him that I will talk to him and get to the bottom of whatever it is he's doing. I didn't put my life on hold for two years to sit with his ass in the hospital to lose him to this bitch now." She eyes me and I fight the urge to knock the shit out of her.

I narrow my eyes at her and speak in a very low and very threatening voice. "I'm not the woman to talk to like that. I'll knock your ass clean into next week, Sandy. By the way, do you think I don't know the address of your family home, idiot? Do yourself a favor and get some fucking psychiatric help before it's too late. You need some help, bad. And as far as Gage goes, you will not be talking to him. I can see he still has a brain injury that he is recovering from and isn't all himself yet. I'll be calling his family to be sure they know the real story. Your little scam is about to end, sweetie."

My grandmother pulls into the driveway and I look past bat-shit-crazy here to see her. Benny looks too and says, "I don't want to call the cops to get you to leave, but I will. Am I going to have to do that?"

She shakes her head and turns to leave then looks back at me over her shoulder. "You can't have them both, bitch. I will get Gage."

I start out after her. "You shouldn't have called me that, Sandy." But I feel a hand on my arm and Benny's holding me back.

He whispers, "Baby, she's not all there. Don't take it personally."

She laughs kind of hysterically and I really want to kick her ass. But Benny's right. It's obvious she's not all there. And now I really believe Gage's story. As farfetched as it sounds, I think he's telling the truth.

My grandmother, who's is in her late sixties, but thanks to a life full of love with my grandfather, looks great. She keeps her blonde hair in shoulder-length waves. Sure, the blonde isn't natural like it once was, but it's not an obvious dye job. Her blue eyes are still sparkly and full of life.

She looks at Sandy as the laughing chick passes by her then looks back at me with a, 'what the fuck,' look.

I nod and wait for her to get to us as Benny isn't taking any chances and not letting me go. "Who is that?" she asks as she gets to us.

"That's a woman who's gone a bit insane. It seems she's the one to blame for Gage leaving me," I tell her as I pull her into a hug. "It's nice to see you. I'm glad you came, Grams."

Benny extends his hand. "I'm Benjamin Worthington, it's nice to meet you."

She lets me go and pulls him into a hug, ignoring his hand. "Nice to meet you too! My, you're keeping my granddaughter in very nice surroundings, I must say. You call me Grams, Son."

HE SMILES AT ME. "Grams it is then."

I take her hand and lead her inside as we see the looney bird has left our place and we can hear her car jetting off down the road. In the great room, I see that Freddy has several trays of appetizers out and a few bottles of wine and a pitcher of what looks like margaritas.

"Margarita or wine, Grams?" I ask as I lead her into the large room where everyone else is gathered and talking like old friends.

Her footsteps falter and I see her eyes are set on Benny's grandfather. When I look at him, I see him getting up and coming our way. He's wearing a smile and an expensive suit.

BENNY'S GRANDFATHER is a very distinguished looking man as one can imagine a wealthy lawyer would look and he does not disappoint. Silver hair is neatly combed and light blue eyes look both strong and inviting at the same time.

I feel a tremble in my grandmother's hand as his grandfather takes her other one and lifts it to his lips, placing a kiss on top. "Hello there, I'm Samuel Worthington. And you must be this little angel's very pretty grandmother. I can see where she gets her great beauty from now."

My grandmother doesn't bat an eye. "She looks like her mother. I'm her father's mother. My name is Rebecca Jennings. It's nice to meet you, Samuel."

His grandfather looks at me and asks, "Might I steal her away from you, Angel?"

I nod and release her hand. "Of course, you may."

He takes her to meet his son- and daughter-in-law and I'm seeing a light in my grandmother's eyes I haven't seen in some time and it has me wondering. A light has sparked in Benny's grandfather's eyes too.

Benny whispers, "Oh my God, Angel. I've never seen my grandfather look like that in my entire life."

I giggle a little and pull him along with me to check on the food in the kitchen and whisper back, "I've seen my grandmother look like that before. When she was looking at my grandfather, though."

Gage jogs up behind us and puts his hand on my shoulder. I turn back and see him smiling. "Hey, Angel, what took you so long at the door? I thought I heard Melissa's voice, but I wasn't about to come see."

I look at Benny who gives me a nod. "Tell him."

Instead of the kitchen, I take his hand and lead him to a small sitting room where we all sit down. I look into his eyes. "Gage, that woman is mentally unstable."

He frowns at me. "I'm well aware of that. What did she say? Did she threaten you?"

"Not really. Not directly. I do think she's going to be a pain in the ass unless we do something about her. I think you should go to the authorities with what's happened. Let them investigate the whole thing." I pat his leg and see something in his eyes that tells me he's left something out. "Do you want to tell me anything else, Gage?"

"I probably should." He looks at Benny and gets up to move away from me. "Hey, can you hold her over here and not let her go when I tell her this. She might try to hit me."

Benny's hand takes mine. "I won't let her hurt you, Gage. Just tell her what you have to say."

GAGE LOOKS LIKE A KICKED PUPPY. "Angel, I kind of lied to you before."

"You did mess around with her before you left, didn't you?" I ask as I hold tight to Benny's hand.

He nods. "I need your help, though. You're one tough chick and I don't know anyone else to help me. That woman is crazy. Even her friend, Patty, told me that she was worried about her mental state."

I find I'm clenching my jaw. Then Benny's hand on mine makes me think that things happen for a reason. "That's the past and I can't hang onto that. I can help you. I do care about you and I can see the accident has taken some of you away. I'll protect you, Gage."

He looks relieved. "Not mad, then?"

"I AM MAD. But, I'm not exactly mad at you. I'm mad at me too. I was hanging on to you for selfish reasons. I didn't want to be alone. Not completely. I've always kept to myself and you were the very first person I let in. I knew we weren't really compatible. I knew I was heading a different direction than you were." I look at Benny and smile. "And although I'm sorry you were hurt in that accident when you left. I'm glad you did leave me."

"Angel, you don't know how good that is to hear. I thought the same thing the entire last year we were together. You were so into your schoolwork and learning as much as you could by watching the mechanics at your uncle's garage that I knew you were destined for greatness. I was destined for just getting by." He smiles at me. "And I knew I would never be enough for you. I knew you'd leave me one day when you figured that out on your own."

I look at Gage. The man I loved first. Not the most, just first and think to myself that he was a good guy. He was a stand-up guy who went to work at a fast-food restaurant so he could stay in this town to date me.

After six months, we moved in together in the little house we rented. He lived in a motel room until that time. He stayed for me and worked as many hours as he could so he could get us a place.

And I did spend very little time at home the last year that we were together. And when I was home, I was holed up in the bedroom, studying or doing online school work. It left him alone much of the time.

Yet, when he left, I was devastated by it. I recall not understanding at all why he'd leave. But now I can see it very clearly.

I ask him, "Gage, did you and she leave together then?"

HE SHAKES HIS HEAD. "No. Everything else I've told you is the truth. She wanted me to leave you and threatened to kill you if I didn't. I was trying to get out of town without her knowing but somehow she figured it all out and found me on the road, I guess. That part I'm unclear on. I know she was there at the scene of the accident because when I was able to talk again, the paramedics who were first on the scene and took care of me, came to see me and told me she was right by my side from before they got there."

"Okay, so we know she was there from the beginning. Gage, are you sure you and she weren't leaving together?" I ask him one more time because he's letting little things out a bit at a time and I'd hate for him to give the police information that's strewn with lies. They would stop pursuing the case if that's how he's going to be.

"I was going to go back to Texas. That's the truth, Angel. And I wasn't leaving you. Not altogether, I wasn't. I was just making sure she didn't hurt you." He looks at Benny and smiles. "Angel and I did a little rough stuff, sex wise. And Melissa was into that too. Only she could take phenomenal amounts of pain and had me do some really hard shit to her. I won't get into the details but I knew Melissa could take any kind of ass whooping Angel could dish out. So I was afraid for Angel, even though she's tough."

My stomach hurts all of a sudden as I think about my Gage and that crazy bitch. Gage sees the look on my face and he looks away. His expression tells me he's sorry. But it doesn't make the pain stop.

Benny pulls me to him and I snuggle into his side. His warmth helps me to try to come to peace with the fact so much was going on behind my back at that time. "It's okay, Baby," he whispers.

No, it's not, okay. But I guess someday it will be.

GAGE LOOKS at me with a sheepishness to his handsome face. A face I used to really like to look at. His rugged jawline with softness around the edges always fascinated me.

His mouth moves into a crooked grimace. "I'm really sorry, Angel."

I nod. "I'll get over it."

Benny asks him, "Gage, did that woman ever hurt you?"

Gage's eyes go very dark. "Yes."

I sit up and am suddenly furious. "Before or after your accident?"

"After," he says then he looks despondent.

I move quickly to sit next to him on the small sofa across from the one we're sitting on. I take his hands in mine and make him look at me. "After you were hurt? What did she do to you? Tell me, Gage!"

He just stares into my eyes for what seems like forever then he says very quietly, "She tied me up when I told her I was leaving. I had pain pills to help with the really bad headaches that would crop up after I woke up from the coma. I still get them only not as often as I did when I first woke up. Anyway, she must've put some of them in my drink or something because I recall telling her I was leaving. Then I found myself waking up in the bed. I was all tied up and tied down to it."

"She drugged you and tied you up. Then what did she do to you, Gage?" I ask as I see in his eyes that wasn't all she did to him.

He looks from me to Benny. "I'd rather not say."

Benny gets up and takes me by the shoulders. "Angel, don't make him relive that. Whatever it was. Don't make him do that just so you can get really pissed at that crazy chick."

Gage nods at me. "You wouldn't look at me the same way. I couldn't take that, Angel."

And now I know I'm going to make that bitch pay for what she did to us both.

23

BLAZE

The evening went by faster than I ever expected it would. My family has turned into a bunch of people I didn't know they could be. Angel and her grandmother have spun some magic, and it seems to have captivated my family.

Guess I'm not the only Worthington to find a Jennings so remarkable. Grandfather couldn't seem to leave Angel's grandmother's side. And it wouldn't surprise me to find him leaving her bedroom in the morning.

We had Gage stay the night too. I have a feeling that crazy chick would be massive amounts of trouble for him if he were to stay at the motel in town. And he does seem to be more than a bit fragile the more time I spend around him.

Angel climbs into bed next to me and snuggles up to me. "Benny, why did you say your family was so stuffy?"

"Because they are." I run my fingertip over her collarbone and kiss the top of her head as she wiggles her body to get in closer to me.

Her hand moves over my chest as she seems to be feeling every muscle I have. "No, they're not. I think you have some kind of a chip on your shoulder about them. Like you just don't like to be told how to act so you really rebelled against them."

I take her hand and kiss it. "I don't like to be told how to act."

"I doubt anyone does. But when you're a little kid, you do have to be taught how to act accordingly. Don't you agree?" She turns her deep blue eyes up to mine and smiles.

Her smile does something to my heart. It flutters and in her eyes, I see my future. "I do. And you're right, I do have a chip. But I came by it honestly. My grandfather has ruled my entire family since the very beginning. I don't know how my mother stood it all these years. He overrode her and Father's every decision."

"But he seems very smart," she says. "I'm sure it's only because he had no other family. He felt very obligated to make sure his son and his son's family were taken care of and learned the things he thought were important."

"Probably." I pull her up on my chest to lie on top of me. Pushing her dark hair back, I say, "He won't be overruling you and me about our kids."

Her right eyebrow cocks to up as her lips curve into a smile. "Our kids. That's sounds oddly enticing. I wonder if our son will have your rebellious streak. I wonder how you'd handle that."

"Don't wish that on us, Baby," I say with a laugh. "If you knew half the shit I've done in the name of nonconformity, you'd shit."

"Yeah, don't tell me about any of it. I won't shit as much as I'll want to smack you around a little bit." She smiles but I think she's being pretty damn honest. "What are we going to do about this Gage mess? We can't keep him safe with us forever."

"My grandfather's wheels are turning on it. He's a lawyer to his core and if anyone can figure out how to press charges that will stick, it's him." I kiss her and she melts on top of me and the conversation is over.

. . .

I ROLL OVER WITH HER, covering her body with mine, savoring the feeling of her soft body giving into mine. Her leg moves up the back of mine and I feel her foot on my ass.

The heat from between her legs calls out to my cock and it grows to life with a want to fill her. I run my hand over her cheek and sigh. "You're so beautiful, Angel."

Her deep blue eyes dart back and forth then she kisses me back. Her lips press hard to mine. Her tongue pushes past my lips and runs over mine

My entire body is tingling. This is like a fantasy come true. A fantasy I never knew I even wanted. The light from the television is the only light there is, and she looks gorgeous in the muted tones.

I run my hands over the soft flesh of her back as her sweet kiss takes me to a world far away from this place. Her hands roam all over my body, leaving electric trails in their paths.

I run one hand between us and cup one of her breasts. She arches a little and her breath catches as I squeeze it. Her mouth leaves mine, and I move down to take a breast into my mouth. My lips press the nipple between them as my tongue flicks over the tip.

She moans as my hands roam over her hips and run around to grip her ass. I'm on fire for her with a dull ache to be inside her.

Her hands travel over my arms, stopping to feel my biceps. "I love your muscles, Benny," she says with a low moan.

I pull my mouth from her breast. "I love your juicy tits."

She giggles and I kiss my way down her body, pushing her legs apart as I make my way down. My heart is pounding as I stop. My face is right at her apex.

Our eyes are locked as my lips touch her clit and she makes a spectacular moan with the sensation. "Benny!" She grabs the sheet and fists it.

. . .

She closes her eyes as I use my tongue to stroke over her stomach then move my mouth down again. My tongue flicks and runs over her clit, making her arch up with a deep groan. "Sweet Jesus, that feels amazing."

I smile and grip her ass, pulling her up to devour her. She can't stop moaning. Eventually, she completely falls apart under his mouth. "God! Benny! Benny!"

My tongue runs inside her and she shivers. Then I move up her body and kiss her hard. I cradle her ass as I press my erection against her. I ache to go inside her but I wait until she's wiggling underneath me. "Benny, please."

I keep the tip of my wanting cock just at the edge and can feel her pulsing with the orgasm I just gave her. My lips graze over hers as I ask, "Do you love me, Angel?"

"Yes."

"Do you want me, Angel?"

"Yes! Benny, please," she hisses as she arches up to try to get me inside her. "I need you! I need to feel you inside me now."

I put the tip inside and she moans like it's the best thing she's ever felt. I pull it back out and she makes the cutest little mewling sound. Then I slam into her and she lets out a bunch of air as it seems I've pushed it out of her lungs.

Over and over I thrust into her so hard that I can feel her breath coming from her mouth as mine hovers near hers. I breathe her in and take in everything she is. Her essence is amazing and I want all of her.

I want all of her forever.

. . .

I CAN'T SEE my life without her being a part of it and slow my hard thrusts, making long, slow strokes as I move one hand up and down her side.

Her body shakes with the chill my touch gives her. She rises up a bit, making our mouths touch. Her tongue taps at my lips and I open them to find hers moving inside as she kisses me with a deep, sweet kiss.

She tastes like the red wine we drank before we came to bed and I run my tongue over hers, tasting the wine mixed with her own natural juices. I roll us over, so she can be on top of me and she sits up, looking down at me as I lift her up and down.

Her dark hair is falling over her shoulders in waves that shine with the television's light. Her tits are magnificent as they bounce with each movement she makes.

"How about you lean over here and pop one of those yummy tits into my mouth, Pumpkin?"

With a smile, she leans over and teases me with just the slightest touch of her nipple to my lips. I growl and raise my head and grab it with my teeth, making her yelp then it morphs into a groan as I bite it and lick the tip until it's as taut as it can get.

I pull more of it into my mouth and suck it hard. Her nails gouge into my shoulders as she moans my name then a string of curse words comes out of her mouth as her body tightens around my cock and she starts to shake with an orgasm.

My cock can feel every little wave and squeeze the orgasm has her body making. I want nothing more than to give her as many of these things I can.

Just as I feel her beginning to slow the squeezing action it has on my cock, I let her tit go and smile at her as I say, "I have a little surprise for you."

She opens her eyes and sits up on top of me. "What is it?"

I lift her up, off me and turn over to take out a set of pink, fluffy handcuffs and a matching blindfold from the nightstand. "You game?"

She nods and smiles. "Oh yeah, I'm game."

"Hands in front," I say as I hold out the cuffs.

SHE HOLDS out her hands then I cuff them. I get off the bed and place the blindfold over her eyes. Picking her up and tossing her over my shoulder, caveman style, I carry her to the closet where I hang her cuffed hands over the hook on the door where her robe usually hangs from.

It's high enough off the ground she has to stand on her tippy toes. "Please tell me you plan on making my ass ache, Benny."

I walk back over to the nightstand and get out a pink gag and one of my belts. I kiss her long and hard. Then stop and ask, "Hand or belt?"

She licks her red lips. "Some of each, please."

"Gag or no gag?" I ask as I run the ball over her lips so she can feel how big the gag is.

"Gag. I want you to make me feel it, Baby. I want to see red covering my ass when I look at it later in the mirror."

Her breathing is already getting heavy again as she grows more excited. "Since you won't be able to talk and use a safe word, when do you want me to stop?"

She takes in a deep breath and says, "This might sound weird, but I really need to cry since I found out that Gage actually did cheat on me. I want you to stop only once you see tears streaming down my cheeks. Because I feel the hurt welling up inside me and I don't want it to fester like it did before. I want it out and gone. Okay?"

I kiss her cheek then put the gag into place and fasten it behind her neck. "You got it, Baby. And for the record, I don't think it's weird at all."

We all have our ways of dealing with tough shit after all.

I run my hands over her ass. It's round and plump and perfect. I take it all in. The paleness of the skin I'm about to turn pink. The way it gets tighter with every pass I make over it with my hand.

I smack it once half as hard as I can. She makes a little moan and I do it again then run my hand over it, finding it warm where I hit it. I pick up the belt and give her a slight slap with it and watch the plump muscles move in waves then I do it again in another place, and once more in another place.

She groans with each one and I look at her to see if any tears are beginning to spill but see no indication of any.

I use my hand to administer more spanks to her flesh that's beginning to turn pink. She's tough as shit and I make a few more strikes with the belt then her groan turns a little high and I look at her face and find the pink blindfold staining with tears.

I stop the spanking and move in behind her. Moving two fingers inside her, I find her not only insanely wet but her insides as quaking with an orgasm.

It makes my dick actually hurt and I lift her up higher and slide my dick into her from behind. I make hard thrusts into her as I kiss her neck, nipping it and sucking it.

Her body is hot and I can feel sobs making her chest heave. I whisper, "Do you want me to remove the gag?"

She shakes her head. I'm sure she's afraid she'll make so much noise someone will hear her crying.

Her body is still squeezing and throbbing with an intense orgasm as I stroke into her and all I can think about is making everything better for her. I keep making deep thrusts into her over and over until I finally cum and send my semen into her hot depths.

Her legs quiver as I do and finally our bodies slow their intense pulsing and squeezing. I pull the gag off then take her cuffed wrists down.

Picking her up, I lie her face down on the bed, leaving the blindfold on as I look in the drawer for the key to the cuffs. I don't see them as I move the few things that are inside the drawer around.

SHE'S CRYING PRETTY HARD SO I stop my search and rub her shoulders as her arms are stretched out over her head. "I have to go downstairs and see if I can find the keys to the cuffs, Baby. I must've tossed them in the trash with the package they came in. That was careless of me and you can take it out on my ass if you want to."

"It's okay. I'm just going to lie here and cry some more. I'm starting to feel better, believe it or not."

Her ass is red so I ask, "You want me to put some ointment on your ass before I go down there?"

She shakes her head. "I like the comfort of the burn. It makes me feel like I'm experiencing the pain of the heartbreak. I know it sounds crazy…"

I stop her as I kiss her shoulder. "No, nothing is crazy, Baby. You want the blindfold off?"

"No. Leave it on. The complete darkness is comforting. And, Benny?"

"Yeah, Baby?"

"Thank you. Thank you for understanding me like I've never been understood before." She lets out a long sigh.

Her red ass makes me feel kind of terrible and I place my lips on it. "You're welcome. You know, you understand me better than anyone ever has too, Pumpkin. And when I get back with the keys or some other way to get you out of those cuffs, I'm going to kiss every inch of your sweet ass and let you know how much I love you and how happy I am that you're mine. I'm sorry your heart had to get broken by that dumbass, but I'm happy you were free when I came along."

"Me too," she says with a whimper.

After I put on a robe, I leave the room to head out to find the damn key.

24

BLAZE

It's dark as I go down the long hallway. I can see the light from the television coming from underneath the door closest to ours. It's the one her grandmother is in and I have to wonder if my grandfather is in there too.

A little further down the hallway, I see the door to my parents' room. It's dark under that door and I'm sure they're asleep already. The next two doors are where my parents' and grandfather's drivers are sleeping. I see no lights on in either room.

The door to my grandfather's room is dark underneath it. Then there's the room we put Gage in and I find it wide open and no lights are on inside of it. Curiosity takes me over and I creep inside to see if he's in here and sleeping with the door open.

There's enough light from the moon as it shines in the window to see the blankets have been pulled back and he's not in the bed. I look at the door to the attached bathroom and see it's opened and there's no light on in there.

Maybe he needed a drink or something.

I head back out of the room and down the stairs, going very

quietly so I don't startle him. As I go down the stairs, I don't hear a thing to tell me he's down here. But it's a big place so he could be anywhere.

Going into the kitchen, I go to the laundry room to look through the trash where I threw the package the cuffs came in. Angel is my top priority. I can come look for wonder boy once I've set her free.

As I open the door to the laundry room, I find Cuddles sleeping in a corner of the large room. She doesn't open her eyes as I come inside and turn the light on.

"Cuddles?"

I can see her little body rising and falling with each breath so I know she's breathing. But damn that's some hard sleeping she's doing.

I know she played pretty hard with Gage but that's too deep for her to be sleeping. I nudge her with my foot and brace myself for her to tear into me with the intrusion.

Nothing.

She doesn't even halfway open her eyes.

A chill runs through me. But I shake it off and start digging through the trash for the package. It's taking too long and I pick up the can and turn it over, making the paper and other paper goods we put in this can for recycling spill out onto the floor.

I look back at the dog and she's still out like a light. When I look back, I see the package the cuffs came in and pick it up. There the little set of keys are. I must've forgotten to take them out.

With a quick tug on the tape that holds them inside the package, I get them out and leave the laundry room and head to the stairs to let Angel out of the cuffs.

I'll come back down after I get her settled.

. . .

"Hey," I hear from the dark of the dining room off the kitchen.

I turn as I recognize the woman's voice.

"How the hell did you get in here?"

Angel

My tears have dried up as Benny seems to be taking a very long time to get back. I'm cuffed and blindfolded, lying on the bed. Being naked as well, I feel extremely vulnerable.

Wiggling around on the bed, I try to get the blindfold to slip off and manage to get it some of the way off. One eye is nearly free, I think.

The door squeaks a little as it opens. "Thank God, Benny. Did you find the key?"

I hear nothing. Then hear not one set of footsteps but two. Then two sets of hands are on both of my arms and I'm lifted off the bed.

"Hey!" I scream.

These hands are small. Not Benny's or any other man's.

I'm drug backward. The carpeting turns to tile. I'm in the bathroom and I hear the water turn on in the tub.

"What the fuck!"

I scream as I feel something slam against the side of my head.

I'm dropped and fall to the floor.

It stings on the side of my head. I'm very disoriented and try hard to listen. Neither of the people speak as I hear water filling the tub.

Steam is beginning to fill the bathroom as I can feel it on my skin and the heat from it lets me know that it is straight hot water they're filling the tub with.

"PLEASE, whatever you want just take it and leave us alone," I say, trying hard not to let my voice tremble.

The urge to scream for someone to help me is a thing I have to keep under control or they may well knock my ass out and then I stand no chance.

It's painfully obvious they plan on putting me in the deep bathtub in the scalding hot water. My mind is racing with what I need to do.

With the blindfold on, I can really hone in on where the two women are in the bathroom. Footsteps echo off the marble floor and the tiled walls.

One is across the bathroom and the other is by the vanity. My heart is pounding hard with fear and I take in some slow breaths to calm it so I can hear better.

My feet are free and even though my hands are cuffed, they're in front of me. I can kick and make some uppercuts with my bound hands.

I'm not dead yet. I know they want me that way, but I still have a hell of a lot of fight in me.

"Who are you? I deserve to get to see the faces of the women who kill me, don't I?" I ask with an even tone to let them know I'm not afraid of them.

FOOTSTEPS CLICK and clack quickly toward me then they stop right in front of me. I feel a hand move over my cheek and the blindfold is nearly taken off but then another set of footsteps moves quickly toward me and I hear a loud smack as the one who's about to remove the blindfold is whacked by the other.

Okay, I bet they aren't getting along so well now.

"No reason for any violence," I say.

I'm picked up by my hair and made to stand up. My toes hit the edge of the bathtub and I can feel the heat from the water below me.

I know I have this one chance, and that's it, to save myself.

No one else can do this for me. I ready myself to fight for my life. Both let my arms go and I hear them take a few steps back. I think they're about to run at me and push me into the water.

God, please help me...

THE COMPROMISE OF THE BILLIONAIRE
AND HIS ANGEL

Book 4

25

BLAZE

The smell of wet dog brings me around and I find myself lying face down on the hardwood floor in the dining room as Cuddles licks my face. I blink a few times to try to focus as everything is dark and blurry.

I guess I need to get up and figure out what's happened to me.

Everything's a big blur. I went downstairs to get something. I can't really remember what it was.

Hey!

I'm tied up. My arms are behind my back and my wrists are tied with something. And so are my ankles.

Shit!

Cuddles takes a few steps back and I can see she's kind of wobbly.

Oh yeah! Now I remember.

I saw Cuddles asleep in the laundry room. I was going through the trash to find the key for the cuffs I put on Angel.

My eyes focus and I see that Cuddles' face is all wet. I have no idea why she would be wet. But I have no idea why I'm lying here on the floor with my feet and hands bound either.

Then a face flashes in my mind and I do recall seeing a woman in the house. A tall, kind of heavy-set blonde.

The blonde from the bar that night! The one Angel decked and knocked out!

What's she doing here? Is she the one who did this to me?

She had to have help!

Looking back and forth and listening very hard, I hear nothing and see nothing. So, I start to roll over and make my way to anywhere but here.

If they left me here, they'll come back here to do whatever else they have planned for me. So here is not a place I want to be.

Cuddles follows me as I roll over and over and I find myself in the great room. Cuddles walks in front of me, her gait is way off. She must've been drugged by the big chick.

I guess I was too. I don't feel where I was hit to get knocked out. And now that I'm becoming more and more aware of things, I can smell something odd.

I suppose they used some type of thing to knock me out. Maybe chloroform or something like that. Cuddles begins to whine and I try to see what she's whining about.

A dark figure is lying on the floor in front of the fireplace. I roll over to it and find it is not moving and I think it might be a man. And he seems to be tied up too.

One more roll has me close enough to see. Cuddles licks the man's face and I can see that it is Gage.

Great! The only two viable males in this house who could possibly protect the rest and we're both tied up and one of us is still out!

. . .

How much worse can things get?

I bite my tongue as the thought crosses my mind. I shouldn't have even thought that.

Angel's still handcuffed, up in our bedroom, naked as the day she was born and completely vulnerable. I have to get up and get to her. But how?

I roll over and hit Gage with as much force as I can and hiss, "Gage! Wake up!"

Nothing.

Cuddles is licking his face like crazy and it's not doing a thing to wake him up. So I lean over and bite his shoulder. I give him a good bite and he stirs a bit.

"Ow!"

"Gage, wake up!" I whisper as loud a whisper as I can.

I don't need us getting found.

"What the hell?" he mumbles. "Why am I tied up?"

His eyes flutter open and his pupils are dilated.

"Gage, someone's in the house. I need your help to get untied. Angel's alone in our bedroom and I have every reason to believe it's her they're here to hurt."

He shakes his head to clear it. "Fuck!" He coughs a little.

"Shh," I hiss at him. "We have to be quiet."

With a nod, he says, "Yeah. It's Melissa and some blonde woman here. I remember now. I came down to grab a bottle of water and found them with Cuddles. Melissa was holding her and that other chick was holding a rag over her little face."

"Then they got you, huh?"

He nods. "Only, I ran out of the kitchen and they caught up to me in the great room." He looks around. "Yep. Right about here is when the big one tackled me and then something was placed over my nose and mouth and here I am."

"How good are your teeth, Gage?"

He looks confused. "They're okay. Why?"

"I'm going to move around and you try to get my wrists free using them." I start to move around the best I can and manage to get my bound wrists near his face.

I feel him trying to loosen the bond. Then he stops and whispers, "It's a bungee cord, Blaze. Try to pull against it. I'll never be able to bite through that rubber."

"If I could get on my feet, I could hop over to a door and use the handle to stretch the cord then I might be able to get out of it. I'm going to need your help," I tell him as I roll around to try to use his body to help get my ass off the floor.

Together, we manage to get me off the floor and I start hopping to the closest door knob. My robe is all messed up and parts of me are hanging out that I'd rather not have doing that. Hooking my wrists over the door knob, I pull and the cord stretches but it hurts like hell.

I have to keep thinking about what the hell they're doing to my Angel to keep pulling them against my skin and finally I can get one hand free.

That's all I need. I pull the cord off my wrists then my ankles and rush to set Gage free.

"We need something to level the playing field against these bitches, Gage. Maybe a couple of long knives. And something to hit them with," I say as we hurry to the kitchen and I adjust my robe to properly cover myself again.

I grab a couple of knives out of the wooden block on the counter and Gage goes into the laundry room and brings back a broom and a mop. "These will work to knock the shit out of them with." He looks down at Cuddles who still looks kind of loopy. "We should put her up. She might get hurt."

"Stash her in the laundry room," I tell him.

. . .

After he puts her up, we take off to go upstairs to see if the women have found Angel yet. I have no idea how long I was out so I'm worried about what we'll find. Or won't find.

I notice all the bedroom doors are closed as we pass them. All except Gage's.

"Gage, is your cell phone in there so we can get the police coming this way?"

He nods and we go into the room. He grabs his cell off the dresser and calls 911. With a quick description of what's happening and the address, I end the call and we leave the room to get to Angel.

I'm praying we make it to her before it's too late. I have this terrible feeling in the pit of my stomach.

We stop in front of our bedroom door and I try the handle.

"Fuck! It's locked," I whisper and lean my ear against the door to try to hear anything.

My eyes go wide at what I hear and Gage leans in to listen too.

"God damn! What the fuck is happening in there, Blaze?"

"We have to get inside!"

26

ANGEL

I can hear the two sets of feet making noise against the tiled floor of the bathroom as they take steps away from me. I have a feeling they're about to push me into this scalding hot water they've filled our deep bathtub with.

Obviously, I can't let that happen so I'm gearing myself up for a fight where I'm at a distinct disadvantage as my hands are cuffed in front of me and I'm also blindfolded.

Here they come, running at me and I duck just as they get to me and take a few steps back. I hear one of them shriek and some water splash as they must've hit the hot water.

The other has turned and I take a swing at her with my bound hands. They connect with what feels like her face and she makes a loud grunt as I knock her backward.

The other girl grabs me by the hair so I throw my hands at her and hit her in the face too. Then I hear the other girl running at me so I do a little hop and kick one foot straight out and it hits her in the stomach.

I can hear the air leaving her lungs as she falls back. The other girl isn't letting my hair go so I give her three quick whacks with my bound hands in succession then she finally lets it go and I take off running as fast as I can to get to my bedroom door.

It's not very fast as I can't see and have to be careful not to fall down or they'll have even more of an advantage over me. A sound comes from the door. It sounds as if someone has hit it.

Then I'm yanked back by the hair and a fist hits me in the face. It infuriates me and I manage to get my cuffed hands over her head and pull her over my shoulder where she lands at my feet with a hard thud.

The girl is big, and that was hard but I managed it and stand up to try to catch my breath. Then the other, girl, who's smaller, runs up behind me and wraps her legs around me as she hits me in the head over and over with her little fists.

I move backward with her until I come to a wall and ram her into it then squish her between me and the wall. The big girl makes a sound like a bull and I can hear her running toward me.

The sound of wood splintering fills my ears then I hear Benny and Gage yelling, "Stop!"

I'm hit by the big girl as she mashes my body between hers and the other girl's. The small girl shouts, "Fuck! You're killing me, Donna! Stop!"

Then the big girl is pulled off me and the blindfold is removed and there's Benny. "Thank God!"

He pulls me into his arms and picks me up and carries me into the bathroom. "I'm shutting you in here while I help Gage. Just wait here, Baby."

I nod and he turns and leaves, shutting the door behind him. I sit on the closed toilet and try to catch my breath. My hands are still cuffed but at least I can see again.

After a few loud whacks and several screams, Benny comes

back into the bathroom with my white robe. He pulls the little set of keys to the pink cuffs out of the pocket of his robe.

My hands are finally released and I throw my arms around him and start crying like a little kid. "Benny, it was horrible."

He holds me and shushes me as he rocks me back and forth. "It's okay. We have them tied up and the police are on their way."

"I was so afraid," I cry as he holds me. His strong arms feel safe and I'm not sure how long it will take before I can leave them.

Then I hear sirens and know the time is at hand for him to have to let me go. "Here, let me get this robe on you." He lets me go and I find I'm shaking like a leaf.

I look at him as he puts the robe on me then runs his fingertips over the place on my face that's beginning to hurt. "One of them got in a hit," I tell him.

He smiles. "It's amazing there's only one. Want to see what they look like, Pumpkin?"

I nod then he takes my hand and leads me out of the bathroom. The first thing I see are the two bitches who broke into our home, lying face down on the floor. Their hands are behind their backs and tied with bungee cords.

It's Sandy and the chick from the bar who I knocked out!

I stop shaking as I grow furious. Walking in between them I look them over as they lie there. Both have quite a few red and swollen places on their faces.

"I don't know how I managed to do that much damage. But I'm glad I did." I squat down next to Sandy and pull her back by her hair so she has to look at me.

"Fuck you, bitch," she says then attempts to spit at me but I hold my hand over her mouth before she can.

"No, mam." I press her mouth hard with my hand. "Now you listen to me. We're pressing full charges on you both. Attempted murder is what you'll be charged with amongst other things. You see, you dumbass, you broke into a house full of lawyers. Not just any lawyers either. The lawyers of the prestigious New York law firm, The Worthington Law Firm. So you can expect to be sent away for a very long time."

I remove my hand to give her a chance to speak but she chooses the wrong words as she says, "Fuck you!"

"No, fuck you, Sandy. Now I need you to tell Gage the truth about things. Tell him how you are the one who ran him off the road that day," I say and yank her head around so she has to look at Gage.

Her eyes go wild as she asks, "How did you know about that?"

I laugh and so does Benny. Then he answers her, "She didn't. You just confirmed her suspicions."

"Fuck," she mumbles.

I look up at Benny as I drop her head and she face plants into the carpet. "So there's two counts of attempted murder then."

He smiles and takes my hand as the first set of police officers comes to our bedroom door with their firearms drawn. "Everyone okay in here?" the taller one asks.

THE THREE OF us nod then I see Benny's parents, my grandmother with his grandfather, and the two drivers looming in the hallway behind the cops. "Maybe I should let them in on what happened," I say and leave Benny and Gage to explain things to the officers.

One of the officers takes me by the arm and asks, "Are you okay, mam?"

I nod. "A little shaken up. It takes more than a couple of dumb tramps to take me out."

He nods and touches the place underneath my eye. "When the paramedics get here, have them look that over, will you?"

"I guess so." I walk away to talk to the people who I hope one day will be my family.

My grandmother hugs me as she whispers, "What happened?"

"Those women tried to kill me. No big deal, let's all go downstairs. I need something to drink. A lot of something to drink." I lead the way down to the kitchen and pull out a bottle of Jack Daniels from the cabinet Benny keeps it in and drink straight out of the bottle.

It burns going down but stops my body from the internal shaking it's been doing for far too long now. Everyone takes seats at the bar and stares at me. I don't know what to say or where to start so I just look back at them.

Finally, Benny's grandfather asks, "Did you take both of those women on alone, Angel?"

I nod and take another drink then say, "I did. I had to. They were going to throw me into a tub of scalding hot water and drown me. Plus, I was handcuffed and blindfolded."

My grandmother's hand goes to her chest. "They cuffed and blindfolded you?"

I scratch my head and wonder if I should tell them. Then it dawns on me that I'll have to tell the cops that too and possibly tell a judge and jury that as well. So I weigh my words before I say, "Not them."

Benny's grandfather rolls his eyes and his mother looks confused as she asks, "Then who did cuff and blindfold you, dear?"

I take another long drink and the whiskey is finally beginning to work as I answer her, "Your son."

She kind of looks like she might faint and her husband wraps his arm around her and frowns as he looks at her and says, "That sort of stuff has to come from your side of the family."

I laugh and shake my head then say, "What a night!"

27

BLAZE

The Manhattan fall air is crisp in the open air section of the church my family attends. I wait at the altar with my grandfather. I never pictured this day would come, or that I'd be the one standing next to him.

The music wells up into the air, surrounding us all with the sounds of a harp and piano as an old song is played. It's what she wanted and since my grandfather met her, she has always gotten what she wants.

On this day, my grandfather is making Angel's grandmother his wife. Seems the two were smitten with each other from the first time they saw one another. Kind of like me and Angel were.

My grandfather moved a hell of a lot faster than I have, though. He asked Rebecca to marry him after only a week. She left her home and went back home with my grandfather.

Gage moved into her house and is taking care of her many animals. She told him he could have the small farm house and the animals. The man is in hog-heaven with them all.

We didn't give him Cuddles but Rebecca had an old bloodhound and Gage loves the thing. They're like best friends.

We go check on him once a week and hang out with him. I'm

paying for him to get physical and mental therapy to help him make what all hope will be a complete recovery.

He's making a living selling the fresh eggs the chickens lay and milk from the three dairy cows she has. I pay the bills for the house, so any money he makes is all his.

He seems pretty happy since he has his truck and now Angel's old motorcycle that she gave him, since she rides with me on my bike or in her new truck. I look for things to go fine for the guy. And having somebody to take over her little farm has made Rebecca happy as well.

Rebecca's presence in my grandfather's life has certainly softened the old snooty fart. It's made life with him a lot easier. And business too, for that matter.

With Rebecca's gentle influence, Grandfather finally saw the wrong in helping that asshole, Bain, with his endeavor to keep the AIDs drug at the high price he set. The government was able to make him lower it so that problem is history.

I stand by his side, holding the wedding ring he's going to place on her finger and watch as Angel walks down the aisle. She's her grandmother's maid of honor and I'm my grandfather's best man.

I thought for sure he'd pick my brown-nosing brother to be his best man, but he shocked us both by asking me. I had to accept. At least that's what Angel told me I had to do.

She's helped me to see how much of a chip on my shoulder I really had. It's made it a lot easier to do the things I want to without thinking I need to stick it to my family at the same time.

We still ride motorcycles. I'm still in the biker club and Angel and I still like to get rough with each other. But I don't make any of it about showing my family that I can be who I want to be. I just am who I want to be.

Seems they have no problem accepting that now. I think Angel and her grandmother are the reasons why. They have an air about them that makes people comfortable.

It's odd but a great odd.

Angel has on a peach-colored dress her grandmother picked out. Her long dark hair is put into a fancy up do, strung with tiny burgundy roses. She looks delicious and I can't wait for this to be over so I can eat her up.

She gives me a nod when she makes it to her place then the music picks up as her grandmother walks down the aisle. I watch my grandfather's lips curve into a smile. A thing I've seen more of since he met Rebecca than I have in my entire life.

Angel was more than surprised when her grandmother found my grandfather just as compatible with her as her first husband was. She'd thought her first husband was the only man who could make her feel so special.

Seems my grandfather can too!

The only thing bad about that is now Angel thinks we should take more time and see other people to find out if what we have is real. She's making me nuts with her idea and I've yet to come up with the right words to make her stop being crazy.

She's told me after today, she's moving into her own place again and giving what we have a break. But there's no way I'm letting that happen. Not ever!

I have two rings in my pockets. The right pocket holds my grandfather's ring, and the left holds the one I'm giving Angel after this is over.

I'm not only going to make the engagement official but also extremely short.

∽

Angel

As my grandmother gets to me, she hands me her bouquet and I take it and hand it back to my younger sister who's gotten up to take it from me. She's very pregnant with her third baby and has already been hounding me that her kids need some cousins.

But I think I'm going to put things like that off for a while. My grandmother thought there was only one man in the world for her and boy, was I surprised when she told me she felt the same magic she'd felt with my grandfather when Benny's grandfather touched her.

So there is more than one person for us after all it seems. What if I marry Benny and the other man for me shows up after that? Then what would I do?

As I turn back around, Benny's eyes catch mine, and he mouths the words, 'I love you,' to me.

I do love him so I mouth the same words back to him.

It's not that I don't love him. It's not like I don't think I'd be happy forever with him. It's just that the new knowledge that there could be more than him who's out there for me has me confused.

Everything is so confusing!

Benny's trimmed his beard down to a very nice manicured look. He still has those whiskers but they've been tamed and his tassel of waves at the top of his head has been trimmed and tamed too.

He's really a sight to see. Tall, handsome, and all decked out in a gorgeous black tux. Last night at the rehearsal dinner, I was the envy of all the New York and Manhattan females who've long held torches for the man who loves me.

He winks at me and purses his lips then licks them slowly as he looks into my eyes. My body goes hot and my little, white, silk panties get wet.

What he does to me is amazing!

So why do I feel like I need to move out and give what we have a break?

Sometimes I think maybe I have something wrong with me. Like I can't believe things can go right for any real period of time. Always waiting for the other shoe to drop.

Like almost getting killed by those two broads. Their trials are coming up soon and it looks like they'll both get what they deserve. Sandy a bit more than the other girl, who ended up being her cousin.

THINGS like that have me thinking that what Benny and I have could end. The other man in this world who is also meant for me could show up and ruin everything. Or worse, the other woman in this world meant for my Benny could show up and ruin everything!

Life might well be spent alone rather than waiting for that shit to happen and blow my perfect world to smithereens.

I feel a tug at my dress and turn back to see my three-year-old niece holding her arms up to me. So even though this is not how rehearsal went, I pick her up so she can get a better look at her great-grandmother getting hitched again.

A bunch of people make that aww sound people make when things are cute. My niece looks a lot like me and when she runs her arms around my neck and hugs me, then lays her little head on my shoulder, I kind of go all melty inside.

I find Benny looking at me and he mouths, 'That looks good on you, Baby.'

The urge to shoot the finger comes over me but all the people watching us has me not going through with that.

Benny has made no secret one day he wants to marry me. One day!

Well, I think a girl should get a bit more than that. I mean, sure he bought a house and my name is on it too. And that should be better than any engagement ring. But the fact is, it's not.

The snooty bitches here have very rudely pointed that fact out too many times to count. I've been introduced as Benjamin's girlfriend and nothing more than that.

I've spotted a few of the women talking in hushed tones about me being far too average for a man of Benny's social stature. And that's true. If he was all about his social place in New York circles, then he wouldn't ever be happy with me.

That's not my cup of tea so to speak.

But Benny isn't about that life. He's about freedom. The outdoors. The open road. That kind of stuff.

Not sitting around a country club, gossiping about what the wanderers did on their European trip that cost them gazillions of dollars.

No, my Benny is a man who likes the smell of an open fire and to sit underneath a blanket of stars in a desolate part of the country. Listening to the sounds that the night creatures make and holding me in his arms as he sings a song to me.

That's my Benny!

I sway with my niece back and forth and find myself gazing at the man who stands across the aisle from me and he looks back at me.

He makes me smile as he runs his hand over his stomach then makes a gesture of it all rounded out and nods at me. I shake my head at him and he smiles at me with those pearly whites of his.

Suddenly, I realize we're at the part where I need to hand my grandmother the ring she'll slip onto her new husband's finger and I have to maneuver my now sleeping niece so I can pull it from the little pouch that's hanging from my right wrist.

I manage to get it out and place it in my waiting grandmother's palm as she smiles at me with infinite patience only the elderly have.

MY ATTENTION GOES to her and my new grandpa as they seal the deal with the rings and then they kiss. It's a long and very smoochy kiss for such old people.

It makes my heart skip a beat as I think about loving someone so completely at that age.

I wonder if I'll still love Benny when I'm as old as she is?

They end their kiss as their guests clap and my side of the family cheers like a bunch of second-class citizens. But Benny's grandfather smiles, and it seems to make him happy.

I don't know how Benny grew up with these people and didn't see this side of them at all. He always talked about how stuffy and snobby they all are. But they're nice.

Do they have little eccentric ways?

Well, yeah. But who doesn't have little idiosyncrasies?

My gran and new gramps walk down the aisle hand in hand then I feel Benny's hand slip over mine as he leads us down the aisle behind them. His lips press my neck near my ear. "I love you, Princess."

I'm pretty sure I'm blushing as heat fills my cheeks and I whisper, "I love you too, Benny."

. . .

My sister's husband catches up to us and takes his sleeping oldest daughter out of my arms, thankfully as she was getting very heavy. Then Benny spirits me away to a small room off the main church.

"Benny, what are you doing? They're about to get in the car and leave," I say as he drags me inside the little room and closes the door behind us.

He presses me against the door and kisses me. It takes my mind off my leaving grandmother and all I can think about is running my arms around him and pulling him closer to me.

When he ends the kiss, I'm light headed and when he gets on one knee, I'm close to fainting. "What are you doing, Benny?"

"Shh," he says as he pulls a shiny thing out of his pocket. He takes my shaking hand and looks up at me. "Angel Jennings, my life began when I laid eyes on your beautiful face. I didn't even realize I was living life as a zombie until I met you. You helped me integrate my two sides and I've never felt more whole. Only I'm not complete yet. Without you, I'm not the whole enchilada that I can be."

I giggle a little with his words and then stop as it all gets very real when a tear falls over his cheek. My heart stops and I want nothing more than to kiss it away. "Oh, Benny."

"Shh," he says to me again. "Let me finish this. My life will never be complete until you become my wife. So I'm asking you, Angel Jennings, if you will do me the great honor of becoming Mrs. Benjamin Franklin Worthington, later on this evening in Las Vegas?"

"Today?" I ask in complete surprise.

He nods. "What do you say, Baby?"

My knees get weak and I go down on them to get on the

same level he is. "I say yes, Benny. Yes, I'll marry you tonight in Vegas."

He slips the ring on my shaking finger then pulls me into his arms and kisses me in a way he's never done before. Soft and sweet yet hard and permanent.

This is all about to be permanent and here I was only a few minutes ago preparing myself for moving out of our house tomorrow.

Things can change so quickly!

28

BLAZE

Little feet pound the pavement as a horde of small children run past us and jump all at once into the swimming pool of the Vegas hotel.

"My God!" Angel says under her breath as the parents of the little munchkins come up behind us. "It's past midnight!"

One of the mothers walks up next to her and says, "I know. That's why we're letting them swim off some of their inexhaustible energy. We all have husbands we'd like to spend a few moments of time with on this vacation."

Angel looks suitably embarrassed by getting caught and apologizes, "Sorry, it's just that I'm beyond exhausted. My grandmother got married this afternoon, and I was her maid of honor then this guy here asked me to marry him and we just got done with that and now we're going up to our hotel suite and I'm kind of crabby."

The woman frowns at Angel then looks at me. "Don't worry. That's how most wedding nights end up, anyway. Both people falling asleep without even touching each other. It's to be expected after such a long day and it sounds like she's had a hell of a long day."

Angel nods. "And I'm so damn hungry for some reason. I've been snacking like non-stop all day and I'm still hungry. My stomach has been so weird feeling. I was thinking it was because of being in my grandmother's wedding but now I'm thinking it might be a virus. A really weird one that makes you hungry."

Another one of the mothers walks up and says, "You know I was that way through my entire first pregnancy. Hungry all the time. Never could get enough to eat."

"Well, that's not my problem." Angel looks at me with a little bit of horror on her beautiful face. "Right? It can't be that! Right?"

I shrug my shoulders. "Wouldn't bother me one little bit if that was the case, Mrs. Worthington."

ANGEL'S EYES move over the kids who are all swimming and jumping off the sides of the large swimming pool. She looks over the one mother of the pack who holds a sleeping baby in her arm like a sack of potatoes. Then she bursts into tears.

The women all look at her with understanding in their eyes and one of them says, "You better get her to the room. She's had it for today."

"Milk and cookies should do the trick," another offers as I take my brand new wife inside the huge hotel.

SHE'S CRYING SOFTLY, but she's still crying as we go inside and get on the elevator. There's one other couple in the elevator who look at her then me. The man asks, "Hard night?"

I shake my head. "Nah, not really. We just got married and this one here just had the idea that she might be pregnant put into her head. That's all."

Angel turns to me and buries her face in my chest to hide

her tears. Then the woman offers, "You can call the desk clerk and they'll send up a pregnancy test. I had to do that on our last trip here. I took one drink of a rum and coke and puked everything up. John told me I needed to take a pregnancy test before I put even one little bit of alcohol into my body. So we went to the room and made the phone call, and thirty minutes later I knew that trip to Vegas was going to be alcohol-free."

Angel gulps back her tears. "Did you cry?"

"Sure," the woman says, as if every woman cries when she finds out that kind of great news.

"So, I am normal?" Angel asks.

The woman nods as the elevator stops and just before they get off she offers a word of encouragement, "Don't worry if you are. This man loves you. Anyone can see that."

The elevator doors close and she looks up at me with red-rimmed eyes. "You do, don't you?"

I nod and kiss the top of her head then pick her up as the elevator comes to a stop at the penthouse then I take her to our suite.

Laying her gently on the bed, I ask, "Should I call and get you one of those things, Baby?"

"I'm on the pill," she says and gets up to go pull them out of her bag. She shows them to me. "See, I've taken them every day just like I'm supposed to."

I take the pack out of her hand and look at the back and my nose wrinkles up instinctively. "Angel, these are a year past the expiration date."

"What?" She grabs the pack out of my hands. Her eyes go round as she looks back at me. "Oh my God, Benny! That means

I could be a couple of months pregnant! I didn't even notice the damn date and I got these and last months at the same time from my doctor. The idiot! Call the desk. Call them now."

She runs to the bathroom and I hear her throwing up. I laugh and shake my head as I pick up the phone in the room. "Hi, I need a couple of things. One pregnancy test and one bottle of non-alcoholic champagne, please."

Just as I hang up, she comes out completely naked and pointing at her stomach. "I thought I was bloated. I thought maybe I was getting a little tummy because I've been snacking so much. Feel this." She takes my hand and places it on her stomach that is a little bit bigger but not much.

"I can't tell, Baby. But we'll be fine either way. You know we will."

She falls backward onto the bed and looks at the ceiling. "This is awful. If I am pregnant, then everyone will think you only married me because of that."

I lean over and kiss her cheek. "Who cares what anyone thinks?"

"It'll make the New York Times. I know it will. I can see the headline now, 'Benjamin Worthington married a nobody because he got her pregnant.' It'll be everywhere."

I have to laugh. "Okay, first thing, that's no kind of headline. Second, it will never make the news. Third, who gives a fuck?"

A knock comes at the door and she sits up quickly. "Go get it and bring me the thingy to the bathroom." She shoots into the bathroom as I go to the door.

The man at the door hands me a discreet brown paper bag and the bottle of champagne and a basket of fruit. He has a big grin as he asks, "Are we happy about this?"

I nod. "Very."

"Great!" he says as he places the things on a small table near the door. "I'll keep my fingers crossed for you guys then."

. . .

AFTER READING the directions to make sure she does this right, I take the test to her. She's chewing at her fingernail as I walk in. "Here, Baby. Pee on this then lay it on this tissue on the counter top. Then I want you to put on one of these fluffy robes and come out to me. In ten minutes you and I will come back in here together and see what it says."

She nods. "K."

I leave her alone because I know she needs a bit of space to do what she has to. Grabbing two champagne glasses, I fill them up and leave them on the table. I sit on the sofa and in no time she's coming out.

A white robe is covering her now, and she looks nervous as hell. I wiggle my finger at her and she comes to me.

Taking her hand, I pull her to sit on my lap. I pull her hair out of the bobby pins that are holding her hair up and run my hands through it to make the long waves hang down.

"You're really beautiful, Angel." I push the robe back and kiss her shoulder.

She smiles at me and runs her hands over my face. "And you are too, Benny,"

I pull her to me and take her lips with a deep kiss. A kiss that lets her know I love her with everything in me. A kiss that tells her everything will be okay. A kiss that tells her I'm happy no matter what.

The kiss gets me hot for her and I lay her back on the sofa and move my body over hers. Her legs wrap around me and I grind against her. A low moan comes out of her, making our mouths vibrate.

One breast finds its way into my hand and I squeeze it as our mouths take us to places only they can. My cock is straining inside the tuxedo pants and I somehow manage to kick my shoes off then her hand finds my zipper and the button keeping my pants on and she frees me up.

Opening her robe, I push it back and press my aching cock into her as she arches up to me. "Benny," she moans as I enter her.

I move my mouth to kiss her neck as I move inside her and make gentle thrusts. "Angel Worthington, you taste delicious." I suck her sweet skin and make her moan and writhe underneath me.

She unbuttons my shirt and runs her hands under it, all over my back. "Your body feels even better now that you're all mine, Benny."

I look at her with a smile and kiss the tip of her nose. "I am all yours, Angel. And you are all mine."

She's so gorgeous my insides ache knowing I get to look at her every day and every night. The way her legs wrap around me has her holding me to her and my thrusts are short.

She runs her hand over my head and looks at me intensely. "We're married, Benny. That's so weird."

"I wouldn't use the word, weird, my Angel." I kiss her cheek. "I'd use fantastic."

She bites her lower lip and says, "Yeah, it's that too."

"You know you're a very rich woman now, Mrs. Worthington. What's the first thing you want to buy?" I ask, as I pump slow and easy into her wet depths.

"I THINK my first purchase is going to be a tattoo of my name right over your heart. What do you think about that?" She runs her hand over the empty spot on my chest and I run my fingertips over the same spot on her.

"If I can see my name right here, then you can put your

name right there," I say then kiss the place just above her plump and juicy left breast.

She nods, "Deal. And I'm putting my new last name across the top of my wrist. Like a built in bracelet."

I smile and kiss her and know I married the right one for me.

Our bodies move together like they were built for this. And suddenly I want all of our clothes off. I pull away from her and pull my clothes all the way off as she watches me.

Then I pick her up and carry her to the bed. I place her feet on the floor and take the robe all the way off then lay her back on the bed and look at her for the longest time.

This woman is mine. To love, care for, and take care of. She is my responsibility and always will be. Instead of feeling a weight on my shoulders, I feel an energy I've never felt before.

Her blue eyes look up at me and her face is void of any emotion as she holds her arms out to me. I go into them and her face fills with light. "I love you, Benny."

I kiss her and know all is right with us.

Angel

THE DAY finally took its toll on us and after we made love, we fell asleep. The light peeking in from the heavily curtained window wakes me up. Benny snores next to my ear as he holds me in his arms.

It's the best sound I've ever heard.

Then the fog clears and I remember what's waiting for us in the bathroom. I nudge him in the ribs and he grunts as he wakes up.

. . .

His warm lips touch my shoulder. His voice is scratchy as he says, "Good morning, Mrs. Worthington."

"Good morning. Do you think you're ready to go see what that test in the bathroom has for us?"

He moans a little as he squeezes me. "I completely forgot about that. All I could think about was you. And how happy I am you're mine now."

I turn in his arms and look at him then run my hand through his dark blonde hair. "I'm happy too. More than I knew was possible. Funny how a little piece of paper makes things feel so permanent."

He pulls my left hand from underneath the blanket and kisses the wedding set on it. "And the rings help too."

I nod and bring his left hand to my lips and kiss the one on his finger too. "Yes, they do."

"Okay," he says as he looks into my eyes and runs his hand over my cheek. "We're happy no matter what the outcome of that test is. Okay?"

I nod. "What else can we be?"

"Well, you could get all weepy again. That's no good," he says with a frown.

I smack him in the arm. "Hey, I might not be able to help that!"

He rubs his arm, "Ow!"

I raise my eyebrow at him and give him that look that says not to mess with me. "Well!"

"Okay. If you have to cry for reasons I'll never understand then do it and I'll try not to laugh at you. It won't be easy, but I'll try." He gets out of bed and puts on the fluffy white robe that's lying over the chair near him and I get out of bed and pick up the one he pulled off me last night from the floor and put it on.

. . .

"Come on, Big Papa," I say as I hold out my hand for him.

He laughs and smacks my ass. "You come on, Big Momma."

I shake my head. "Baby, there's not a woman on the planet that likes to be called big anything."

He laughs again. "Got ya. Come on, Lil' Momma."

So into the bathroom we go to see what we're doing here. Partying like rock stars or like pregnant people.

My heart's pounding so hard that's basically all I can hear as my pulse fills my ears. And I close my eyes as Benny opens the bathroom door. He flips on the light switch and we lean over the counter top and I open my eyes.

"What's that mean?" I ask as I didn't read the directions, and he did.

"What does a plus sign usually mean, Baby?" he asks me with a smile.

"Positive," I answer. "But, is that like a positive sign I'm not pregnant? You know, like this test is positive you are not pregnant."

He shakes his head. "Come on, Baby. You know what a positive result is. Don't act dumb."

His arms surround me and he leans his forehead against mine. I run my arms around him and we just hold each other like that for a long time. Like longer than I ever recall holding anyone like this in my life.

Finally, I can speak without the threat of crying, "Benny, we sure hurry up and do things, don't we?"

"We sure do, Baby," he says then kisses my lips with a light kiss. "We sure do."

29

BLAZE

The squeaking of the rocking chair as it moves back and forth over the hardwood floor in the great room makes a comforting sound that's not only putting our six-month-old son to sleep but also his very tired daddy.

The fireplace is in full blaze and the warmth it's putting out is making things way too comfortable not to take a well-deserved afternoon nap. It's quiet since Angel's in her shop creating a masterpiece of artwork on the gas tank of the bike she's putting the finishing touches on.

It's her very first design, and she's doing all the graphics by hand. We're taking it to Milwaukie to the Harley Davidson plant next month to see what they think about her design.

It's too lightweight for me but men like me are not who it was designed for, anyway. Angel designed it for people who weigh less than a hundred and fifty pounds. And are not terribly tall in stature either.

And she's making it pretty. This first one is designed for a woman. She's going to make another one of the same body style and frame but use graphics and colors for a man.

. . .

To say I'm proud of her just isn't enough. She's managed to make a baby inside her while finishing her degree and starting her first motorcycle design. Then she built it with her own two hands. She had a little help from me and a couple of men I hired to help with the heavy lifting, of course.

Then she had our son after twenty-seven hours of labor. To be honest, I'm not sure how she did that at all. She's like a miracle woman!

After only four weeks of recovery time, she got back to work on her motorcycle while I took over most of the care of little Woodrow Wilson Worthington. We call him Woody. Grandfather came up with the name and Angel thought it would be a great tradition to keep up.

I wasn't so keen on it, but we've learned how to make compromises. I get to name any daughters we might have. Although, Angel said it's going to have to be a few years before we try for another kid so she can get the horrible labor she had with Woody far out of her mind.

Cuddles comes into the room, jumping and acting like a young puppy which means someone is here. The front door opens and I hear people walking inside. Then Angel's voice floats out of the entry room and into the great room, "He's going to be so surprised."

Picking my head up off the back of the chair where I was resting it in hopes of a nap, I see Angel coming into the room with Gage walking next to her and carrying a little box that seems to be making a cheeping noise.

A wide smile covers his face as he looks right at the sleeping baby I'm holding. "Uncle Gage brought little Woody a friend." He puts the box down where I can see inside of it and I see the thing making the incessant cheeping sounds.

Woody stirs and is fully awake within seconds as he hears

the sounds too and has to see what it is. Gage picks the little yellow chick up and holds it out to Woody.

He nearly climbs off me to get away from the thing as he looks terrified. "It's a baby chick, Woody," I say quietly to him.

He looks at me as if my words alone make it safe. I'm like a God to this little guy!

I pet the little thing on top of its fluffy tiny head and my son follows me. Then he giggles and my heart fills with that crazy stuff that makes it feel wiggly and full of happiness.

One little giggle out of him does it to me every time. I hope it always does.

GAGE IS BEAMING. "I knew he'd love it. What are you going to call him, Woody?"

Angel rolls her eyes. "Gage, he can't talk yet. He's smart but not that smart yet. So let's call it, Yellow Chick."

Gage rolls his eyes right back at her. "No way. That's a lame name. How about, Pecker?"

I let out a laugh, "Ha! No. I'm not going to have my son going around calling out, here, Pecker. Has anyone seen my Pecker?"

"Oh, yeah. Didn't think that one out," Gage admits.

His physical therapy is coming along great and he's a hundred percent back to his former self like he was before his wreck. But the mental therapy is taking a bit longer.

Although Angel did have to admit he wasn't up there in the high points where intelligence was concerned before his wreck. She said it was his muscles and handsome face that got to her, not his brain.

So he may be back to normal for him, anyway.

The baby watches the little chick peeping like crazy and he starts popping his mouth, making a little popping sound. Angel and I look at each other and we both say, "Pop Pop!"

Gage nods. "I like it. Pop Pop it is." He holds his hand up as he's managed to teach our baby how to high five.

Woody holds up his hand and they both laugh as they do a little baby version of it. Woody laughs like it's the funniest thing in the world and it makes Angel and I laugh too.

This kid has been more fun than I ever knew a kid could be. Oh, he's also been a horror show. Especially the diapers in the beginning. My God, those were horrible!

Angel really put it to me with those awful things. Seems like the smell was so awful it was always about to make her puke. So she'd shout out that she needed help and would quickly abandon me with the terrible task of finishing the diaper change.

She really is a little bit of Heaven and a little bit of Hell, in more ways than one!

But I wouldn't have her any other way.

Gage holds his hands out for Woody to come to him and as always he does. He loves his Uncle Gage. And their friendship which started right off the bat has been a huge help to Angel and me.

We have a reliable babysitter anytime we ask for one and I think it might be the right time to ask so I can take my wife out on a little motorcycle ride.

As I rock back and forth in the rocking chair, I reach up and pull Angel down to sit in my vacated lap. She giggles and runs her arms around my neck. I kiss her lips as Gage takes the baby and sits with him on the floor to play with Cuddles and the new baby chick.

"What do you say to a bike ride with your old man, Baby?"

She leans her head on my chest and sighs. "You gonna let me drive this time?"

"No," I say with a chuckle. "You're going to ride bitch like you always do. And you're going to like it." I kiss her lips again and she kisses me back a bit harder.

She pulls back and says, "Damn it, I love your ass."

I run my hand along her side and over her hip. "I love your sweet ass too, Lil' Momma."

She gazes up at me with those deep blue eyes and flutters her thick dark lashes at me. "Can we stop at the Tasty Freeze for an ice cream cone?"

I nod and she smiles. And I have to wonder if just her smile alone will always make me feel this way.

30

ANGEL

The wind is cold on the sunny yet cold, late November afternoon. I ride behind my husband and use his body to shield my face from the freezing air. But he wanted to take a ride with me and I rarely tell him no to that.

Plus, he said he'd get me an ice cream cone and I rarely say no to that too!

But I find myself thinking back to the summer and I do recall bitching about how hot it was then. Seems I like spring and fall and that's about all.

It's hard to believe we celebrated our first wedding anniversary last month. The year flew by. Even being pregnant didn't make it feel like forever although the pregnancy itself did feel that way.

Odd how time works.

Benny takes a turn to the left instead of the right and heads away from town. And in no time I see he's taking us out to a little-known spot, one that we found when we went riding when we first got together.

The trees get thick and the road narrows as we pull into a small park. No one's here, like usual. He goes through the entrance and heads to the back of the park where the secluded area is and my heart starts to race because I know what Benny likes to do in this little secluded area we found back then.

He stops the bike and holds his hand out for me to take and get off first. Then he gets off and pulls something out of the compartment at the back of the bike.

"A BLANKET, HUH?" I ask. "Nap time, or what?"

He shakes his head and takes the blanket and my hand and leads me through the thick woods until he finds the spot we found that's perfect. A tall pine tree shoots up in the middle of the mix of Aspens and looks surreal against the tiny bits of blue sky that can be seen out of the thick canopy of the evergreen.

He spreads the blanket and sits on it, pulling me down with him. He has me on my back in no time and his body is next to mine as he looks at me. I run my hand along his muscular arm as he holds himself up on it.

"I love the way you look in this light," he says in a husky whisper.

"You do, huh?" I pull him to me and kiss him.

He twirls his tongue around mine for a few moments then pulls back and looks at me again. He runs his hands through my hair and just gazes at me. "You know you're extremely special, don't you?"

"I think you are," I say and move my hands up over his wide shoulders.

My eyes close as he moves in and takes my lips with his. The instant they touch a fire rips through me and my arms move over his broad shoulders then through his hair.

He pulls me tighter to him and my breasts press against his hard chest. His heart is pounding so hard in his chest I can feel it on my own.

Mine speeds up and matches the pace of his. Heat seems to be whipping through my veins.

When his lips leave mine, I keep my eyes closed, savoring the way his mouth mingled with mine. Loving the taste that lingers on my tongue. Uniquely Benny and me.

I want this man like I have never wanted anything in my entire life. My body is so drawn to his, even now we hold onto one another as if the other is a life preserver in an ocean full of dangerous waves.

My mind spins and my body heats as his lips touch mine again and his tongue touches my bottom lip. I part my lips and his tongue pushes through them and slides along mine.

A pulsing sensation begins in my crotch as he moves his body so I can straddle him. He presses his growing erection to my core. I feel myself growing wetter by the second.

His makes a deep moan, igniting a desire in me I didn't know could be so raw and powerful. His body grinds into mine and I grind right back. The rubbing back and forth on my leather pants has me shaking with need.

Now he really starts grinding against me and I can feel his hard cock pulsing and growing with every move he makes. His kiss grows hungry and frantic as if he needs me to live or something.

I wrap my legs around him and rake my nails over his back then run my hands over every leather covered muscle and try to memorize this whole thing for a future reference for my daydreams.

I need him now. I need all of him. This making out isn't going to cut it this afternoon under this tree. And by the way he's breathing hard and heavy and pulling at my body, I can see he needs me too.

His mouth leaves mine, and he reaches under my shirt and around me to unclasp my bra. "I just want to feel you breasts freed from this thing. They're so soft and supple and amazing."

Benny pushes my T-shirt up and takes a tit in his hot mouth as his hand rubs the other and I moan with how it feels. His touch is sending little volts of electricity through me and my insides begin to pulse.

THE WAY he's sucking my tit makes my stomach clench with each hard pull he makes on it. I groan in ecstasy as I look at the sky through the tree tops, "Benny." It's all so intense and unreal.

My body begins to shake as he continues to grind into my core and the way he's moving has my clothes moving over my clit and I shriek as I orgasm.

His mouth leaves my breasts, and he trails kisses up my neck. "I love you."

I feel terrible that my body was able to finish in a sweet climax and his is left wanting more. Needing more.

"Turn over. I want to finish you, Benny."

He looks at me with lust-filled eyes and he makes a low growl as I push him back and move my body over his. I kiss his chest and down his stomach then unbutton and unzip his leather jeans and release the beast inside.

Although I'd like to take a minute or two to admire the long length as it stands at attention for me and the girth of it as it pulses with impatience to feel my mouth, I know that it is cold out and waiting could be uncomfortable for him. So I press my lips to the bulbous tip and he lies back with a loud groan, "That feels amazing!"

And I haven't really done anything yet!

As I slide my mouth over him, I run my hands around his cock. Up and down I move them right behind where my mouth leaves.

He tastes like Heaven and the way his soft skin feels as I move my mouth over his hard as a rock cock is a mixture of sensations I like very much.

I find only half of him is fitting into my mouth so I push myself a bit more and take him down my throat. I gag a little then it slips on down and the sounds he makes lets me know he's kind of enjoying it.

Moving up and down his cock, I run my tongue along the underside and move one hand to touch his balls.

They feel wonderful in my hand as I gently squeeze them and play with the little hard ball-like things inside. They instantly swell in my hand as a bit of juice comes out of the tip of his cock.

I love the way it tastes and moan. Benny moans too and his hands tangle up in my hair. "Your cock-sucking skills are amazing."

A little more juice comes out and I speed up the process and before I know it he's shouting curse words and his hot juices are shooting down my throat.

HIS GROAN of appreciation makes the leaves shake on the trees it's so loud and deep. I pull my mouth away from his cock and give him a smile.

"Now for that ice cream, I was promised."

He laughs. "I'd have thought what I just gave you filled you up. You sure you have room for ice cream, Baby?"

I get up as I nod and hold my hand out to help him up.

"Benny, Benny, Benny, there's always room for ice cream. Now come on, and take your wife to get some of that creamy goodness."

He gets up and pulls me to him and kisses me with a soft kiss. His tongue thrusts through my lips and he makes a low moan as our tongues run over the others. Then he eases the kiss and says, "I love the way my creamy goodness tastes in your sweet mouth, Princess."

I have to giggle and feel a blush heating my cheeks. "Me too."

I wonder if it will ever stop being this good. I hope not!

31

BLAZE

"I don't like this one bit, Gage," I overhear Angel telling her old boyfriend who's finally found himself a girlfriend after two years of staying single and us being his only friends.

His past with the crazy Sandy chic, who now resides in prison along with her cousin, Donna, had him gun-shy for far too long. And now it seems that my wife isn't a fan of this new chick he found on the internet.

I mosey on over to the kitchen where I hear their voices coming from and find them looking at each other with scowls on both their faces as our little toddler walks around trying to open all the child-safety-locked drawers and cabinets.

Easing into the kitchen, I pick up our now one and a half-year-old, Woody, and he immediately pulls my beard. I've been letting it grow again, and he's kind of mesmerized by it and keeps wanting to see if it can come off.

"Blaze, would you tell her that lots of people meet on the internet now?" Gage asks as he looks to me for some kind of hope.

"Angel, lots of people meet now on the internet," I say but I know my wife and it doesn't really matter what anyone else says about things she's sure of. And she's sure this woman, who's about to be here, is some kind of a kook.

"Lots of people get killed by crazy women too. And Gage was almost a statistic, as was I and you for that matter, Benny! No!" She stomps her little boot covered foot. "No, Gage!"

"She's already on her way, Angel. She'll be here any minute. I gave her this address so you can meet her before I take her to my place. And I expect you to give her the same kind of welcome that I gave Blaze here," he says then crosses his arms.

I laugh and look out the window and see Cuddles running around the yard with the chicken who's now full grown. He turned out to be a rooster who's mean as hell. And upon closer inspection, I see they aren't playing as much as the rooster is chasing the poor dog.

I breathe a sigh of relief as Cuddles ducks under the fence, leaving the rooster alone in the backyard. We really need to set that bird free!

Then Angel's shrill voice fills the kitchen and Woody holds his little hands over his ears, "I will do that then. I guess you don't recall nearly getting into a fight with him the first time you two met."

Gage looks a little shocked.

"Blaze and I have always been the best of friends. I don't know how you remember it but he and I got along from the get-go and that's what I expect from you."

"I keep forgetting about your memory problems, Gage. Sorry." She looks at me for a little help and all I can seem to do is shrug my shoulders.

"Give the chick a shot, Angel," I say as I bat my eyelashes at her. "For me. Please. Gage needs a life too, sweetheart."

Ever since we found out just how much irreversible damage

was done to Gage's brain a few months ago, Angel has become his fierce protector. And God help anyone who thinks they can attempt to pull anything over on the man.

The doorbell chimes and Angel races Gage to the front door. I come along behind them, holding Woody and making faces at him to make him laugh. I love this kid's laugh!

GAGE MANAGES to beat her and he opens the door and there stands a woman. Not a chick, a full grown older woman. Pretty and nice looking but at least twenty years older than Gage.

Angel stares at her as Gage reaches out and takes her hand. "Dana, it's nice to finally meet you face to face."

She smiles, revealing a really nice set of dentures. She has to be in her early fifties, I think. A bit early for dentures but who am I to judge.

I wonder if he realizes how much older she is than him.

He pulls her into a hug and she squeals with delight. "Oh my, Gage! You're even more handsome in person!"

Angel steps back and looks them over as they hug and she looks kind of shocked as she mutters, "Um, hi."

Gage lets the woman out of his tight hug and holds her hand as he looks back at Angel. "Angel, this is the woman I've been telling you about. This is Dana Braxton. Dana, this is Angel, my self-proclaimed guardian."

Angel doesn't even attempt to conceal her thoughts from the woman. "Hey there, Dana. Did Gage's ad on that dating site say he was twenty-eight?"

"It did," she says as she pats his hand. "We talked over the phone too and he told me. He also told me his sad story and my heart just went out to him. I'm a bit of a nurturing soul. My last kid just left for college in the fall and I'm an empty-nester. When I found Gage here, well, I knew I'd found the man I'm supposed to take care of. My husband died three years ago and I've been very lonely."

"How many kids do you have, Dana?" Angel asks as she crosses her arms.

"Six," the woman says without blinking an eye. "I love having a big family."

"You like kids, huh," Angel asks adding a little tap of her boot on the hardwood floor to accent her words and how she's really not cool with this.

But she's not looking at Gage who's beaming at the woman. She's shorter than he is. Her hair is shoulder-length, blonde, and cut into a bob-like hairstyle.

He likes her a lot from what I can tell. She's okay for her age, but damn!

THE WOMAN NODS enthusiastically then looks at Woody. "Is that your son?"

I walk up to her. "Hi, I'm Benny and this is Woody."

Our son holds out his arms to her, which is not a thing he does with strangers. She takes him and coos and he coos back at her. And all the while Gage looks at her with adoration.

I wrap my arm around Angel's shoulders, and she looks at me with such a scowl on her pretty face. I give her a little squeeze and whisper, "Invite her to stay for dinner."

She shakes her head a little and I squeeze her shoulders a little more and nod. Her eyes go narrow and she finally says, "We're having a roast for dinner. I don't suppose you like roast."

Dana looks away from Woody and smiles. "I love roast."

"Oh," Angel says then frowns. "I don't suppose you'd like to eat with us?"

"I'd love to. If you're inviting me." Dana looks at Gage. "Is that something you want to do, sweetie?"

He nods. "Angel makes a good roast."

Dana looks back at Angel. "If you're inviting me, then I'd love to stay for dinner."

With a deep sigh, Angel says, "Great. I'll be in the kitchen."

Dana hands the baby to Gage and winks at him. "I'll help you, Angel. Gage has told me all about you and I think it's fascinating that you make motorcycles. I ride too."

"You're shitting me!" Angel says, making me cringe.

Gage just laughs and looks at me. "She'll have Angel wrapped around her finger before you know it."

I nod and wait for the women to get all the way out of earshot then say, "She's a little older than you, you know."

He nods and follows me as we move along to join the women in the kitchen at a slow pace. "I know that. But there's something about her. I don't know what it is."

"I doubt she can have kids," I say and watch his reaction to see what he thinks about that.

Gage stops and looks sheepish for a second. "I've been keeping something from you guys. It is part of the reason I hang out with Woody so much. In the accident, some real damage was done to my private area. I'm sterile. No kids are in my future, anyway. And I really do like Dana."

"Why didn't you say anything to us about that, Gage?" I clap him on the back and feel terrible for the man.

"It's not a thing I like to talk about. I'm sure you can understand."

When we get into the kitchen, he puts Woody down and the kid goes straight to Dana. He's a great judge of character so I think Gage may be onto something with the woman.

Dana picks the baby up and keeps on doing what she was doing like it's not a problem at all rinsing off baby carrots as she holds him. And after six kids, maybe it's not a problem.

Angel looks at our son and shakes her head and I know she's thinking he's a little traitor. She asks Dana, "Guess with six kids, you have a lot of grandkids, Dana."

"You'd think so," Dana says with a nod. "But do you know, every one of those dang kids of mine are going to medical school and waiting to start their families until they're finished? My oldest son got married last year to another dang doctor."

Angel stops peeling potatoes and looks at the woman with skepticism. "Do you expect me to...?"

Gage cuts her off. "Look, Angel, here she is at the oldest one's wedding." He takes his cell phone to her and starts showing her the pictures of Dana with her apparently very intelligent kids.

Angel taps her foot as she looks at picture after picture of the woman with her family. She doesn't bother to look at Gage and see how his face is all lit up as he looks at the pictures.

Angel spins around and looks at Dana. "Okay, I have to say something."

"PLEASE DO," Dana says. "I'm an open book, dear. And I'm very pleased to see Gage has someone who looks out for him so well. His own family doesn't do half the job you're doing."

"Wait," Angel looks at Gage. "How does she know your family? You never ever took me to meet them. Damn it!"

Gage laughs. "My mother cleans her house, Angel."

Angel narrows her eyes. "Oh. Well, you said you met on the internet."

"And we did," Dana says. "His mother told me about her son and his tragic story and told me he was on this dating site. And when I put in my information into the site, he was one of the ones it said I'd be compatible with."

"But you're so much older than he is," Angel says very bluntly.

I find myself cringing again and hiss, "Angel Worthington!"

She looks at me with an incredulous expression. "Well, she is."

Dana nods. "I am. But he and I have not only similar experiences in life but also interests too. I love to play video games and ride motorcycles too."

"You like to play video games?" Angel asks as if there is no possible way that could be true.

Gage laughs. "She does like to play games. We've played a lot online. She's totally cool. You'll see."

Dana's cheeks go pink as she says, "Oh, Gage! You, flatterer."

Gage gets off the barstool and goes around and takes her up in his arms. His lips touch her cheek and Angel's mouth drops open as he says, "You are cool. And gorgeous and sexy and I'm so damn happy to finally get to actually touch you."

Angel goes to the fridge and pulls out a few beers. She pops one open and chugs it then opens another before she offers, "Anyone else want a refreshing beverage?" Then she burps and we all laugh.

Seems like my Angel is having problems letting Gage just be Gage.

ANGEL

I climb into bed with Benny after putting the baby to bed and still can't wrap my head around Gage with the old lady. "Benny, why would he want her?"

"Come on, Baby. He has his reasons. I get that you don't

understand that but the woman checks out. She's very wealthy. Maybe the whole thing where she's stable and can't have kids either has him liking that about her." He fluffs his pillows and lies back on them.

"What do you mean, can't have kids either?" I stare at him and he freezes like a deer in the headlights.

"Huh?" He acts stupid.

"Benny, what do you know?" I pinch his shoulder and he lets out a yelp.

"Damn! Okay, stop torturing me!"

"Gage told you he can't have kids?"

He nods. "It's not like he told me not to tell you but I doubt that he wants me to."

"Why wouldn't he tell me that? And how long have you known this? And why haven't you told me sooner? And..."

He grabs me and kisses me. I'm sure to get me to stop asking questions. When he releases me I'm a little out of breath because that's just how badass our kisses are.

"He didn't want anyone to feel sorry for him. It happened when he was in the wreck. I only found out today when you and Dana went to the kitchen and this is the soonest I could possibly tell you." He holds me in his arms and looks at me.

"Poor, Gage." My eyes go misty. "That fucking Sandy is so lucky she's in prison right now because I would fucking kill her if she was free. Can't you sue her for that?"

"Sue her? She doesn't have anything," he says as he lets me go and I fall onto his wide chest and hug him.

"Life just isn't fair for him." I run my hand over his naked chest. "I feel so responsible for not being more available to him when he and I were together. I should've done so many things different. I'm not saying I would've stayed with him or anything but maybe those awful things wouldn't have happened to him if I had been different."

"Is that why you became his crusader when you found out everything that Sandy did to him? You feel responsible?" he asks me and pulls me up to make me look at him.

I NOD. "You have no idea what that feels like to know because you were so wrapped up in your work and school that you let someone hurt someone you love. It feels terrible. If I could go back in time, I'd change it all. Gage wasn't a bad guy."

"Life is life, baby. For whatever reason that happened to Gage isn't for you to understand or take the blame for. He did mess with the chick. He wasn't a complete innocent." He pulls me back down to rest my head on his chest and runs his hands up and down my arms.

"And what if this woman is crazy too?" I ask as I nuzzle his chest.

"Then at least you and I are going to be around and we can watch out for that. He needs to make a life for himself instead of his revolving around ours." He rolls me over onto my back and looks down at me. "I love the guy. I do. And that's why I'd like to see him get to share his life with someone. Really share it. If you care about him, then you should want that too."

"I DO WANT that for him. But with someone more age appropriate. I like Dana. She's funny and nice and damn it, she is cool too. But that age difference is ridiculous!"

"And if it were a fifty-something man with a nearly thirty-year-old woman, then what would you think? Because I'll have you know that we not only hobnob with couples like that back in New York but also in the motorcycle club. You've never said a word about any of them." He just stares me down and waits for me to say one word against what he's pointed out to me.

"Damn it, Benny," I whine. "You're right. I'll give this woman the benefit of the doubt. But I'll be on top of this. If I see anything the least bit weird. Well, weird is going to happen with how I look at them. But I mean that looks like he's being done wrong or she's crazy. Well, she does have to be a little crazy to want to spend her golden years with a man nearly half her age. But I mean anything that…"

His mouth crashes down on mine and I get his drift. Stop talking and kiss him.

I can do that. I can do that for a long, long time.

32

BLAZE

My hands run up her arms and I pull her in close to me as I gaze into her deep blue eyes. "You are so beautiful." My lips touch hers and I'm lost.

On a mission of their own, my hands travel over her shoulders and down her back and then I take her sweet, plump ass in them and pull her to me as I press my growing erection against her soft core.

She shudders and wraps her arms around my neck. Her legs go around my waist as I pick her up.

She strokes my tongue as I stroke hers and it feels right. Angel in my arms always feels more than right.

Four years after Woody's birth, Angel finally said that we can have another baby. This is our first attempt at getting her pregnant and I'm getting this woman primed and ready.

Her body is shaking as I lie her back on the bed.

I slip first one thin strap of her silky blue nightgown down then the other. Her breasts are bare and I take them all in. My eyes roam over them then I touch them using only the tips of my fingers.

Goosebumps raise across her flesh as her nipples grow and

harden. She moves her fingertips up and down my arm and watches me as I take in her gorgeous body. A body I hope to see changed very soon as she grows our next child inside her.

My hands run over both her plump and firm tits. It sends heat through me as she gasps at the immediate reaction my touch gives her body. I climb up next to her on the bed and place my mouth on one as I play with the other.

My tongue makes lazy circles around her taut nipple. One long suck I make. "My God, that feels amazing," she moans and runs her hands through my hair.

She hasn't felt amazing yet!

33

ANGEL

Warmth spreads over me as his mouth leaves my breast, trailing kisses up my chest. His piercing blue eyes meet mine and his intensity has me quivering.

It's been no secret he's wanted to have another child for some time now. I can see it's going to be his mission to impregnate me as soon as possible. And I have a feeling he's going to keep me satiated until we see a plus sign on one of the dozens of pregnancy tests that the man has already bought.

A WILDNESS in him comes out through those steely eyes and it thrills me. With one quick motion, he pulls his T-shirt off and I find myself gazing at his perfectly muscled chest.

My hand moves over the tight muscles. A six-pack and pecs that won't quit, ripple as my hand moves over them. His pecs are large and look powerful. A thing I know they are as I've seen this man pick things up that weigh crazy amounts. He's so strong and virile and it makes me so wet for him.

"My God, you're gorgeous, Benjamin Worthington. You sure

you want to have another baby? You know a little one takes away a lot of our sex-life."

He nods and makes a deep growl. "I'll deal with that. I want to see your stomach filled with my seed."

"Okay, Conan! That didn't sound barbaric at all," I say with sarcasm-laced words.

He grins and gets off the bed, dropping his pajama bottoms, releasing his huge gift. My eyes go wide as it seems larger somehow. He must really be excited about having another kid!

He pulls my nightgown the rest of the way off and slides my silky panties off me. I lie naked in front of him as he looks me over and I chew on my bottom lip in anticipation of what he plans on doing to me next.

His fingers trail lightly over my chest, down my stomach and it makes the muscles tighten. An electric current flows in the wake of his touch and my body is on fire now.

My brain starts to spiral and I can only focus on the way he's making my body react to his touch. Only the tips of his fingers are on my skin yet I can feel it all over my body.

He makes another deep growl. "You are beyond gorgeous, baby."

MY HEART POUNDS and my body quivers as he climbs back onto the bed and spreads my legs and gives me a smile before his mouth is on me. My hands fist the sheets with the intense reaction my body has to him.

His tongue taps my clitoris and I nearly fall apart. "Oh, hell!" My breath is already coming in gasps.

The heat of his mouth on me and the wetness of his tongue are insanely good. He has my legs pulled up so my knees are bent and then his hands go to my ass and he squeezes it.

Pulling me up to take more of me in, his mouth goes

ravenous on me. It has my insides a liquid mass of intense pleasure.

All too soon I find myself screaming out as my body falls apart under his mouth and my hands go to his hair. His tongue goes inside me as he laps up the juices my body has released. He moans and growls and seems to love it.

The way he's being so animalistic has me going crazy for him. I should've let him get me pregnant a long time ago.

He's very good at it!

Benny's eyes go soft, and he changes his entire demeanor as he kisses me with a gentle and sweet kiss. My arms move around his neck on their own. My heart skips a beat with his soft touch after being so rough before.

He lies on the side of me and moves his fingertips over my stomach, trailing down until he finds my still pulsing clit. He strokes it and makes his way down my heated and wet folds.

I arch up to him as he continues to stroke me softly while he kisses me. The fire inside me builds and his gentle touch is making me crave so much more.

His tongue flows smoothly over mine then he pulls his mouth away and looks into my eyes. "I love you, Angel."

I stroke his cheek and gaze into his eyes. "I love you, Benny."

He moves his body over mine and slowly enters me as I pull my knees up to allow him to move in deep. Then he kisses me again as he makes gentle strokes into me and it makes me moan, wanting more from him.

Slow and easy he shows me only gentleness and I feel so loved by him.

His body is all over mine and moves so slowly I can feel the fine hairs on his chest as they graze me. My breasts squish under his hard muscles with every stroke he makes.

His mouth leaves mine then he trails kisses down my neck and gives me a little nip then more kisses. It sends a wave of heat all through me.

Inside me, a wave is cresting. His body moves back and forth over mine and his hard cock moves in and out so slowly it's tormenting me. "Faster," I moan.

His growl makes my insides quake, and he moves faster as he takes one of my legs and pulls it up so he can go into me deeper. His teeth graze my neck then he bites a bit harder, and it sends me right over the edge.

I cling to him as my body climaxes and scream his name over and over.

He grinds into me as he continuously growls low and steady as I buck underneath him. Then his body stiffens and liquid heat pours into me.

We both make low moans as our bodies take what they need from the others. And I feel amazing with him like this.

He's brought more to my life than I ever knew I even wanted. I wrap my arms around him and hold him tight to me. Then tears start to fall over my cheeks and I'm silently crying.

HE MUST FEEL the wetness on his cheek as his face is touching mine. He pulls back and kisses the tears away. "Why the tears, Pumpkin?"

"That was beyond beautiful to me, Benny. The whole thing was so completely amazing. You've made my life like something out of a fantasy novel and the way you touch me makes me feel more than human." I run my hand over his face. "You are real, aren't you?"

He chuckles and kisses the tip of my nose. "Oh yeah, I'm real."

I laugh a little. I know I'm being crazy. "Okay, the romantic stuff is over. I can see it makes you uncomfortable."

He holds me still underneath him. "I love the romantic stuff and you know it. I just don't want you going to that place in your head where this is all too good to be true and stuff like you do from time to time. This is just life. Our life together. It's not magic or fantasy. It's just life."

His cock makes one last jerk inside me and I have to laugh. "There you go. Got it all out now?"

He kisses my cheek then rolls off me. "Yep. Now let's talk about names for our daughter. I like Penelope."

"No way," I say as I roll onto my side only to have him roll me right back onto my back.

"I read about this," he says as he puts a pillow under my ass, lifting me up so my pelvis is tilted back somewhat. "You need to stay in this position for a while. I think thirty minutes should do it. We need my magic potion to sit on your basket of, could one day be people, eggs. You know, to ensure fertilization. Now, why don't you like the name, Penelope?"

He props his head up on his hand and looks down at me as he strokes my stomach. I guess he thinks he's mixing up the magic kid brew inside me.

"I think that name is perfect for a pet but not a kid. Not one of ours, anyway." I put my arms behind my head and lay back and try to relax since he won't be letting me move anytime soon.

"Well, how about Jax?" he asks as he watches his finger moving over my stomach.

"No. That's a boy's name. How about, Bonnie?"

"No." He moves his whole hand over my stomach, lying it flat out on it. "How about, Serendipity?"

I shake my head and run my hand through his dark blonde wavy hair. "They'll call her Sara. I'm not sure I like that. What are we going to do if it's another boy?"

"Sell, him," he says with a chuckle and I smack him upside the head. "Oww!"

"Don't even joke about a thing like that."

HE LAUGHS AND SAYS, "If I wasn't worried about shaking the baby stew you have going on in your insides right now, I'd toss you over my lap and give you a good spanking, Mrs. Worthington."

The thought makes my ass tingle and I say, "Oh, Benny. Start with that the next time then. You just made me ache to feel your strong hand on my ass."

"Damn it, Angel. You just made my dick hard!" he growls. "And we need to let this baste for a while."

"I think you're trying too hard. Come on. I can lie still like this the next time. I promise I won't talk naughty then. And you can make me be still even longer if you want."

He looks at me for a minute as he rubs his palms together while he contemplates his answer. Then he smiles and says, "Nope. You have to stay still. But we can start with a spanking next time. And you'll stay still after that too."

I moan and run my hand over my tit to entice him. "Don't you want a taste of this?"

He shakes his head. "Not right now, I don't."

SLOWLY, I ease my hand off my tit and down my stomach then over his and I touch only the tip of his cock, that's not soft at all. "You sure, you don't want to smack my ass a little then take me from behind?"

He closes his eyes and moans as I move my fingertip over the head of his cock. "You're an evil temptress."

I make an evil laugh. "And I need a good spanking to bring the good girl out in me and put the bad girl to bed. But not until you've shown that bad girl who's boss around here." His dick shoots up and I know I almost have him where I want him.

"God damn it!" he shouts as he flips me around and I end up lying face down over his lap. "But after this time, you have to lie back with your ass up on the pillow for a whole hour. Agreed?"

His hand comes down hard on my ass and it heats up and sends crazy heat through me. "Yes," I hiss. "Again."

He smacks my ass again and I go all wet inside. He does it again and I cry out for more. Over and over, he makes my flesh sizzle then he flips me around again and I'm on my knees with him behind me.

This baby making thing is going to be quite a workout it seems!

34

BLAZE

The smell of alcohol makes my nose itch as I stand by Angel's head while her doctor, an old guy who smells like coffee, has his head in her nether regions with some kind of thing that's supposed to let us see our kid.

But he hasn't managed to bring the image up yet and went back in to reposition the device. It's not a pleasant thing to witness your wife being so completely open to another man. But it is an evil necessity in bringing kids into our world.

HE COMES BACK out from under the blue sheet that's keeping my wife covered from my view, anyway, though I have no idea why. His face is a little red from the heat I guess and he looks at the screen that begins to de-fuzz and then some blobby stuff appears in shades of gray. "There we go," he says.

I look really hard and I don't know why he said that. There we do not go. "Doc, I don't see a thing I recognize. And I've been down there a lot." I laugh at my own joke and Angel smacks me in the ribs and frowns at me.

With a shake of her head, she utters one word that shuts my comedic line up of one-liners down, "Don't!"

I nod to show her she's won this round, but that just means she'll have to listen to them all once we're alone.

The doctor points to the screen. "You see that there?"

Angel and I make humming sounds as if we know what he's talking about but neither of us does. So I ask, "What is that there, Doc?"

He looks at us as if it's as plain as the nose on his face. Which is kind of bulbous and on the red side and I think my wife's obstetrician might be a heavy drinker.

He taps the screen with his finger. "Right there! It's a little round head."

"I do see a circle but I see another one right next to that so I don't think it's a head, Doc." I squint and try to see the rest of a body and do see something like that dangling off the round thing he said was a head but I see the same thing dangling under the other round thing and he didn't call that a head.

"What do you think the other round thing is, Mr. Worthington?" the doctor asks.

I shrug my shoulders. "No idea."

Angel starts crying and then she points at the screen. "They're twins and they look like they're joined in the middle."

I shake my head. "No, Angel. Not twins. He didn't say that, Baby."

The doctor looks at me with a no-nonsense look in his pale blue eyes with many wrinkles around them. "It is twins."

"What do you mean by that?" I ask in complete confusion.

"There are two babies. And it does look as if they're joined at the abdomen. I'll have to send you to a specialist. But it looks as if you're having conjoined twins."

. . .

"WAIT ONE MINUTE HERE. There are two babies in there and they're attached to each other?" I ask just to be really sure I understand this. "Because we only wanted one, and we didn't want anything stuck to it. Especially not another entire person."

Then the real waterworks start flowing from Angel and she's bawling. "You had to make me stay in that damn position and let the juices simmer! And now look what's happened! There are two of them and they're stuck together. Oh, Benny! What are we going to do?"

The doctor pats her on the shoulder. "No need to cry, Mrs. Worthington. You'll have the best doctors to care for you and these babies. And the simmering thing didn't cause this. Don't blame yourself."

She sniffles and wipes her nose with the back of her hand. "I'm not blaming myself, I'm blaming him." She sticks her finger out at me and I have to point at myself.

"Me! Why only me? I mean I didn't hold a gun to your head and make you keep your ass up on that pillow for an hour after each time we had sex. You did have something to do with this fiasco, you know." I begin to pace and have no idea what we're going to do with a couple of kids who'll be stuck together for the rest of their lives.

"Simmer down, guys," the doctor shouts at us. "Whatever the hell you two did, didn't have a thing to do with this. Now, I'm going to schedule you an appointment with the specialist and by next week you'll have a plan of action. Okay?"

We both nod because what the fuck else can we do at this point. And as I look at my wife, I can see she's never letting me get her pregnant again.

Well, fuck!

Angel

Now in my third trimester with the twins who are joined at the abdomen, Benny and I are at an appointment with the specialist who is going to be doing surgery on the babies while they're still inside me. She says she's done this type of thing before on a woman in Africa who had the same exact thing happen to her.

So I ask the specialist as my pale husband looks at me, "Okay, so you've seen this before. Can you tell me if the other woman also did this thing where she got her bottom up on a pillow after sex to let the semen essentially sit on top of the eggs?"

"You just sound ignorant, Angel," Benny snaps at me.

We've had an ongoing argument about this since we found out and he refuses to take any kind of responsibility for it. But I'm determined to get him to see this is all his fault.

The specialist laughs a little. "That's not even physically possible, Mrs. Worthington." She looks at my chart and then back at me. "It says here that you hold a Master's Degree in Engineering."

I nod and smile. "Yes, I do." I hold my head up high and look at Benny as I think she's about to be the first person to finally back me up.

"Well, then you should know a little about human anatomy, I should think. There is no possible way to get semen to sit on the eggs. They're in your fallopian tubes until your body releases them. Your body released two, and that's how this happened." She looks at me over her glasses and wrinkles her nose. "So, stop trying to blame this man for things which are not under his control."

. . .

Well, fuck me!

I look over at Benny and frown, "This one is not about to let me get away with shit, is she?"

"I like her," Benny says with a smile. "I like her a lot."

I lie back and rest my head on the pillow and look up at the ceiling and try hard not to cry. I want so desperately for this to be someone's fault. If it isn't, then it means things are starting to go bad for us.

Just like I knew they would one day!

Several other surgeons join us in the small examination room and it feels really stuffy in here all of a sudden. Benny stands by my right shoulder as they pull the open in the front gown away from my huge belly and draw on it with a black sharpie.

They discuss how I'll be cut open only a little and how a small camera will be shoved up inside me. The cameraman smiles at me as he says, "Hi, I'm Doctor Larson. You can call me, Shane. I hate formalities. Can I call you, Angel?"

"Sure, why not?"

His smile gets even bigger. "I think this is an exciting time in medical history and I'm so glad to be a part of it. Aren't you?"

"Not really." I look away from the idiot so I don't say anything mean to him. He will have a camera inside me after all. I don't need him taking pictures of me at any bad angles just to get back at me.

He just keeps talking even though it's obvious that I don't want to have a conversation right now, "I'm going to save all the video so you can see the whole operation when you wake back up. Isn't that going to be so cool?"

"The coolest," I say then Benny takes my hand and picks it up and kisses it.

He can tell by the tone of my voice that I'm getting more and more upset by the minute. "It's all going to be okay, my Angel. You'll see."

If it's all going to be okay, why do I feel so fucking scared?

Blaze

WITH THE COMPLICATIONS of the pregnancy, I moved us to New York and we're staying at my parents' home until after the twins are born and stable.

We're having girls so I get to name them both, per Angel's permission, of course. But I want her to help me because I think she's never going to have any more kids.

This is taking such a toll on her. The girl carries around so much responsibility on her narrow shoulders for anything bad or hard that happens in the lives which surround her.

Gage and Dana got married last year. She finally let Dana take over as Gage's fierce protector. But that was only after giving her explicit directions on what it means to be his protector.

Angel still blames herself for what happened to Gage. No amount of talking can get her to stop. And now she's blaming herself for the twins and their problems.

She's going into surgery today and she's sitting in our suite with Woody sitting next to her in the large rocking chair I bought her. I can see by the way that she's holding her jaw so tight that she's afraid this might be the last time she gets with our son.

As with any surgery, the doctors had to advise the patient there's a chance she could die or one or both of the babies, which they call fetuses, could die during or even after the surgery. Angel signed the papers yesterday accepting that fact.

. . .

I'M TRYING to only think positive thoughts. Angel's grandmother and my grandfather are going to be at the hospital with me as we wait for her to have the surgery that hopeful will lead to the twins being separated.

That gives them a better chance at making it through the surgery and leading healthier lives.

I listen as I hear Angel saying something to our son, "You know, Son, no matter what happens I love you and always will."

"I know, Mom. You know what?" he asks as I see him run his little hand over her cheek.

She shakes her head and runs her hand over his dark hair. He looks so much like her, only a male version. "What, baby?"

"Everything's going to be okay. My sisters are tough. I know they are. Because I'm really tough, Mom. Do you 'member when I fell off the swing and scraped my knees all up and blood was everywhere?"

She nods. "Yes, I cried, and you didn't."

He nods. "Yeah, you do 'member. Mom, why did you cry?"

"I cried because I had bought the swing set and I felt like I had done that before you were big enough to enjoy it safely. I cried because you got hurt and it was all my fault. And you were so brave with your little bleeding knees and it made me mad at myself for putting you on the swing you weren't ready for."

"KIDS GET HURT, MOM." He reaches up and wipes a tear from his mother's cheek and I try hard not to cry too.

"I know, Baby, but it's a mommy's job to do her best not to let them. You know what I mean. I made a mistake putting that swing set up too soon," she says then kisses the top of his head. "I've made lots of mistakes and I'm sorry, Baby."

"Do you think having my baby sisters was a mistake?" he asks her and I can see him searching her eyes.

She waits a while before she answers him. "Woody, of course not. I think I wanted something too bad, though. I didn't think about what all could go wrong. And now there will be two little girls in the world who have to undergo life-threatening surgery before they even breathe their first breath. And that's because I couldn't manage to keep their bodies apart."

"That's not your fault," I say in a whisper as I move in behind her. "Things just happen, baby. None of it is your fault or anyone else's for that matter. Bad things happen, Pumpkin. I thank God we have the money and resources to do the best we can for our babies. What more could anyone ask for?"

I run my hand over her shoulder and can feel the tension in her body.

She runs her hand up and rubs it over mine. "I know you're right. I do."

"Woody, give Mommy kisses. I need to get her to the hospital. You'll stay here with Grammy and Grampy while we're gone. You can visit Mommy when she wakes up after the surgery, okay Buddy?" I ask as I lift him up and put him down on the floor.

He nods and wipes his eyes where a few tears have managed to escape the tough little man.

After I help Angel up, he grabs her around her knees and hugs her tight. "I love you, Mommy. You be good, okay?"

She runs her hands over his head and the tears start flowing out of her. She can only nod and look at me to help her not to freak the kid out.

I run my arm around her and she buries her face in my chest. "Mommy will be good and you be good too. I'll call as soon as she's awake and your grandparents will bring you down to the hospital."

Staying positive is getting harder and harder to do as the time grows closer.

But I have to be strong for my family. Now more than ever...

35

ANGEL

It is funny how no one tells you things might not always go according to plan when bringing life into this world. If this had been part of the plan, then I'd have said, no thank you, to it.

But I wasn't given any idea this could happen. Planned or not, I'm getting prepped for surgery. My little babies are all snuggled up, holding each other inside of me.

The little things aren't expecting sharp instruments to be cutting through their soft skins and stomachs, separating them merely an hour from now. They're just a couple of peaceful beings right now whose world is about to be shook up.

I lie here and I can blame myself forever but it won't change a damn thing. It won't change the fact my daughters will be born with scars. It won't change the fact one or both might not be born at all. And it won't change the fact that all three of us have a chance of not making it through this surgery.

The surgery isn't a necessary thing. This is not a life or death situation. I chose this. It was either to do it in the utero or do it after they're born or not do it at all.

. . .

The scars will be less visible and they will have less chance of complications if my body and immune system can sustain them after the surgery. So I'm taking the chance to give them theirs.

I've bulked up on my vitamins and made myself as healthy as I can be to help give them the extra boost only I can at this point. So I can kick myself and blame myself but the fact is I have to get a hold of myself and stop doing that.

I have to be strong and brave for my little girls. And if something does happen to me, then I trust Benny to raise our son without me. I did pick a great man to marry and have a family with.

I just hope we get to continue on this journey together. And I pray our daughters will both be joining us.

The nurse leaves after getting me all hooked up to the lines and then I see my husband coming in, followed by my grandmother and his grandfather.

I smile as big as I can to let my grandmother know I can do this. Her expression is filled with worry and I'm glad that she has her husband to help her through this.

"Hi, Grams, and Gramps." I hold out my arms and they both hug me.

Kisses are placed on each of my cheeks by them then there they are, looking at me like it might be the last time they get to see me. Gram's bottom lip quivers as she says with a shaky voice, "You stay strong for me, you hear me?"

I nod. "I'm trying, Grams."

"We'll be right here until you three are alright and safe. I'll take good care of Benny for you," she tells me.

I notice Benny's grandfather can't seem to say a word. Which is highly unusual. He kisses my forehead and takes my grandmother's hand and leads her out of the room.

Benny sits down on the side of the bed and takes my hand. I run mine over his and his thumb touches the place the needle from the IV goes into my hand.

I lick my lips and swallow back the lump in my throat. "Benny, if I don't..."

He quickly puts his finger to my lips. "Don't even say it, Angel. You know I'll take care of Woody. So don't even say it."

"But I want you to know that I'll be okay if you move on..."

His mouth stops me from saying another word as he kisses me. He always has known how to make me shut up.

My mind goes blank with his kiss and suddenly I realize the nurse put something in my IV and everything is going black. He kisses me still and away I go.

Blaze

SITTING in between my grandfather and Angel's grandmother, I can't help but think about how far apart he and I were before I met Angel and how she brought me and my family closer than we had ever been.

If I had never met her, I'd probably be still hating this man who I've come to really love. If Angel and I had never, met my life would have been so different.

I don't really like to think about such things but with her in such a compromised state, I have to look at things and really appreciate her being in my life.

She is stubborn and can be a she-devil at times. Then she can also be the sweetest, kindest, and loving person at other times. She's a paradox of feelings and emotions and I never know what part of Angel I'm going to get at any time.

Sometimes she's the rock in the family and other times she's the drowning chick who's screaming and calling out for help.

Grabbing onto me with a panic that threatens to sink us both. She's perfect!

AND RIGHT NOW SHE'S asleep and our babies are being separated from each other. I wonder what they're thinking. If they can really comprehend anything at all.

I find myself praying that they're asleep and as unaware as their mother is, of what's happening to them. The phone rings in the waiting room we're in and I jump up to answer it.

A female voice says, "Hello, Mr. Worthington?"

"This is him." I find myself crossing my fingers and hoping for great news.

"I'm calling to inform you that the surgeons have successfully separated the babies. Their vitals are nearly back to normal. Mrs. Worthington is taking longer to get back to normal. Her blood pressure has spiked." She clears her throat and my chest gets tight as I wait. "She may have suffered a small stroke with the spike. We won't be able to do a CT scan until the operation is completed. Once it is, though, she'll be transported to radiology where that will be done. It means another hour longer than we thought. Someone will call you when that's done."

Then she hangs up and I stand here in shock.

"What did they say, Benjamin?" Grandfather asks me.

"UM, uh, she might have had a stroke," I mumble then place the phone back down.

Her grandmother grabs her chest. "What? No!"

I nod. "Her blood pressure spiked pretty damn high, I guess. They'll have to do a CT scan once the surgery is finished to find out if she did have one or not." I have to go to the bathroom.

I try to walk out of the room but my grandfather gets up and grabs me by the shoulders and pulls me into his arms. "No, you don't. I'm here for you, Son."

His arms are so strong and so comforting and I find I'm crying like a little kid in them. "Grandfather, I can't live without her."

He sways back and forth with me. "I'm sure you won't have to."

"What if something happened to her brain? What if she's not the same when she wakes up? What if she's not capable of taking care of the babies? What will I do then?"

"We'll get her therapy to get her back on track. That's all we'll have to do. You have a family who will jump in and help you both with your children. That's what families do for each other after all, Benjamin. We're here for you all." He pats my back as I sob and cry so much harder than I ever have before.

Not even when I was little, do I recall crying like this. Then it hits me that I have to be strong for Angel and our kids now. So I suck it up.

I can fall apart later. Right now they need me to be their rock. I pull out of my grandfather's arms and pat him on the shoulder. "Thank you, Grandfather. Thank you for being here for me and my family at such a hard time. Thank you for showing me what it means to be the man of the family. Without your influence, I'd have no idea of how to be a man, a husband, or a father."

"You've become a man I'm proud to call my grandson, Benjamin. No matter what happens, I know you can handle it the best way possible." He takes my hand and pulls me back to sit down between him and Rebecca.

I see how pale she is, and it suddenly dawns on me how

frightened she must be for her granddaughter. I take her hand and hold it. "I'm sure she'll be fine. I think that girl always runs on higher octane than most, anyway."

She nods her head and looks at me. "I'm sure you're right. She has always been a little high strung and quick tempered. Maybe that spike looked big to them but not so much to her."

I nod and hope we're right about that.

Because I don't know what I'd do without her being her anymore.

Angel

A BRIGHT LIGHT flashes into my eyes as someone asks me, "Mrs. Worthington, can you see me?"

"No," I answer in a scratchy voice that makes my throat hurt very bad. "There's a light in my eyes."

The light goes away and there's a shadowy figure in front of me. "Good."

"Her voice sounds clear," I hear some man say from the corner of the room. "The scan is up on the monitor, Doctor."

I watch the blurry figure move away from me and go towards a box with gray fuzzy stuff on it. I close my eyes to try to get the blurriness to go away as I listen to them talk.

"Okay, I see no damage," the doctor says.

"Damage?" I ask. I open my eyes and blink and things start looking normal. "To what?"

He comes back to me and looks down at me then removes the strap that's holding my head down. "You had a spike in your blood pressure. We had to check for signs of a stroke. How do you feel?

"Like shit, to be honest."

He laughs and moves the bed up just a little. "Yeah, that's normal. Can you think and focus?"

"Yes." I look around and can see everything clear. "So, how'd the surgery go? Are my little girls two separate kids now?"

He nods. "It all went really well. The interns are going over the video in the gallery right now. They're excited to see the procedure. I think you'll be really happy to see your babies when they arrive. I foresee little to no scarring. It's amazing really."

"What about my husband?" I ask. "And did you guys tell him about thinking I had a stroke?"

He nods and I feel awful. "You need to hurry up and let him know I'm fine. He'll be worried sick. I can't imagine what all went through his head. What torture."

He looks over at the nurse. "Go get her family, will you?"

The nurse hurries out and I ask, "So when can I get the hell out of here?"

"AFTER THE BABIES ARE BORN," he says.

"What?" I shake my head. "That's like a month away."

"Didn't your doctor tell you that?"

"No. Damn!"

The door opens and Benny comes in alone. "Angel?"

I nod and he comes to me and leans over the bed, rubbing my shoulder and I see his eyes are all red and his nose is too. "Benny, you've been crying."

"YOU'RE DAMN right I have. I was worried sick about you." His hand rubs my shoulder harder like he's trying to tell himself I'm really okay.

"Sorry," I say with a little smile. "I didn't mean to scare you."

He kisses my forehead. "Well, you did. And I don't want you to do that anymore. I'm never going to ask you to do this again. This will be our last pregnancy."

"Hold up there, Big Daddy." I take his hand in mine and give it a little squeeze. "That's jumping to conclusions. We can see how things go. I'm not getting on that wagon just yet."

"I thought you'd be the one telling me that, to be honest. I was just wanting you to know I'm onboard with that idea. My heart nearly gave out, and this thing isn't even all the way over yet." He kisses my forehead again. "I'm not cut out for this."

I laugh then stop as it hurts pretty damn bad. "It's just life, Benny. I had a dream while I was under. And in that dream, there was another son. He looked like you. I can't think of not having another kid right now."

He pats my shoulder and smiles. "Okay then. I'm leaving that all up to you, Sugarplum."

"Good."

Somehow I think everything's going to work out fine.

BLAZE

"Hush, girls," I hiss as Serenity and Harmony run into the nursery where I'm rocking the latest edition to our little family.

"Daddy, I want to hold him. You've been hogging him for over an hour," Serenity gripes as she puts her hands on her hips.

The girls look just like me only with feminine qualities. They just turned sixteen last week and think they're grown.

Harmony holds out her arms. "No, Daddy, give him to me. She held him last. Oh, and Mom wants you, anyway. Woody took your old Harley out last night and he accidentally ran over something. She wants you to see what happened before she fixes it."

I set my jaw and get up out of the rocking chair. It's the same large wooden chair I rocked all of my kids in. Harmony sits down, and I put little Ronald Reagan Worthington in her arms.

Grandfather has passed on, but he told Angel his favorite president was Ronald Reagan just before he died. She was adamant our last son would carry on the tradition he started. We call him Ronnie.

Her grandmother joined my grandfather in the hereafter only three months after he left us. I guess she just didn't want to go on without him.

I MAKE my way down the stairs and out to the shop to find Woody and Angel looking over the bike I had when I meet the mother of my children and love of my life.

"Gross!" I shout as I see blood covering the front fender. "What the hell, Son?"

Woody shrugs his shoulders. "I think it was a jack-a-lope, Dad."

"It bent the rim a little, Baby," Angel tells me. "I have one I can swap it out with. But I wanted your permission first."

I look at her with a lopsided grin. "Baby, when will you understand that I completely trust your judgment where any bike of mine is concerned? You are the top designer of the lightweight Harley, you know. Your call is always great with me."

She smiles back at me and nods. "Okay then. If you're sure."

I WALK OVER and pull her into my arms as Woody makes a face. "Geez, when will you two get too old for this mushy crap? I'm out of here. Sorry about your bike, Dad."

Angel cocks her head as she asks, "Are we ever going to get too old for this, Benny?"

"I sure as hell hope not, my Angel." I kiss her and her sweet mouth still takes me to the place it always has.

Beyond this place and time to another world where only she and I exist. And hopefully, it always will.

AND WE ALL lived happily ever after...
   The End

ABOUT THE AUTHOR

Mrs. Love writes about smart, sexy women and the hot alpha billionaires who love them. She has found her own happily ever after with her dream husband and adorable 6 and 2 year old kids.
Currently, Michelle is hard at work on the next book in the series, and trying to stay off the Internet.
"Thank you for supporting an indie author. Anything you can do, whether it be writing a review, or even simply telling a fellow reader that you enjoyed this. Thanks

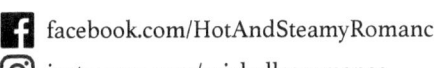 facebook.com/HotAndSteamyRomance
instagram.com/michellesromance

©Copyright 2020 by Michelle Love - All rights Reserved
In no way is it legal to reproduce, duplicate, or transmit any part of this document in either electronic means or in printed format. Recording of this publication is strictly prohibited and any storage of this document is not allowed unless with written permission from the publisher. All rights are reserved.
Respective authors own all copyrights not held by the publisher.

❦ Created with Vellum

www.ingramcontent.com/pod-product-compliance
Lightning Source LLC
LaVergne TN
LVHW021652060526
838200LV00050B/2322